FR

Trina Bahati

MY FAKE

FOREVER

Peach Tree Flings Book 1

Isla Drake

Copyright © 2022 by Isla Drake

All rights reserved.

No portion of this book may be reproduced in any form without written permission from the publisher or author, except as permitted by U.S. copyright law.

For everyone working hard to make your dreams come true. Keep going. But don't forget to take some time for self care. Sometimes that self care is just letting a hot guy rail you in a beach house.

CHAPTER 1

Luke

I stand at the window, gazing out at the muddy river flowing by, just yards from my office. Most days, staring out at this view calms me, pulling me away from the chaos of my day and to a more peaceful place. That's not the case today. Even the morning sunlight glinting off the slow-moving water can't take my mind off the meeting I'm about to endure. I dread these weekly meetings with my father more than anything. They're rarely productive and usually only serve as an excuse for him to berate me for whatever I've done recently to tarnish the company's reputation.

It's usually some imagined faux pas or slight that exists only in his head. I generally endure the meetings, keeping my comments to a minimum so they'll end as quickly as possible. My record escape time is 7.5 minutes. That had been a good day. I sigh, turning away from the window and the view that has failed to calm my nerves today. I know today's meeting won't be nearly so quick to end. I've been away for two weeks, something with which my father made certain to voice his displeasure. Not that I've ever cared what the old man thinks of me. But I've mostly stopped intentionally riling him in recent years, discovering that I can get more from him and the company if I stay on his good side.

But this trip couldn't be helped. When my new brother-in-law had called to tell me that he and my sister were on their way to the hospital to give birth to my niece, I'd dropped everything and boarded the first flight to North Carolina. I'd arrived at the hospital in time to join the other members of my sister's new family in pacing the waiting room for another 3 hours. That's when I'd learned how long labor really can be. My father had called me so many times that I'd finally turned my phone off and stuffed it into my pocket, ignoring him completely. It had been worth it, though. Seeing Mya and her husband smiling down at their baby girl had brought a lump to my throat and I'd had to blink my suddenly stinging eyes. Holding my niece for the first time had been worth all the anger I know I'm set to face today. Squaring my shoulders and blowing out a breath, I stride from my office and head for the elevator.

When I enter my father's office, he's sitting at his desk, looking as powerful and imposing as always. The wall of glass behind him looks out over the same view of the river as my own, much smaller window. Though I doubt if Charles Wolfe ever takes the time to enjoy the view. When I was younger, the sight of him in this office used to fill me with awe and a sense of pride. That was before I'd realized what a true bastard he really is. Now, looking at him just fills me with dread that I'm forced to interact with him at all. But it can't be helped. As long as I work for his company, I'm stuck dealing with him on a regular basis.

I wish I could quit and start my own ad firm, but I don't have the financial backing for that. Yet. In less than a year, I'll be old enough to access the trust left for me by my grandfather. When that happens, I'm leaving Wolfe Industries behind and creating my own company. I've been quietly laying the foundation for it for the past few years, fostering relationships with powerful individuals who'll be assets when I no longer have the Wolfe name backing me. I just need to bide my time until my 30th birthday. Then I can use my trust to start the kind of business I've always wished Wolfe Industries could be.

I stand there, waiting for my father to look up from his reports and acknowledge me. This is another game we play where we each try to outlast the other. He used to win every time, but over the years I've grown more patient while Charles has become more easily annoyed. Or maybe his age is finally catching up with him and he's realized he doesn't have as much time as he used to. Either way, I've gotten very good at standing on this rug in front of his desk, waiting.

When he finally lowers the report in his hand and meets my gaze, there's no hint of fatherly affection in his expression. I may as well be any other employee at this firm for all the recognition he shows when he looks at me. But that stopped bothering me long before I came to work here. Charles Wolfe has love for himself, his image and this company. He doesn't let pesky things like family get in the way of his goals. My sister is living proof of that. None of my thoughts show on my face, however. I keep my expression carefully neutral as I nod a greeting.

"I see you're finally back," he says in lieu of an actual greeting.

I dip my head in a nod again.

"Good," he says. "Your place is here. Not off in some shithole town with that woman."

I grit my teeth, but I'm not able to bite back the retort. "'That woman' is my sister, whether you choose to acknowledge her or not. And her daughter is your granddaughter. Quite possibly, the only one you'll ever get." I know it's a mistake as soon as the words leave my lips. He'll count my retort as a point in his favor, pleased that he was able to get a rise out of me.

I see a spark of victory in his eyes before he sneers dismissively, indicating his feelings on the matter. Mya doesn't exist to him, and he hates me reminding him of the daughter he abandoned. The only bloodline that matters to him is the one with the last name Wolfe. I sometimes wonder if I have other illegitimate siblings I haven't discovered yet. If so, I hope they're happier where they are. Being a part of this family never made anyone happy. My mother has spent the last 32 years in a loveless marriage based on convenience. She seems to have resigned herself to it, even if she's never been truly happy. In fact, I can't remember a single time when I've seen my parents pleased to see one another.

After spending the past two weeks with my sister and her new family, coming back to Georgia had been a bit of a letdown. The obvious love and happiness the King family members have for each other is such a departure from everything I grew up with. It's something I wouldn't have thought real if I hadn't seen it for myself. And now that I have seen it, I don't know how anyone could settle for a marriage like my parents have. It's so cold and distant. The Kings are so full of life and laughter, teasing and silliness. It's so far removed from everything I've ever known that it had been a shock to my system at first. But the family had welcomed me as one of their own, no questions asked. I'm Mya's family, therefore I'm their family too. It had been that simple.

I hadn't wanted to leave Mya and the tiny dark-haired baby that had stolen my heart. I'd taken one look at my niece and fallen head over heels in love with her. I'd surprised Mya and even myself by how much I wanted to just hold her and count her tiny fingers and toes. I'd had to battle with the rest of the family who all seem to be just as spellbound by the tiny princess. But eventually, the real world had beckoned, reminding me that I couldn't hide from my responsibilities forever.

Technically, it had been my father calling. Repeatedly. More specifically, his assistant had called me with twice daily reminders of every conference call and board meeting I was missing by 'lazing around with my poor relations'. That quote had pissed me off more than I'd let on. But I'd learned over the years that showing emotion when it comes to Charles Wolfe leads nowhere. As a matter of fact, it generally indicates weakness in his eyes. So, I'd brushed off his insults and made it clear that I'd be back in my own time, regardless of his wishes on the matter. That had only infuriated him even more, which I'd seen as a bonus. After two weeks, however, I'd forced myself to return home, promising my sister I'd visit again as soon as possible.

Returning to Savannah and to the family business had been harder than I'd anticipated. Seeing the cold, calculated look in my father's eyes when he conducts business is a far cry from the easy-going smiles I'd grown used to in Oak Hill. But it's time to shake off the end of vacation blues and get back to work. Charles Wolfe is a man who senses any type of weakness and pounces on it, no matter if I am his only son. I take a seat across from him and cross one ankle over a knee, making sure to look unbothered. I can tell by the slight tightening of his eyes that it annoys my father. Good posture indicates good breeding, after all. At least, that's what he's always preached at me. Which is why I go out of my way to slouch as much as possible in his presence. He doesn't remark upon it. Instead, he picks up a folder and holds it out for me to take. I hesitate for only a moment before reaching over and taking the folder from him.

"You missed a few things while you were gone."

He says it casually, but I detect a note of satisfaction in his voice. I'm instantly suspicious. What is he up to? He's watching me, waiting for me to read the file in my hands. For some reason, I don't want to. I can tell by the calculating look in his eyes that whatever is in this file isn't going to be something good. If he's happy about it, it's probably something awful. That's just the kind of man he is. I look away from my father and down to the file in my hands. The feeling of dread grows as I read.

When I finally understand what I'm reading, I feel like I've been punched in the gut. He's shutting down the small business department. My department. I'm not sure why I'm so shocked. He's made it clear since I first pitched the idea of taking on small business clients that he's against it. They're not lucrative enough to matter to him. They're not big enough names. They don't draw enough flashy attention to the company. I think about the half dozen people I've had assigned to that department and wonder what they'll do now. I don't bother to hide my fury as I meet his gaze.

"What the hell?" I say. "You went behind my back and shut down my projects?"

He waves a hand dismissively. "I warned you that your little charity projects weren't worth the time and energy spent on them."

"They haven't had time to—"

He cuts me off with a raised hand. "It's done," he says. "Those are the projected savings for Wolfe Industries without these anchors weighing us down."

My jaw is clenched so tightly I'm worried it might snap. I'd chosen those accounts with strategy and care, banking not on their current wealth, but on their futures. They might be small now, but with the right marketing and direction, they could be huge. And Wolfe Industries would have locked them in as clients before all the big names begin clamoring for them. But my asshole father can't seem to look toward the future. It was my vision that brought his crumbling company into the modern age. Why doesn't he trust me to continue that?

"Don't worry," he sneers, cutting into my thoughts. "No one is losing their job. I know how much you hate firing people. They'll be absorbed into other departments."

I feel a mild sense of relief at that knowledge, even as disgust for my father rolls through me. I'm surprised he gave any thought to the employees this move will affect.

He damned sure didn't think about the businesses who are counting on us to deliver these ad campaigns for them. For a lot of them, this can mean the difference between the business failing or thriving. But Charles Wolfe doesn't think about others. He's only ever been concerned about his bottom line.

He straightens and reaches for another folder on his desk. It's clear this discussion is over. He's made his decision and he won't be swayed on the matter. Typical. I don't know how he managed to run this company before I came to work. My grandfather built it and it was thriving before my father took over. His stubborn refusal to see the bigger picture and to look toward the future had nearly run Wolfe Industries into the ground. It had been my vision that brought the company from the brink of bankruptcy to where it is today. But my father refuses to acknowledge my part, publicly or privately. We both know the company would crumble if left solely in his care. But his pride won't allow him to admit that he relies on my help. Instead, he makes sure I know who's in control every chance he gets. Today's news just reinforces that. Part of me wonders if he'd done it in retaliation for me leaving so abruptly to see Mya. I'd like to think he wouldn't do something like this for such a petty reason, but I don't doubt he'd stoop that low.

"What do you know about Arthur Mitchell?" he asks, surprising me with the abrupt change of subject.

Though I'm still pissed at him, I know him well enough to know that we've moved on from the topic of my dismantled department. It won't help me to bring it up again right now. I'll have to come up with some other way to get those clients back on our roster. With a sigh, I begin reciting the few facts I know about Arthur Mitchell.

"Self-made billionaire," I say. "He owns a shipping company, which is where he made the bulk of his money. He's made sound investments over the past 20 years which is how he turned his millions into billions. Rumors are that he's looking to start his own luxury airline. But that's just speculation at this point. He's also a bit of a recluse, avoids most public outings and keeps to himself."

I sit back in my chair, returning to my relaxed posture as my father nods in what might be approval.

"Right," he says, returning his gaze to his desk. "Well, you're having lunch with him Monday at Harbor Oaks."

Shock hits me and I bolt upright in my chair. "What? How? Why?" Charles shoots me a look at my lack of articulate speech, but I can't worry about that right now. I'm still reeling over the fact that I'm having lunch with Arthur Mitchell.

"You'll be there to represent Wolfe Industries." He looks as me as though that should be obvious. I know he wants me to pull the information out of him. It's why he's dragging this out. Normally, I wouldn't give him the satisfaction, but the surprise of his announcement still has me off my game.

"Why am I meeting him?" I ask, ignoring the little flash of smug satisfaction in my father's eyes.

He takes a second to stack the papers on his desk as though we're talking about the weather or something equally benign. Finally, he looks up at me and speaks.

"The rumors are more than that," he says. "Mitchell is looking to expand his empire to include a private luxury airline complete with private airports. He doesn't want his guests to mill about with the thousands of idiot families on their way to Disneyworld or the Grand Canyon."

I can hear the disgust in his tone at the idea of families taking vacations together. I'm not surprised as our family never took a single vacation when I was growing up. My mother and I would spend summers at our house on Tybee Island when I was young. Sometimes my father would join us for a weekend, but not often. Not that either of us missed him when he wasn't around.

The summer I turned 16, my father put an end to my summer trips to the island. That's when I started joining him at the office. And when I finally realized what a bastard he truly is. With a start, I realize he's still talking. I pull myself out of memories of the past and back to the conversation.

"He's looking for a local company to liaise with his PR people," Charles says. "He doesn't want to piss off the locals. I can't understand why he cares so much. It's not like they're his target customers. Most of them can't even afford to fly first class." The disgust in his voice makes me clench my jaw to keep from telling him off.

I take a breath to calm my anger before speaking. "You're saying he's thinking of Wolfe Industries as his liaison?"

He shrugs. "At the moment, he's undecided. It's your job to convince him to sign with us." His eyes narrow as he pins me with a sharp glare. "Don't fuck this up."

I allow a humorless smile to curve my lips. "As always, these father/son talks are inspiring," I say, rising to my feet.

He rolls his eyes and gives a little wave of his hand. I've seen that move enough to know I'm being dismissed.

Before I turn to go, a thought occurs to me. I feel a hint of excitement course through me. I look at my father who's already turned his attention back to the files on his desk.

"If I land Mitchell," I say, gaining his attention once more. "I want to reinstate the small business department."

Charles doesn't look up from his papers. "No."

I grit my teeth and force myself to take a deep breath. I know how Charles Wolfe operates. He never gives in immediately. In any bargain, he needs to feel like he's coming out on top.

"With the right marketing, those accounts are going to take off in the next five years," I say. "It's only going to make Wolfe more money."

I can see the slight hesitation, and I pounce on it. He knows I'm good at what I do, whether he wants to acknowledge that or not. He can't deny my outstanding track record.

"With Arthur Mitchell as our client, Wolfe will be the leader on the east coast," I say.

"What makes you so sure you can get him to sign with us?" he asks with a derisive sneer.

I hide my annoyance at his doubt. "Because I'm the best closer at this company," I say. "You know it as well as I do. If I say I'll get him, I will."

"Mitchell isn't like your little bar owner friend in that Podunk town," he says. "He's elite. He's richer than anyone you've ever worked with. And he doesn't put up with bullshit. You know his reputation."

I nod. "Of course. I can handle him."

He studies me for a long moment. I can tell the exact moment he makes up his mind. His shoulders drop the slightest bit, and he dips his head in a single nod.

"Fine," he says on a sigh. "If you get him to sign, I'll let you have your little pet projects back. Not that you'll have time for them."

He returns his gaze to the papers on his desk. This time I know I've been truly dismissed. I leave before he can call me back and change his mind.

CHAPTER 2

Piper

I smile and wave at the four older gentlemen sitting on the benches in front of the café. They're permanent fixtures on those benches. I see them every day on my walk to work, and I wave at them every day. And every day they avert their eyes and pretend not to notice me. I sigh when, as one, they all four direct their gazes to the newspapers in their hands. Must be a riveting article in the Peach Tree Gazette today. I sigh and continue walking. One of these days, I'll get a smile from one of those old men. I'm determined to keep trying until I do.

"Are you still there?"

My sister's voice comes through my phone, pulling me back to our conversation.

"I'm here," I say.

"Good," she says. "I thought maybe you'd died of boredom or something."

I roll my eyes at her idea of a joke. She's more of a city girl. She doesn't understand why I moved to a town this small.

"Layna, I'm fine," I insist for what feels like the hundredth time. "I love it here."

I hear her heave a sigh through the phone. "You're just telling me that so I won't worry."

I smile, knowing she's partly right. I don't want my big sister worrying about me. She worries too much already. She always has. I know she does it out of love. It's why I try not to get too annoyed with her about it. She practically raised me, after all. She's the reason I finished high school and got into college and she's the reason I have my business now. Such as it is. I grind my teeth at my own thoughts. Piping Hot Brews is a business. Even if it's not exactly successful yet. I tell myself for the millionth time that it will be. It just takes time for people to come around to new things in a town this small.

"I don't know why you won't come back to Atlanta," Layna says, rehashing an old argument.

"We've been over this, Lay," I say. "I'm happy here in Peach Tree. I know it's hard for you to understand, but I love the small-town life."

"I can breathe here," I say, sucking in a deep breath of smog-free air and blowing it out loudly.

Layna sighs again, but this time it's in resignation. She knows I'm not changing my mind. Stubbornness seems to be the one trait we both inherited from our late mother. When we make up our minds about something, we don't back down without a fight.

"How's business?" she asks, shifting to the one subject I'd rather not discuss.

I can't lie to my sister. I've never been able to. For one thing, she can see right through any lie I try to tell her. For another, I've always been a terrible liar. I get sweaty and red-faced if I try. So, I don't. Instead, I try for a bright tone when I answer.

"Not bad," I say, knowing she can hear what I'm not saying.

There's a beat of silence before Layna speaks again. "I don't know why the people in that town are so damned stubborn. If they'd just try your coffee and pastries, they'd know how amazing you are. Is this because you didn't name the place after a damned peach?"

I laugh. "I think they're just set in their ways," I say. "Not used to change. They'll come around."

"If you say so." Layna sounds skeptical.

I try not to let her lack of confidence bother me. I know it's not me she doesn't have faith in. It's the rest of the world she's convinced will let us down. Not that she's had a lot of reasons to think otherwise. Losing our mother at a young age changed my sister and me in different ways. She stepped up and became the responsible big sister, looking out for me any way she could. As for me, I came to the realization that most people, if given the chance, will let you down. Layna has been the one exception to that rule. She's always been there for me, no matter what. Which is just another reason I need Piping Hot Brews to be a success. I don't want Layna's faith in me to be misplaced. I don't want to let her down.

"I promise, Layna," I say. "It's just a matter of time. I'll have them eating out of my hand in no time."

I can hear Layna trying to inject a hint of optimism into her voice. "I know you will, Piper."

As it does every morning, my gaze lands on the town's water tower and I can't help but stare at it as I walk. It's massive, round and painted to look exactly like a peach. Right down to the blush-colored line down one side that's meant to look like the indention most peaches have. The first time I saw the giant, peach-colored monstrosity, I laughed for five full minutes, tears streaming down my face. I'd snapped a picture and sent it to Layna with the caption, "I guess subtlety isn't their thing."

Within seconds, she'd texted back. "Please tell me that's not really the water tower. What's the school mascot? A giant eggplant?"

That had set off a fresh round of laughter until I'd remembered that I was outside, on a public street and if people thought I was crazy, they might not want to buy my coffee. I'd sobered up and assured Layna that the giant peach-shaped water tower was absolutely real, and that the school mascot was actually a bear. Today, I manage to hold in my laughter when I look at the tower, but I can't stop the smile that curves my lips. This town definitely has its quirks.

"Shit," Layna says, pulling me out of my musings. "I'm going to be late. I gotta go, Piper."

"No worries," I say. "I'm almost at the shop anyway." I still have a few blocks left of my walk, but my sister will feel less guilty if she doesn't think she's rushing me off the phone.

"We'll talk soon?" she asks.

"Absolutely."

I end the call and slip my cell into my back pocket, enjoying the morning sunlight. It's not unbearably hot yet, but the humidity is already in high gear, and I know this summer will be a scorcher. I pass a woman pushing a toddler in a stroller and give her a smile and a wave. She doesn't exactly shun me, but the look she gives can't truly be called a smile. Her lips curve slightly in my direction, but she looks away immediately, pretending to soothe the perfectly happy toddler.

I sigh. I've been in Peach Tree for nearly 9 months. You'd think the locals would eventually realize I'm not going anywhere and start to welcome me. I thought small towns were supposed to be friendlier than big cities. So far, I'm not seeing that. Well, that's not exactly true. I see plenty of happy, smiling, welcoming faces all over this town when I go for my daily jog. Those smiles just aren't directed at me. It's clear I'm considered an interloper. I'd moved to town and bought the old diner which had been closed for nearly 5 years. I'd seen the potential in the old building and I knew it would be perfect for my coffee shop. Apparently, the people of Peach Tree hadn't agreed. I'd been met with accusatory glares when I'd taken down the old sign proclaiming the building to be the "Peach Blossom Café" and replaced it with the one I'd had made for "Piping Hot Brews". Maybe Layna was right, and I should have kept the peach theme going and chosen something that fit the town rather than playing off my own name. I'd thought it clever at the time, but maybe I'd been wrong.

As I do every day on my walk to the shop, I survey the town, taking in the storefronts and businesses getting ready for the day. I wave at the young man flipping over the sign in the front window of Peachy Clean Dry-Cleaning service. He gives me a strained nod and turns away quickly. I bite back another sigh. As I approach the Peach Pit Boutique, a woman comes out carrying a large sign and an easel to display it.

I hurry my steps, intending to help the woman with the awkwardly large sign. As I reach her, however, she immediately shakes her head and shies away from my help, the large sign nearly slipping from her hands.

"Let me help," I say in what I think is a polite tone.

"That's okay," the woman says, her voice slightly strained. "I've got it."

Before I can reach for the sign again, the woman hurriedly places it onto the stand and straightens. "See?" she says, gesturing toward the slightly off-kilter sign. "No problem." She gives me a tight-lipped smile and hurries back inside the store.

I stand there for a moment, wondering just what this town seems to have against me. With a sigh, I eventually turn away from the Peach Pit Boutique and the crooked sign and continue down the street toward my own place of business.

"Don't mind Jenna," a female voice comes from my right.

I glance over and see a woman standing in the doorway to Peach Tree's one and only beauty shop. She's sporting shoulder-length blonde hair with hot pink streaks scattered throughout and wearing a black tank top and a pair of ripped jeans. I cast her a questioning look and she tilts her head back toward the boutique.

"She's terrified of the elders," the woman says. I assume that was meant to clear things up, but it only leaves me more confused.

"The elders?" I question.

The woman studies me for a moment before seeming to reach some sort of conclusion. She sighs and gives me a sympathetic smile.

"I forget what it's like to be new in this town," she says. "You need someone to give you the quick and dirty. I guess that'll have to be me."

I'm still standing there on the sidewalk in front of the beauty shop, no doubt with a look of utter bewilderment on my face. This is the most any of the town's people have spoken to me at one time since I opened my shop.

"I'm Harlow St. James," the woman says, holding out a hand.

"Piper Brooks," I say, shaking the offered hand.

She smiles, a genuine smile, that lights up her face and makes her green eyes sparkle. "Piper. Piping Hot Brews," she muses. "Clever."

I'm still slightly confused, but I smile at the compliment. "I thought so," I say. "Not that the rest of this town agrees."

Harlow waves a hand and rolls her eyes. "Don't let them get to you," she says. "The only word-play they're interested in is in reference to that damned fruit."

I manage to stifle my laugh. "I noticed the ongoing theme," I say in a dry tone.

Harlow's gaze goes past me to peer around at the businesses lining the main avenue and shrugs. "I'd like to believe there's a reason for it, but I think it all boils down to conformity. It's easier to go with the flow around here, so most people do it."

I study the pink tips of her hair and the tattoo I can see peeking out from behind the strap of her tank top.

"I'm guessing you don't buy into that?" I ask.

Harlow laughs. "What gave me away?"

I look at the sign on the window of her shop. In curling gold script, it reads simply, "Harlow's". I nod toward it.

"Not a peach reference in sight," I say.

She follows my gaze and nods. "I had a bit of an advantage though," she says, leaning toward me as though imparting a secret. "I was born and raised in this town."

I nod. "I figured it was something like that," I say. I glance back down the street, imagining unseen eyes peering out from the windows of the shops and businesses behind me.

"Are you going to be shunned for talking to the city girl?" I ask.

Harlow waves a dismissive hand. "I'll be fine," she says. "I've got the only salon in town. I also won over Miss Dottie three years ago when I fixed her hair after she went to one of those chain salons. Now, I'm the only person she'll let touch her hair. So, I'm practically untouchable." She shrugs as if I'm supposed to understand the significance of that statement.

"Miss Dottie?" I ask, letting my confusion show.

Harlow looks at me with something akin to pity. "You've got a lot to learn about this town, city girl."

Opening the door to her shop, Harlow flips the sign back over to read 'closed' before closing the door behind her and looping her arm through mine.

"Come on," she says with a smile. "I've got some time before my first client. Let's go check out this coffee shop of yours and I'll fill you in on a few things."

Slightly overwhelmed by this woman's take-charge attitude, I just nod.

"Um, okay," I say, leading the way.

It takes less than five minutes to make it from Harlow's shop to the front door of Piping Hot Brews. Harlow doesn't stop talking the entire time. By the time I lead the way inside, I've learned that Harlow has owned the beauty shop for five years and has lived in Peach Tree for most of her life. She lived in Atlanta for a few years but moved back when she decided to open her shop.

We make our way inside and I wave a greeting to Stevie, Piping Hot Brews' lone employee, a quiet young woman fresh out of high school. Stevie hasn't said as much, but I think she's going to leave in the fall for college. That would leave me with zero employees. Not that I'll be able to afford to pay someone if this place doesn't start making more money soon.

Oblivious to my internal monologue, Harlow waves and smiles at Stevie. "How's your mom?" Harlow asks.

Stevie's expression brightens and she returns Harlow's smile. "She's good. She was just saying how she needs to book an appointment soon."

Harlow's smile grows even brighter, if possible. "Tell her to call or text me anytime and I'll make time, even if I'm booked up."

Stevie nods. "Yes, ma'am."

I watch the interaction with some fascination. That's the most information I've heard Stevie volunteer since she accepted the job here. I always got the feeling she feels like she's betraying the town by working for me. She's never been particularly warm toward me, even if she's never been downright rude to me. She's friendly with the few customers we do get, but nothing like what I just witnessed with Harlow. I narrow my eyes at the woman standing beside me.

"How did you do that?" I ask in a low voice.

Harlow looks at me, brows raised in question. "Do what?"

I dip my head in Stevie's direction where the girl is busy loading one of the grinders with fresh beans. "Get her to smile and talk to you," I say, like it should be obvious. "She hardly says 2 words to me in a day."

Harlow smiles, shaking her head. "That's because you're an outsider," she says. "You might as well be a damned Yankee to the people of this town. You're from the big city. People here don't trust the cities. They're set in their ways. You have to show them that you're just as small-town as they are." She leans closer and speaks the next part in a lower voice. "Even if you're not."

I roll my eyes, suddenly defensive. Every southerner knows that being called a Yankee ranks right up there with the phrase, 'Bless your heart'. It's downright offensive.

"Please," I say. "I'm from Atlanta, not New York. I'm a southern girl through and through. I even spent summers with my grandparents out in the country, too. I'm not just a big city girl."

Harlow shrugs. "You don't have to convince me. I don't judge people based on the same criteria as the rest of this town." She lifts a strand of pink hair and waves it in my direction. "And, in case you haven't noticed, I also don't go out of my way to worry about what they think." She sighs. "But, like I said earlier, I'm nearly untouchable in this town."

"Yeah," I say. "You mentioned someone called Miss Dottie?"

From the corner of my eye, I notice Stevie pause in the act of pulling a carton of milk from the refrigerator, her gaze going to me and Harlow. I glance over at her and she resumes her activity as though nothing had happened. But I'd seen it. I mentally file that information away.

Harlow's attention is on the chalkboard menu above the counter. I'd taken hours designing and drawing it. I'd thought it would be eye-catching, a conversation piece. So far, the only eyes that had seen it have been mine and Stevie's.

"I love the menu," Harlow says, pointing up at it. "Did you draw all of that?"

I follow her gaze to the colorful renderings of ocean creatures adorning the black chalkboard and nod. "I thought it was a fun idea," I say with a shrug. "Not that it matters. There's no one here to see it." I sigh. "Do you want a coffee?"

Harlow studies the board for another few seconds before nodding. "I'll have an iced mocha latte with an extra shot of espresso and whipped cream."

I smile. "Coming right up."

I move to walk behind the counter, but Stevie waves me away. "I've got this," she says. "You want your usual?"

I nod. "Thanks, Stevie."

I turn back to Harlow who's gazing around at the rest of the shop, turning a small circle as she takes everything in. Not for the first time, I try to see the place as she must be seeing it. I try to see it as a customer. The seating areas are comfortable and arranged to make each setting feel like a private little nook. There are bookshelves along some of the walls filled with paperbacks and signs encouraging people to take a book or leave a book. The lighting is bright enough for people to see to work or read, but low enough that it's not hard on the eyes.

"You transformed this place," she say, finally. She points to one corner of the large room, smiling. "My friends and I used to camp out in a booth over there after school and gossip about hot boys." She points to a cozy leather chair near the opposite wall. "There used to be an old jukebox over there."

All at once I understand. This place used to mean something to Harlow. Does the rest of the town feel the same way? Do they see me as some interloper who stole a piece of the town's history? *Shit.* I've been looking at this as a business venture, but the people of this town see it as something more. No wonder they hate me. Harlow notices my stricken look and her eyes grow wide. She waves her hands, shaking her head.

"Oh, no!" she says, rushing toward me. "It's nothing like that. My mom had a second job here in the evenings. After school, I'd come here and sit in one of the booths in the back and do my homework. This place was kind of a shithole." She makes a face of disgust. "I'm honestly shocked it never got shut down by the health department."

She gives a little laugh and reaches out to squeeze my arm. "I'm probably the last person left in this town with a single fond memory of this place. And that's just because so much of my childhood was spent waiting for my mom to get off work so we could go home."

She gives a little laugh like it's no big deal, but I think I see a hint of sadness in her green eyes. I know I just met this woman, but I feel an immediate connection to her. Like maybe I'm making my first friend in Peach Tree. I give her a smile.

"You had me thinking I'd destroyed some kind of town monument," I say.

She shakes her head, a small smile on her face. "I'm the only one left," she says, looking around the room.

Something about the way Harlow said that makes me want to pull her into a hug. Which is ridiculous considering we just met, and I don't know anything about her. But her voice had sounded small and sad, not at all like the bubbly woman who'd talked my ear off on the walk here. I open my mouth to speak, but Stevie calls out before I can, announcing that our coffees are ready. As if a spell has been broken, the melancholy look leaves Harlow's face, and she lights up. Her eyes brighten and she smiles widely in Stevie's direction.

"Thank the gods," she says, making her way over to the counter to take her cup.

I decide to let it go. Whatever had caused that look on Harlow's face is clearly something she doesn't want to discuss. She strikes me as the type of person who doesn't hold back unless there's a reason. If she wanted to say something, she would. Besides, we just met. It's too early to start diving into our deep, dark pasts.

"This place really does look amazing," Harlow says, lifting her cup to her mouth. She takes a long sip from the cup, eyes going wide.

"Holy shit!" her eyes dart to Stevie, then back to me. "This is delicious. Seriously." She takes another longer sip. "What's the secret?"

I laugh. "I'd tell you, but I'd have to kill you."

Harlow shrugs and takes another drink from her cup. "Might be worth it."

I take a sip from my own mug as I lead Harlow over to a table in the corner. "I'm glad you like it," I say, taking a seat. "Since you're probably the only person in this town who's tried it."

She takes another long sip. "That's a damned shame," she says. "Because this?" She points down at her coffee. "Is the best iced latte this town has ever seen."

I feel a sense of pride wash over me. Yes, Stevie had prepared the drink, but I'd been the one to teach her and the recipe is my own. I'd been the one to choose each ingredient and procure it for the shop. Hours of research had gone into the right beans and the right roast for each to achieve the exact right coffee drinking experience. I look around the empty shop and sigh. Too bad only Harlow will ever know if all that work paid off. I feel a hand on my wrist and look up to see Harlow giving it a light squeeze. Her eyes are sympathetic.

"They'll come around," she says, as if reading my mind.

I nod. "I just hope it's sooner, rather than later. I can't afford to keep this place open indefinitely without making any money."

"Well, you just gained a loyal customer in me," Harlow says, hefting her cup in a salute.

I lift my own mug and smile. "I'm not sure you can drink enough iced lattes to single-handedly keep the lights on around here." I laugh.

"Probably not," she concedes. "But some of my clients are the most influential women in this town. I'm going to be telling everyone who'll listen how great your coffee is."

Curiosity hits me again and I remember her comment from before about the mysterious Miss Dottie. "What were you saying about Miss Dottie?" I ask, realizing that she'd never gotten to the bottom of that statement.

Harlow's gaze turns serious as she looks at me. "Just how much do you really know about the town you moved to, Piper Brooks?"

"Clearly not as much as I should," I say.

Harlow leans toward me across the table. "Allow me to educate you."

Over the next half hour, Harlow fills me in on the unofficial hierarchy of the town of Peach Tree. I learn more about the inner workings and behind-the-scenes action than I ever wanted to know. For instance, the mayor might be in charge on paper, but he's not the one who runs Peach Tree. It's his mother who pulls the strings. Mayor Thompson is a lifelong bachelor. His mother, Miss Dottie, lives with him. Everyone assumes it's so he can help her and be there for her as she ages, but Harlow is convinced that the woman is more capable than she lets people believe. Either way, she's the one who dictates what happens around Peach Tree.

"So, if you want your shop to succeed," Harlow says. "You have to win her over."

"Does she like lattes?" I ask, jokingly.

Harlow shakes her head. "She doesn't drink coffee. Just tea."

I deflate slightly. The shop does sell tea, but I don't know as much about it as I do coffee. It only takes up a small portion of the menu. I don't think I can afford to devote the time and money into specialty teas. But it's something to think about. I stop my rambling thoughts. What the hell is wrong with me? Am I really thinking of tailoring the entire shop's menu to suit one woman on the off chance that she'll decide to stop in? I sigh. Yes. I am. I'm desperate. By my calculations, I've got enough savings to keep this place afloat for a few more months before I'll have to admit defeat. But I'm not going down without a fight. By the time Harlow leaves to head back to her salon, I've learned more about Peach Tree than I thought possible.

CHAPTER 3

Luke

I'm early to meet Arthur Mitchell at his country club. I prefer to arrive early to business meetings. It's something I've always done. It shows the client you care enough to make them a priority. Also, showing up first allows me time to compose myself and makes it feel more like I have a home field advantage. That doesn't help me today, however. Mitchell is already seated at a table when I arrive nearly a half hour before we're scheduled to meet. A smiling hostess leads me through the dining room to a large table where I see Arthur Mitchell already seated and sipping iced tea.

Damn. Clearly, he also likes to be early to business meetings. I smile as I approach the table, making sure to hide the nerves I'm feeling. I'm about to sit across the table from one of the wealthiest men in the country. I still can't quite believe it. This is the deal of a lifetime for Wolfe Industries. If it works out, it will be the most important deal of my career. No pressure.

Mr. Mitchell stands when I approach the table. He doesn't smile as he greets me, shaking my hand with a strong grip.

"Mr. Mitchell, sir," I say. "It's nice to finally meet you. Luke Wolfe."

He gives me an appraising look, seeming to size me up before we take our seats.

"I'm hoping it's not a waste of my time," he says. "The last guy I met with had no vision."

I smile, not letting his words bother me. "That's not the case with me, sir."

He narrows his eyes. "We'll see about that."

A familiar feeling rises in me, and my nerves settle. It's the same feeling I get every time I have a hard-to-please client. Determination. I know Arthur Mitchell is going to be a challenge. A man like him doesn't get to be where he is by accepting every deal laid out before him. I'm going to have to impress him. Lucky for me, I came prepared. I reach into my briefcase and pull out the proposals I've created for this meeting.

Mitchell still looks skeptical, but he takes one and follows along as I lay out my vision for this partnership. Over the next half hour, I do most of the talking with Arthur asking the occasional question to clarify something. We order lunch. He laughs at one of my jokes. By the time we finish our club sandwiches, he's asked me to call him Art. Holy shit. This is going to work.

Art orders us a round of drinks after lunch. A server has just placed them on the table before us when I see Art turn to smile at someone behind me. He stands and I turn to follow his gaze, standing when I see a woman approaching.

"Melody, dear," Art says with an indulgent smile. "How was your morning at the spa? Relaxing, I hope?"

The woman leans in to kiss Art's cheek, her lips barely touching his skin. She scoffs, waving a hand. "If you can call it that. I don't think they know the meaning of the word here."

We're at the most luxurious resort in the state. The spa here has an outstanding reputation. I'm not sure what Melody is accustomed to, but I can only assume her experience today was an anomaly. I've done my homework, though. I know that Art has been married to Melody for the past two years. She's only a few years older than me, blonde, petite, attractive. Art is nearly 20 years older than she is. Which doesn't mean anything on its own, but when you add in the man's wealth, it does point to a few reasons why she might have married him. But that's all speculation. She turns her gaze on me as if just noticing I'm there, though she had to walk past me to get to Art.

"Oh, hello," she says, her gaze moving from my head to my toes and back up again. The look has me feeling like I need a shower. "Who's this?"

Her voice has shifted from the annoyed tone of before to a low purr. Art puts an arm around her shoulders, attempting to pull her to his side, but she stiffens and keeps a few inches between them as she turns all her focus on me.

"Mel, honey," Art says. "This is Luke Wolfe. He and I are thinking of working together while we're here in Georgia."

"So nice to meet you," Mel says, smiling as she holds out her hand.

I shake her hand and release it as quickly as possible, but I don't miss the way Mel's grip tightens on mine before I can pull my hand away.

"Lovely to meet you, Mrs. Mitchell," I say. "Your husband and I were just about to wrap things up. I won't keep him from you much longer."

The woman actually bats her lashes at me. I didn't think people really did that.

"Oh, don't be silly!" She swats a hand in my direction, but I manage to duck out of her reach before she makes contact with my chest. "I'm happy to join you two."

That sounds like the last thing I want, but Art smiles happily and pulls out a chair for his wife. I can't very well refuse now. So, I give her a polite smile and take my seat. Art and I try to steer the conversation back to business and my proposal, but it's clear that Mel isn't interested in that. She keeps monopolizing the conversation, bringing up topics like her massage and how she hasn't felt so relaxed in ages.

"I do love a man who's good with his hands," she says, shooting me a wink while Art is talking to our server.

Each time I look over at her, it's as if her chair has moved closer to mine. By the time Art calls for the check, I'm no closer to convincing him to sign with Wolfe Industries than I had been at the beginning of our meeting. But Mel has somehow managed to get close enough to me that I can feel her foot rubbing on the back of my calf. Part of me wants to believe she doesn't know it's my leg. Maybe she thinks it's the chair or the table leg. Yeah. That's it. She can't possibly be rubbing my leg under the table while her husband sits across from us. Can she?

I get my answer when Art excuses himself to use the restroom. The hand on my knee is unmistakable. My eyes shoot down to where Mel's hand is resting, but somehow the rest of me is frozen in surprise. She must interpret my hesitation as agreement because I watch as her hand begins to slide upward. The movement is enough to jolt me from my surprised stupor and I jump to my feet. Thinking fast, I pull my phone from my pocket and pretend to answer a call.

"Hello? Oh hi, honey!" I smile widely. "I'm at a business meeting right now." I pause as if listening and nod. "Okay, but just for a second." I turn to shoot Mel a look of apology. "I'm so sorry," I whisper, ignoring the glare she throws my way. "I have to take this." Then I walk out of the dining room.

What the hell was that? Why had I just panicked and pretended to be talking to a significant other? I've never done anything like that before. I've had women flirt with me before. Not all of them had been unmarried, either. But I've never had a married woman be so bold with her husband seated five feet away. My instincts must be getting rusty because I did not see that coming. None of my research on the Mitchell's indicated infidelity. But clearly, Mrs. Mitchell has no qualms about trying to sleep with men she's just met. The idea of that fills me with a kind of sick horror.

Mel is pretty enough, in a plastic kind of way. But I've never been attracted to that Barbie doll look. Not that there's anything wrong with it. It's just not for me. But even if she was my type physically, there's no way I would act on it. For one thing, she's married. To one of the richest men in the world. He could have me killed and no one would ever find my body. Not that he'd seemed overly bothered by her behavior. Maybe he's used to it? Or he's oblivious. She'd definitely timed that wink for a moment when he'd been distracted. For another thing, her behavior is a total turn-off. There's nothing wrong with a woman who knows what she wants and goes for it. But it's a good idea to know if what—or who—you want wants you back. And I don't want her.

I just need to make it a point to keep my distance from her for the rest of the meal. With any luck, Art and I will close this deal within the week, and I won't have to see her again. When I think sufficient time has passed that Art will be back from the bathroom, I make my way back to the table. Thankfully, Art is back in his chair when I return.

"I'm so sorry about that," I say with a smile. "Can't keep my girl waiting." When I slide my chair out to sit, I make sure to pull it away from the table at an angle so it puts more distance between me and Mel. I need to stay far away from that woman before she gets the idea that I like her attention.

"I know how that goes," Art says with a nod. "Listen, I hate to cut this short, but I have a video conference call with Tokyo in a half hour. I thought your proposal had a lot of potential. Better than others I've read through in the last month."

"Thank you," I say with a smile.

"But I'm not quite convinced," Art adds, tempering some of my excitement at his previous comments. "You should come by the house for dinner next week," Art says. "We can talk more about your plans for my money."

"Oh yes," Mel says, her eyes lighting up with excitement. "We'd love to have you."

Something about the way she says it makes my skin crawl. It sounds more like she'd like to have me as the meal. I don't want to offend Art, but there's no way I'm going anywhere near that woman's home. She's liable to eat me alive.

"That sounds wonderful," I say with a smile that I hope looks convincing.

Art pulls out his phone and scrolls through it for a few seconds. "I'm afraid Thursday is the only night I'm free," he says. "I'm trying to finish all these projects before our big beach vacation." He turns to Mel and shoots her a wink.

Mel smiles at her husband before turning back to me. "Come on, Luke," she says. "What do you say?"

I know what I should say. I should agree to the dinner and impress the hell out of Art when I go. It should be easy. But I hesitate.

"I can make sure to have your favorite meal prepared," Mel says, leaning closer.

She uses her arms to press her breasts together, giving me an eyeful of her cleavage. I know without a doubt that this woman is already making plans to get me alone once I'm in her house. And there's no way I'd be able to convince Art I was innocent if he walked in on her with her hand in my lap.

I open my mouth to politely decline, citing a prior engagement, but what comes out is, "I'm so sorry, but I have plans with my girlfriend that night."

Where the hell did that come from? I don't have a girlfriend. I'm not even dating anyone. Why am I trying to get out of this dinner? I need this deal to work. So, his wife is a little pushy. So, what? I can handle her. And now I've made up a girlfriend?

Art chuckles. "I know what it's like to put your lady before all else," he says. "It's why I let Mel convince me to take this trip out to the island for two weeks. She says I work too hard."

Mel either doesn't hear her husband or she's choosing to ignore him. She shoots me a disdainful look. "Girlfriend? It's not like you're married. This is an important business matter."

I dial up the charm, shooting them both a winning smile. "Ah, but she's important to me. Far more important than my career, I'm afraid."

I don't know where the hell this is coming from. I sound like a lovesick idiot. Art seems to be buying it, though. Even if his wife doesn't seem to care.

Art looks immediately enthralled. It's clear he's a big romantic at heart. "If she's more important than your career, she's got to be something special, Wolfe."

"Oh, she is," I say, lowering my gaze as if I'm being coy.

"Then why is she still just a girlfriend?" Art asks with a wink.

I keep my gaze lowered. I hope it comes off as shy and aloof, but the truth is that I'm stalling. *Because she doesn't* exist, I think. But I can't say that. After a moment, I say the one thing I think might satisfy Art and get Mel off my back.

"That's the thing, Art" I say. "I've been trying to find the right moment to propose."

"Hot damn, boy! Why didn't you say so?" He slaps me on the back. "You should bring her to dinner next week.

I'd like to meet the woman who's got you thinking of settling down."

Panic slams through me. I can't bring my girlfriend to dinner. I don't have a fucking girlfriend! What the hell am I going to do?

"I'll have to check in with her," I say with a grin. "You know how women are when you throw last minute plans at them."

Art rolls his eyes. "Don't I ever."

Mel glares at her husband, but if Art notices, he doesn't let on.

"We wouldn't want to get you into trouble," she coos at me. "If she's unavailable, you're certainly still welcome to come."

I just smile, though I'm panicking inside.

"Call her and ask her," Mel says.

"What?" Panic slams into me. I can't call her. She doesn't exist.

"We don't mind," Art says with a wave of his hand. "Ask her if she's able to make it to dinner Thursday night."

Thinking fast, I glance at my watch and wince.

"She's actually at work right now," I lie. "She called me with an emergency question, but she's super busy today. I'll talk to her as soon as I see her later this evening."

"Of course. We understand." Art says. He glances at his own watch and stands. "We've got to be going now. We look forward to seeing you and your lovely young lady Thursday night. My assistant will be in touch with the details."

I stand, smiling. "Absolutely. Wouldn't miss it for the world."

They're gone before I can understand what the hell just happened. Had I really just made up a girlfriend on the spot? And promised to bring her to dinner next week? I'm so screwed.

Luke

When I show up at Linc's house later that night, his brother Cole opens the door. He gives me a nod of greeting before moving aside to let me in.

"Come on," he says. "I'm having a beer out back. Linc's putting Ella to bed." Cole walks toward the back door and I follow.

My mind is still reeling with everything that happened today at lunch. Everything I said. The lies I told. What the hell happened? This isn't like me. I don't lie. Not in my business, and not in my personal life. I've always prided myself on being honest in all my dealings. So, why had I fabricated a serious girlfriend out of thin air? I'd panicked. That's all I can think. I know how important it is to get Art to sign with Wolfe Industries. So many companies' futures are riding on the outcome of this deal. I can't afford to screw it up. That's why I'd lied.

Cole and I make our way outside and the sultry night air hits me. It's hot, but not as bad as I know it'll be when summer is in full swing. Tonight, it's bearable, even with the humidity. At least the mosquitoes aren't swarming yet. With a sigh, I flop down into the patio chair. I take the beer Cole holds out to me with a nod of thanks.

He looks at me in confusion. "Linc didn't tell me you were stopping by," he says.

"That's because I didn't tell him," I say, twisting the top off the beer.

Cole raises a brow. He knows me. He knows I rarely do anything without a plan. The simple act of me stopping by unannounced tonight is huge.

"You okay?" he asks.

"I'm so screwed," I say on a sigh.

Linc chooses that exact moment to walk out onto the patio, so he hears my pronouncement. He gives me a look with raised brows, taking in my untucked shirt, missing tie and what I assume is wild hair from me raking my fingers through it all afternoon.

"You look a little more defeated than usual," he says, reaching for his own beer.

I glare at his bright tone and teasing smile. "No need to be so happy about it," I grumble.

Linc laughs. "I'm not," he says. "It's just weird to see you this unraveled. What happened?"

I take a long pull from the icy beer in my hand and look at my best friend. "I need a girlfriend."

There's a long beat of silence before the laughter starts. My jaw clenches and I look up at the darkening sky, waiting for it to subside. Linc manages to get control of himself before Cole does. I glare at the younger of the two brothers.

"You finished yet?"

Cole wipes at his eyes and nods, still smiling. "Almost," he says, chuckling once more.

I roll my eyes at him and turn my attention to Linc. As the older of the two brothers, he's always been slightly more mature and level-headed, especially after he became a father while he was still in college. He'd stepped up and taken on the role of single parent with the utmost seriousness, surprising all of us with how well-suited he is to the role. It's been 8 years since Ella was born and it's obvious to anyone with eyes that Lincoln Prescott is wrapped around her perfect fingers.

The same can be said for Cole, Linc's younger brother. Since becoming an uncle, Cole has grown up a lot and become a better man, even if he's still sowing some of his wild oats. Linc and I tease him about his wild ways every chance we get. But the truth is that most of Cole's exploits are on the tamer side these days. He's even opened his own business and has mostly stopped his man-whore ways. Mostly. Cole's bar was the first business I took on as a client in the small business division at Wolfe Industries. With Cole's vision and my marketing expertise, we'd turned The Peach Fuzz into a popular spot. It has the potential to be even more successful if things keep going the way they are now.

These two have been my best friends since college, and I know that no matter what happens, I can count on them for anything. Just as they know the same can be said of me. That doesn't mean we don't give one another shit every chance we get. Still, I know that when I need reason and logic, Linc is the brother to ask. I turn to him now.

"Why, exactly, do you need a girlfriend?" Linc asks, his eyes narrowed.

I blow out a breath and prepare to tell my two best friends how badly I screwed up today.

"Remember that big client I needed to land? The one that was going to get my dad to reopen the small business division?" I'd told them both that much when I'd seen them two days ago.

When they both nod, I continue. "Well, I met with him today over lunch at his country club. He seemed like a decent man. Maybe a little overbearing. He was a little particular, but nothing I can't handle. And he was really unhappy with his last ad firm. Things were going great until his wife showed up."

"What's wrong with his wife?" Cole asks.

I feel a wave of annoyance mixed with disgust as I remember the predatory way she'd looked me over when her husband had excused himself to go to the bathroom. Not to mention the hand on my thigh. Just thinking about it is enough to make me want a shower.

"For starters," I say, "It's clear she's got a lot of influence when it comes to her husband's business dealings. And then there's the fact that she was blatantly flirting with me."

Cole shrugs. "What's the big deal?" His eyes go wide as if he's just thought of something. "Oh, wait. Is this your first time?"

I roll my eyes. "Fuck off. She's not my type."

"Too old?"

"Too terrifying," I say with a dramatic shudder. "Too predatory. I felt like a fish swimming away from a hungry shark. Besides, even if I was into her, which I'm not, she's married. Even I have a line I won't cross. She may not care about her vows, but it's clear her husband adores her. I'm not going to be the reason someone's marriage falls apart. Plus, I want this man to like me. I want him to trust me. I don't think sleeping with his wife is the best way to go about it."

Cole sighs. "Probably not."

Linc leans forward. "What does this have to do with you needing a girlfriend?"

"That's the part where I screwed up," I say, rubbing the back of my neck. "She invited me to join them for dinner next week. At their house. She was very insistent."

Linc shrugs. "That's not unheard of, right? A business dinner?"

I shake my head. "It's not. The hand she tried to slide up my inner thigh was new, though."

"Oh, damn," Cole says. "She tried to give you a handy at the country club? With her husband sitting right there?"

I cringe a little at the memory. "I'm not sure what she was planning. I managed to wiggle out of her grasp." I close my eyes. "I may have also panicked a little and said I had dinner plans with my girlfriend that night."

They both laugh.

"It gets worse," I say. "When the she-beast rolled her eyes at the word 'girlfriend', I decided to double down. I went on and on about how amazing this non-existent girlfriend is and how great we are together."

"You don't have a girlfriend," Cole points out unhelpfully.

"No shit," I say. "That's why I said I need one."

Linc and Cole stare at me, confusion on their faces. I take another swig of my beer.

"You haven't heard the best part," I say. "To get her off my back—"

"And off your cock," Cole mutters.

I roll my eyes, but I secretly think he's not far off in his assessment. "Whatever," I say. "To get her to believe that I'm in a serious relationship, I might have told them I was practically engaged."

Cole's eyes grow wide. "What the fuck for?"

"Because, asshole," I say. "I hoped it would get her to back off."

Linc shakes his head and gives me a pitying look. "If she doesn't care about her own *actual* marriage, what makes you think she'll care about your potential fake one?"

I scrub my hands over my face. "I don't know," I say. "I told you I panicked. It's like someone else took over and spoke for me. The words just came out of my mouth, and I was like an innocent bystander. I don't even know what made me say it. I'm not even dating anyone right now. The closest I came was that stupid dating app. After the way that went down, I haven't tried again."

Cole laughs at my expense. He'd thought it was hilarious when he found out I signed up for a dating app. He'd heckled me about it for weeks. I'd done my best to ignore him at the time. Hell, I don't even know why I signed up in the first place. I think my visit to Mya when I'd found out she was pregnant got to me more than I'd expected it to. Seeing so many happy, healthy couples had made me suddenly feel incredibly alone.

I've always liked my privacy, my solitude. But after that weekend in North Carolina, I'd realized that all my casual hookups and flirtations were meaningless.

Nothing was ever going to come of those interactions. I'd end up miserable and alone if I didn't do something different. Or worse, I'd end up in some loveless arrangement like my parents have. No, thank you. I'd seen my sister happy and settled, even after the crappy hand life had dealt her, and I'd been jealous. No, not jealous. Envious. I envied that happiness. I wanted it for myself. I hadn't been able to stop thinking about it.

So, one night after a few beers, I'd been scrolling social media and an ad for an online dating app had popped up. In my slightly buzzed state, I'd created a profile. I scrolled through the eligible women the app thought might be my type for several minutes. I'd quickly grown discouraged with the results. There were plenty of women who were around my age. They were attractive enough and a lot of them had similar interests, but none of them had piqued my curiosity. Except for one.

She had long, dark hair and brown eyes that seemed to be laughing at something only she knew. I wanted to hear that laugh. After several minutes of indecision, I'd clicked the button to signal my interest in her before closing the app and going to bed. The next morning, I'd been shocked and confused to find that the cute brunette had responded. She'd sent me back a little winky face that indicated she was interested too.

"Remind me what happened with that date," Linc says. "What was wrong with her?"

I sigh. "Nothing. At least, I don't think so. We talked online. We seemed to hit it off, so we made a plan to meet for coffee. But the day of our coffee date, Van called me to tell me Mya was in labor, so I left for North

Carolina. I sent her a message apologizing and asked if we could reschedule, but she ghosted me. Not that I blame her. She probably thinks I'm an asshole."

Linc gives me a look that says he might agree with that assessment. "Did you at least tell her why you were cancelling on her at the last minute?"

I open my mouth to answer, but then realize that I don't actually know what I said to her. I was so excited and nervous for Mya that everything after the call from Van is a blur.

"I don't remember what I said," I finally tell Linc.

He shakes his head as though he's disappointed in me. "Dude. No wonder she didn't answer your messages afterward. Dick."

I wave away his comments. He's probably right. I think back to that day and try to remember details from nearly three weeks ago. I can't remember exactly what I'd said to her in those hurried messages while I'd been packing and trying to book a last-minute flight. I probably hadn't been as tactful as I usually am. I wouldn't be surprised if she does hate me. I can still picture her profile picture. That dimple in her left cheek. I'd liked her. A lot more than I'd thought possible from a few chats online. But I blew it. Cole barks out a laugh, pulling me from my musings. I realize that while I've been daydreaming about the missed coffee date, Linc and Cole have been tossing ideas around about how I can get out of the dinner.

"You could always say you and your fake girlfriend broke up," Linc suggests.

I shake my head, but Cole speaks before I can. "Nah," he says. "The wife will probably just try to fix his broken heart with her pussy."

I force away the mental image that comment leaves in my head. The last thing I need is to picture Melody Mitchell or her private parts. I shudder.

"Hire an escort," Cole says as if it's a perfectly logical thing to suggest. I turn to stare at him. From the corner of my eye, I can tell Linc is doing the same. I'm pretty sure my expression is one of confusion. But Linc? He's wearing the face of a disappointed father. I've seen it enough to recognize it.

"What?" Cole asks with a shrug. "It's an idea. You hire a woman to pretend to be your girlfriend for the weekend. She keeps the cougar off your back, and you can woo the rich guy. Easy."

Linc takes a deep breath and lets it out slowly before speaking. "As a father of a young girl, I'm going on record as being against this idea. I'd like to still be able to look Ella in the eye when she grows up without her thinking I was a party to some prostitution scheme."

Cole rolls his eyes. "I wasn't suggesting he pay her for sex. Get your head out of the gutter." He points a finger at his brother. "Besides, they're called sex workers now, not prostitutes. Get with the times."

Linc punches Cole's shoulder. "Either way, dumbass. It's a bad idea."

I shake my head and reach for my beer. "Even if I wanted to, which I don't, I can't just hire someone," I say, shooting down the idea. "There's no way that would work. They'll see right through it."

Linc narrows his eyes at me. "You're right," he says. "You can't hire someone. You need someone authentic. Someone real. Not an actress or someone who's getting paid to pretend to like you."

Cole shrugs. "So, pick one of your women friends and ask them to pretend for you."

I roll my eyes. "Little problem there," I say. "I don't have any women who are my friend."

Cole takes another sip of beer. "That's because you end up banging all of them."

Linc lets out a loud cackling laugh. "He's not wrong."

I roll my eyes again, ignoring their taunts. I want to argue, but we all know it's the truth. I don't have any women friends. Most of the women I know, I've slept with. Unless you count Mya's new sisters-in-law. They like me well enough, but none of them are single. And I seriously doubt any one of them would be willing to come to Georgia and pretend to be my girlfriend. Even if one of them were, I'll bet my right arm that the men in their lives would kick my ass just for asking. No. There's no one I can ask.

"What about an ex?" Cole asks. "I'm friends with all my exes."

It's Linc's turn to roll his eyes. "That's because you never have real relationships. Just casual hookups or friends with benefits. It's easy to stay friends with someone if you start out that way."

Cole shrugs with a grin. "You're not wrong."

I sigh, raking a hand through my hair. "All my exes move in the same social and professional circles as my father. There's no way he wouldn't get wind of something like that. It wouldn't stay secret for long. I need someone who's not from Savannah. Someone who isn't part of that social scene. Someone my father can't get to because it's someone he'd never think I'd be with."

"Good luck finding her by next week," Cole says, finishing his beer and pulling another from the cooler at his feet.

I sigh and shake my head. I've put myself into an impossible situation by lying to a potential client. This isn't like me.

"I know," I mutter before finishing off my own beer.

When Cole reaches for another one from the cooler, I shake my head.

"I'm driving."

Cole nods and leans back in his chair. Linc has been silent for several minutes now, so I turn to face him. Of the three of us, Linc is usually the quietest. He thinks before he speaks and doesn't let his mouth get him into impossible situations. I wish he could think me up a way out of this one, but he's even quieter tonight than usual. Finally, I blow out a frustrated breath.

"If no one has any miracle fixes for my mess," I say, "I'm going to head home."

"Sorry, man," Cole says with a shrug. "I've got nothing. Unless you want to ask Callie to be your fake girlfriend?"

I shoot him a look that makes him laugh. "I don't want my ass kicked that badly."

Cole just grins. "But it would be funny."

Callie is the only female bartender employed at Cole's bar. She makes the best drinks and has an amazing way with the customers. She's barely 5 feet tall with magenta hair and a musical voice. Callie is tiny and adorable and looks in need of protecting, but she's far fiercer than she seems. She's also the only woman I've ever known Cole Prescott not to hit on. That might be because she and her wife Jenna have been married for nearly 5 years. And Jenna is terrifying when she's angry. Even if I thought Callie would be the perfect fake girlfriend, there's no way in hell I'm risking Jenna's wrath.

"I'll pass," I say as I get to my feet.

Cole shoots me a look of fake annoyance. "You're no fun," he says.

"Thanks for the beer," I say.

Just before I round the side of the house, I hear Linc speak.

"What are you going to do about your girlfriend needs?"

"I'll come up with something," I mutter.

I always do.

CHAPTER 4

Luke

I don't know what made me come here this morning. I hadn't slept well last night. After I'd gotten home from Linc's, I'd pulled up the dating app, but Piper's profile had been deleted. I'd nearly texted her, but I thought it might be too late for her to respond. Besides, I didn't know what to say anyway. I don't even know why I'm looking for her, except that I still feel guilty about the way things went down. So, I'd gone to one of my social media apps and searched for her there, curious to see if she was on there. It hadn't taken long to find her.

I had a moment where I wondered if I should even be trying to find her at all. She'd made it clear that she doesn't want to talk to me, even if she hadn't specifically told me to go away. I've never been the kind of guy to push my attention on a woman who's not interested. But that's not what I want to do. I just want to apologize in person. And okay, part of me just wants to meet Piper. We'd hit it off before I screwed it all up. Who knows? Maybe there's something there. So, I'd kept scrolling until I came across her place of business on her public profile. Public. Meaning she's okay with the public seeing it, right? Granted, the only things posted are in relation to her coffee shop. Piping Hot Brews. I'd smiled at the cleverness of the name. I love a good play on words.

When I'd seen the address of the shop, I'd laughed out loud. I'd been 10 minutes away from Piping Hot Brews earlier at Linc's house. The shop is located on Main Street in Peach Tree. I've probably passed by it dozens of times and never gave it any notice. Small world.

When I'd woken this morning, the first thing I wanted was a cup of coffee. Thinking of coffee made me remember Piping Hot Brews, which made me think of Piper. Before I could let myself dwell on the decision, I was showered, dressed and out the door. Now that I'm sitting in my car outside of the shop, I'm starting to second-guess the decision to come here. What if she's still pissed about our date? What if she thinks I'm a crazy stalker for showing up here out of the blue after not speaking for weeks? This is a bad idea.

But I find myself climbing out of my car anyway. On the way here, I'd rehearsed my apology speech a half dozen times. Each time became more detailed and over-the-top. It was a coffee date, for crying out loud. It's not like I left her at the altar. A simple, sincere apology should be good enough. Right? I don't have time to consider it further, because somehow, I'm opening the door and walking inside.

For a Saturday morning, this place is surprisingly empty. As in, totally empty. I look around at the cozy seating area, wondering where all the customers are. The shop is welcoming. There's a pleasant aroma of coffee and pastries. Soft music is playing. It's downright inviting. So, where are the patrons? Before I can think too much about it, I see her standing behind the counter, a welcoming smile on her face. The sight of her hits me like a punch to the gut. She's even prettier in person. I don't know why I hadn't expected that. Her dark hair is pulled back into a ponytail and she's wearing a pale blue apron with the shop's logo printed on it. An apron shouldn't be sexy. Right? I step closer to the counter and smile back at her. I can see the exact moment she realizes who I am.

I watch Piper's face as recognition dawns. Her confusion shifts to surprise, then to full-blown shock. She quickly tries to mask her expression, but it's too late. I'd seen it. And she knows I did. Since I didn't come here to toy with her, I give her my best smile.

"Hi, Piper," I say. "Great shop you have here."

Her mouth opens and closes, then opens again. Closes again. Her brows draw low over her eyes.

"Luke?"

I nod. "The same."

The confused expression doesn't leave her face. "Why? How? Huh?"

Shit. Now I'm second-guessing this whole thing. What if Piper thinks I'm some crazy stalker? She'd never told me where she works or what town she lives in. When we'd made our plans to meet, we'd picked a neutral location in the city. Now, I'm here in her place of business, grinning at her like an idiot.

"I can explain," I say, though I'm not sure how I plan to explain my presence here. I really hadn't thought this through.

"Explain," she says, drawing out the word until I'm not sure if it's a question or not.

"Why I'm here," I say.

I figure the most pressing issue is to reassure Piper that I'm not a lunatic who tracked her down at her place of business to try and get her to give me a second chance. Even though it seems that's exactly what I am. Shit. I give her another smile that I hope will soften her toward me, but it only succeeds in turning her expression more wary. Great. This is going well.

"Why are you here?" Piper says finally.

She still sounds wary. I wouldn't be surprised if she has the police department on speed dial.

I decide to tell her the truth. Well, most of it.

"To apologize. I felt bad about our canceled date," I say. "When you didn't answer my texts, I went back to our chat in the app, but it said you'd closed your account."

She nods. "Because I realized I don't have time for dating right now. And since my first and only foray into online dating didn't go so well, I decided to cut my losses."

Ouch. That stings.

"I'm sorry," I say. "I feel terrible about how I handled that. But my sister was in labor and when her husband called, I panicked. I dropped everything and booked a flight. I was on the plane about to switch my phone to airplane mode when I remembered our date." I wince. "That sounds bad. Like you were an afterthought, which you weren't. I was really looking forward to meeting you."

I realize I'm probably not helping my case. Piper stands there, silently studying me for several seconds before I see her shoulders relax slightly. She tips her head toward the little dining room.

"Come on," she says. "Let's have coffee."

My smile spreads wide and fast across my face. She points a finger at me and gives me a severe look.

"You better have some damned cute baby pictures on your phone."

I grin even wider. "Prepare to feast your eyes upon the cutest baby girl in North Carolina," I say, following her.

CHAPTER 5

Piper

Luke? What the hell is Luke doing in my shop? We haven't spoken in weeks. Not since he canceled on me at the last minute with a text. I'd been irritated at first, but then I'd realized that it was probably a good thing. It just isn't meant to be. I'm too busy with the shop and my own mess of a life to try and add dating to the mix. That's when I'd shut down my profile on that stupid online dating app that I'd stupidly signed up for. I don't know why I did it in the first place. I think I'd been lonely. In a moment of pure weakness, I'd let my sister's words get to me.

"Piper, I know you," Layna had said. "You're not built to be solo. You're going to get lonely, all by yourself in that little town where the only eligible bachelors are over seventy. At least Atlanta has possibilities that don't require a walker to get around."

I'd laughed at her jokes, but she hadn't been far off the mark. Most of the single men in Peach Tree are widowers who have more years behind them than ahead. Not exactly in my age bracket. So, I'd decided to put myself out there. I'd created a dating profile and tried to be open-minded. And all it had done was get my hopes up and leave me disappointed. Again.

I don't know why I'm still talking to him now. Except for the fact that he's ridiculously hot and charming. That smile had nearly melted my panties right there. I don't know why he's here or whether I should be worried he's a crazy stalker. But I do know I can't seem to look away from those blue-green eyes and that sexy grin. And yeah, maybe I do want to see pictures of his niece.

I watch as Luke looks around the coffee shop, taking everything in. I feel oddly nervous to hear what he thinks, though I'm not sure why. I don't need his approval. But he does work in marketing, I remind myself. His opinion might be valid. I watch as he seems to evaluate everything from the uniforms to the menu to the chairs we're sitting in.

"This place is really amazing," he says, finally meeting my gaze. "You should be proud of it."

"Thanks," I say, trying to act like the small compliment doesn't make me absolutely giddy. But I can feel the blush as it heats my cheeks. Damn this pale complexion. If Luke notices, he has the good manners not to mention it. Instead, he turns his attention to the shop, his sharp gaze taking in everything around us.

"It's just missing one thing," he says, turning back to me.

Confused, I wrinkle my brow. "What's that?"

He leans closer with a smile. "Customers," he says in a low voice. "I know there aren't any other coffee shops in town. There's just the little diner on the other side of town. It's just after 8am. This place should be standing room only. So, where is everyone? Did you piss off the mayor or something?"

I sigh, giving Luke a wry smile. "Just Miss Dottie," I say. When he just looks confused, I wave away the comment. "This town doesn't like outsiders," I tell him. "They haven't been the most welcoming."

Luke's lips purse and he nods before taking another sip from his cup. For the second time in a half hour, I hear the little bell above the door chime signaling a customer. Since it's not a sound I'm used to, I whip my head around to see who's here. My lips curve into a wide smile when I see Harlow's blonde curls shot through with those bright pink streaks. She meets my gaze and gives me a wave as I stand to make my way over to the counter.

"I'll be right back," I tell Luke who only nods.

I can see the questions in Harlow's gaze as I approach her. She's looking from me to Luke and back with raised brows. I shoot her a glare and point toward the counter. She turns in that direction, but not before I see a hint of laughter in her green eyes.

"Not a word," I mutter through clenched teeth.

"Who's the sexy CEO?" Harlow says in a low voice.

I roll my eyes as I get to work making her usual latte. "He's not a CEO," I hiss. "At least, I don't think he is," I add. "I'm not sure what he does for a living. Something in marketing in Savannah."

Harlow shoots a not-so-discreet glance Luke's way. He notices and gives her a small nod over the rim of his cup. I feel my cheeks flame hot.

"He's hot," Harlow says, turning back to look at me. "Are you two banging?"

If I thought my cheeks couldn't get any redder, I was wrong. I think the tips of my ears match the fire hydrant outside.

"Shut up!" I hiss, swatting at Harlow.

She shrugs, unbothered by my outrage. "If you're not, you should be."

At Harlow's words, I feel a shiver of desire coil tightly inside me, making me suck in a breath. She's not wrong. Hadn't I already thought about how gorgeous Luke is? I wonder what he's hiding under that suit.

"Looks good in a suit, too," Harlow says, shooting me a wink. "Bet he looks better out of it."

Is this woman a mind reader? Geez. I finish making her coffee and usher her toward the door as she tries to hand me cash.

"Wait," she says. "I haven't paid."

"Consider it a gift," I say brightly. "See you next time!"

Harlow shoots me an annoyed look that promises that this conversation isn't over yet, then she leaves without further comment. I turn back to where Luke is still sitting, having watched the whole scene with an interested expression.

"I'm not an expert," he says, "But I think not taking payment is the wrong way to make your business a success."

I smile. "That's Harlow," I say. "She's pretty much my only friend in town. She'll be back tomorrow and I'm sure she'll pay double for her latte or find a way to sneak the cash into the tip jar for Stevie."

Luke nods. "It's good to have friends," he says. His voice turning serious now. "I really am sorry about the way I handled things. I hope you can forgive me?"

"There's nothing to forgive," I say, meaning the words. It's not like Luke and I were a couple and he stood me up. He'd canceled the date, rather than leaving me sitting there waiting for him. Sure, it was rather last minute, but it's not like there were any real feelings involved. I give him what I hope is a convincing smile.

Luke returns the smile and dips his head in a single nod. "Good," he says. "I was hoping we could start over." He gestures to the coffee cups on the table. "Since we've already had coffee, maybe we could have dinner. Tomorrow night?"

I open my mouth to politely decline, but the pang of disappointment I feel makes me hesitate. I don't know why, though. Yes, Luke is handsome and charming and makes my lady bits go pitter patter. But hadn't I just decided that men are more trouble than they're worth? Hadn't I recently come to the realization that I don't have time to focus on dating right now? So, why do I want so badly to say yes? Why does the tiniest bit of attention from a hot guy have me debating throwing my own goals aside for the chance to date him? What's wrong with me? Using a will power I'm shocked I possess, I force myself to shake my head. I paste a smile on my face.

"I appreciate the offer, Luke," I say. "I think you're a great guy, but I don't think I'm in a place to date anyone right now."

I watch as his expression shifts from hope to disappointment to acceptance. He nods, giving me a small smile.

"I understand," he says. "I guess I missed my window."

I grit my teeth to keep from recalling my own words and begging him to do unspeakable things to me on this table. Instead, I give him a tight smile and ignore my own raging hormones.

"I'm sorry," I say.

Luke shakes his head. "Don't be. Never apologize for how you feel."

He says the words lightly, but they hit home for me. How many times have I felt the need to apologize for what I want or how I feel? Far too many times over the years, and usually to men who haven't cared enough to respect my feelings. Something about hearing Luke say those words makes something squeeze inside my chest. Before I can come up with some clever response, I realize he's rising to his feet preparing to leave.

"Wait!" The word leaves my mouth without any sort of forethought from my brain. I'm not sure why I even want to stop him. I just know I don't want him to leave yet. I realize that he's looking at me expectantly, waiting for me to say something. I clear my throat, trying to give myself time to formulate a response.

"Maybe," I start, "Maybe we can be friends?"

I want to crawl under the table as soon as the words leave my mouth. Friends? I want to be friends with Luke? I'm pretty sure friends don't picture one another naked. They probably also don't imagine scenarios where the other one's face is buried between their legs. But that's exactly what I just imagined when Luke licked his lips before smiling at me. Is it hot in here? Maybe I need to have the thermostat checked.

"Friends." Luke repeats the word as if deciding how he likes the idea. There's a hint of amusement on his face.

"Is that funny?" I ask, feeling a little defensive.

He huffs out a small laugh. "Just a little," he admits. "But only because I was talking to my best friend last night and he accused me of having zero female friends." He shakes his head. "And he wasn't wrong." He says the last part a little ruefully.

"No female friends," I muse. "Just exes?" I say, teasing.

Now Luke does laugh and damn it. The sound has my insides doing somersaults.

"Guilty," he says.

I scrunch my nose in a grimace. "I have a confession," I say. When he gestures for me to proceed, I do. "I don't have any guy friends either. It just felt like the thing you say when you turn down a date."

Luke laughs again and it's more than my insides doing somersaults this time. Holy shit, this man is a danger to society. Just his laugh can turn me into a puddle. I cross my legs discreetly, hoping he can't tell how uncomfortable I am right now.

"Well, you could be my first," he says with a smile. "Woman friend," he clarifies.

I tamp down all the X-rated images his words evoke and smile. "And you can be mine," I say. "Guy friend, I mean."

Luke nods and holds out a hand for me to shake. "Deal."

I reach out and take his hand. The moment my skin makes contact with his, I know I've made a mistake.

Friends? How the hell can I be friends with a man when just the feel of his hand on mine sends a jolt of heat to my core? His long fingers envelop my hand, and I feel his thumb stroke lightly against the back of my hand before he releases me. Neither of us says anything as he turns and walks out of the shop, leaving me to wonder what the hell just happened.

CHAPTER 6

Saturday afternoon

Luke: *Hey.*
Piper: *Um, hi.*
Luke: *How's your day going?*
Piper: *Not bad, I guess. How's yours?*
Luke: *Could be better. Then again, it could be worse.*
Luke: *This is okay, right? Texting? Friends text.*
Piper: *Yes, friends text each other.*
Luke: *And you did say we could be friends.*
Piper: *I did say that.*
Luke: *Man, I think I'm totally nailing this friends thing already. 10 points for Gryffindor! [lion emoji]*
Piper: *[eyeroll emoji] Who says you're a Gryffindor?*
Luke: *This online quiz I took.*
Piper: *You're too cocky to be a Gryffindor. At best, you're a Ravenclaw. But more likely a Slytherin.*
Luke: *[shocked emoji, crying emoji] You're calling me a death-eater? That's harsh, Huff.*

Piper: *Huff?*

Luke: *Short for Hufflepuff. You're definitely a Hufflepuff.*

Piper: *Did you text me for a reason?*

Luke: *I notice you're not debating your Hogwart's house. Is this because I'm right?*

Piper: *No comment.*

Luke: *Ha! I knew it!*

Piper: *Hufflepuff is a perfectly respectable house, thank you. Besides, it's the only house that didn't get involved in all the drama. [badger emoji, black heart emoji, yellow heart emoji]*

Luke: *Gotta go to a board meeting. [sad face emoji] Later, Huff.*

Piper: *[unamused face emoji]*

Monday morning

Luke: *Hey, Huff. How's your morning?*

Piper: *Is this going to be a thing, now?*

Luke: *Looks like it.*

Piper: *Fine. But don't be mad at whatever nickname I come up with for you.*

Luke: *Bring it.*

Piper: *You asked for this. Just remember that.*

Luke: *Do your worst.*

Piper: *Challenge accepted.*

Monday evening

Piper: *How was your afternoon?*

Luke: *As exciting as one might expect.*

Piper: *That bad?*

Luke: *The worst. I think I fell asleep at one point.*

Piper: *I definitely don't miss those days.*

Luke: *The days of board meetings and suits?*

Piper: *Yep. Good riddance.*

Luke: *What did you do before you were a coffee connoisseur?*

Piper: *Corporate accounting.*

Luke: *Ouch. That sounds more boring than my board meetings.*

Piper: *Haha. It was. Which is why I left that world for the exciting world of coffee.*

Luke: *I'm not sure how great of an accountant you were, but I've had your coffee and I'd say you made a good choice.*

Piper: *Thanks. Though I'm not sure the people of Peach Tree agree with you.*

Luke: *Business not doing so hot?*

Piper: *You could say that. I'm not sure if it's because I'm an outsider or if it's the lack of fruit in the shop's name.*

Luke: *I did notice an overwhelming peach theme happening in that town. What's that about?*

Piper: *[shrugging emoji] Beats me. But it's everywhere. You should see the water tower.*

Luke: *Haha. Believe it or not, I have. What were they thinking?*

Piper: *No clue, but someone should tell them.*

Luke: *Maybe they did it on purpose?*

Piper: *I can't imagine why.*

Luke: *Listen, marketing is kind of my thing. If you ever want to run anything by me or if I can help, let me know.*

Piper: *Thanks, but I don't think I can afford the likes of Wolfe Industries.*

Luke: *I'll give you the new friend discount.*

Piper: *I'll keep that in mind. Thanks.*

Luke: *Any time.*

Luke

I read over the last few messages between me and Piper and smile. A plan begins to form in my mind, but I don't know if it's smart or insane. Cole had said I should get someone to pretend to be my girlfriend for this dinner. And Linc had said I needed someone genuine and real. Piper would be perfect. And we're friends now, right? I ignore the way the word seems to rankle when I think about it in regard to Piper. Friends aren't supposed to want to sleep with one another. And that's exactly what I keep imagining when I think of Piper.

Shaking off the thought, I go back to my dilemma. I still haven't figured out what to do about this dinner with the Mitchells. They're expecting me at their house in 3 days with my girlfriend. And I still don't have one. I glance at Piper's name on my phone again, debating. If I ask her and she thinks I'm crazy, this might be the end of our short-lived friendship. But if she says yes, it could solve my problem. Maybe I could pitch it as a business arrangement. Her coffee shop is clearly struggling. She'd said so herself. And I've officially reached full-blown desperation. I need this deal to work. And I need a girlfriend to make that happen. Piper needs customers in her coffee shop. I can help with her marketing. This can work.

CHAPTER 7

Piper

I flip the sign on the door to 'Open', though I'm not sure why I bother. Peach Tree is too far off the highway to get business from people driving through. And it's clear the locals are still avoiding the place. I pick up my e-reader and settle into one of the overstuffed chairs. It's going to be another long day of no business. But I've barely read a chapter before the bell over the door rings, startling me. I look up to see Luke standing there.

My heart trips in my chest at the sight of him, even as my brain struggles to understand why he's here. He looks good. He's wearing a charcoal gray suit with a deep blue tie. It's clear that he's heading to work. So, why is he here? He lives and works in Savannah. Why would he drive all the way to Peach Tree just for coffee?

He gives me a panty-melting smile as I approach.

"Morning," he says in a pleasant tone, as if it's not at all odd for him to be here.

"Morning," I say, letting him hear the confusion in my voice. "This is a bit out of your way, isn't it?"

Luke's smile is sheepish, and his gaze drops from mine for a moment. "Yeah. I didn't come just for coffee."

I fight down the surge of excitement I feel. The idea that he came all this way just to see me is absurd. But why else is he here? He's your friend, remember? I try to remind myself that friends don't make out with other friends. But no matter how many times I repeat the mantra in my head, I can't stop staring at his mouth and wondering what it would be like to kiss him.

Somehow, I manage to shake off the fantasy and bring my focus back to reality. Luke is just standing there, politely waiting for me to get my shit together. Why can't I focus when I'm around this man? I seem to be able to carry on a conversation through text with no issue. But when he's standing in front of me, I turn into a bumbling idiot. I clear my throat and force a smile.

"Why did you come here?" I ask, hoping my question sounds like a polite inquiry rather than an interrogation.

Luke seems to be steeling himself for whatever he's about to say. This worries me, though I'm not sure why. We barely know one another. What can he possibly do or say to worry me?

"I came to ask you for a favor," he says. "Well, it's more of a business deal between friends, since you'll benefit as well."

My confusion must show on my face because he sighs. "I'm not doing this right. Can we sit?" He gestures to the chair I'd just vacated, and I nod.

Once we're both seated, Luke gives me another of those devastating smiles and I feel my stomach flutter a bit at the sight.

"Sorry," he says. "I know showing up here out of the blue seems strange. Especially twice in one week."

I wave a dismissive hand. "It's okay."

Luke takes a deep breath and blows it out. "I have a business dinner with a potential client on Thursday night. This is the kind of client who can change the entire face of Wolfe Industries. Charles Wolfe, my father, has tasked me with getting this client to sign on with us."

I don't miss the way Luke's voice had shifted slightly when he'd said, "my father". I wonder if there's some animosity between the two. But I don't interrupt. I want to find out where Luke is going with this.

"You've heard of Arthur Mitchell?" he asks, brows raised.

I roll my eyes. "That's like asking if I've heard of the queen of England or the moon. Everyone knows who Arthur Mitchell is."

Luke nods. "Right."

Something occurs to me, and I blink at him. "Wait. Is he the potential client?" When he nods, my eyes grow wide. "You're having dinner with *the* Arthur Mitchell? Holy shit!"

"Yep," Luke says. "We actually had lunch last week. He's a nice guy."

I'm still reeling over this new information, but Luke continues.

"That's kind of why I'm here," he says. "During that lunch, I may have alluded to having a girlfriend."

"Alluded?" I ask, eyes narrowed.

Luke's face flushes. It's the first time I've seen him embarrassed. Why is that so attractive?

"More than alluded," he says. "I told Art that I'm madly in love and on the verge of proposing."

I blink at him. "You call him Art?"

For some reason, this makes Luke laugh. "That's what you're focused on?"

I shrug. "Seems like a big deal to me."

Luke sighs. "He wants me to bring my girlfriend to dinner in 3 days."

"But you don't have a girlfriend," I say slowly.

Luke shakes his head, his gaze focused on me. It takes me longer than it should to piece together what's happening. Why he's here. Why he came here in the first place.

"When did you say you had lunch with him?" I ask, keeping my voice casual.

"Last Thursday," he answers. "Why?"

I feel like an idiot. He hadn't apologized because he cared what I thought of him. He'd only come here looking for someone to go along with his lie to one of the richest men in the world.

"Two days before you came to see me," I say, crossing my arms over my chest. "Weird coincidence."

Luke closes his eyes briefly before speaking. "I know how it looks," he says. "But that's not why I came here that day. I meant everything I said. I really did come here hoping you'd forgive me and go to dinner with me. I hadn't thought beyond that. I wasn't thinking about work when I came here. I swear. But I've been wracking my brain for days for a solution to my screw-up with Art, and I've got nothing."

He rakes a hand through his hair, clearly frustrated. I want to believe him, but it's too convenient to be a coincidence.

"Cole told me to hire an escort," he says. "I even searched online. But it just felt sleazy. And none of the women I saw seemed believable."

I feel a surge of feminist outrage at his comment. "What's that supposed to mean? Just because a woman is an escort doesn't mean she's not good enough for you."

Luke shakes his head. "That's not what I meant. They were all beautiful and polished, but none of them seemed real. I couldn't imagine a scenario where I could pretend to be in love with any of them."

Silence hangs in the air for several seconds before I say softly, "Luke, why did you come here this morning?"

I already know the answer, but I want him to say it aloud.

Luke sits up straighter. "I came here to ask you to be my fake girlfriend," he says. "Long enough to get Art to sign with Wolfe Industries. In exchange, I'll help you market Piping Hot and make it a success. I'm good at what I do, Piper. You've got a great shop. It just needs the right exposure."

Knowing Luke's intent and hearing him say the words aloud are very different. He wants me to pretend to be his girlfriend. Does he realize how insane that sounds? Things like this happen in romantic comedies, not in real life.

"You know this is crazy, right?" I say.

He nods. "If I had any other option, I'd take it."

"Why did you lie about a girlfriend, anyway?"

Luke sighs. "Art's wife," he says in a miserable voice. "She's a bit aggressive with her flirting."

It's clear he's trying to be tactful. "How aggressive?"

He meets my gaze. "Hand on my inner thigh while her husband was sitting across from me," he says.

The disgust must show on my face because Luke just nods. "I didn't want to be outright rude to her," he says. "But I also don't want anything to do with a married woman. Art seems oblivious to the way she acts. It's obvious he's totally in love with her. So, I lied about being in love too. I thought it would send a message to Mel that I was off-limits."

"Seriously?" I ask. "You thought you having a girlfriend would stop a potential adulterer from trying to get in your pants?"

Luke sighs. "Yeah, my best friend said the same thing. Look, I panicked. I don't know how it happened. But I'm stuck now. I can't show up at their house without my loving girlfriend or that woman will eat me alive and blow the biggest deal of my career."

I sigh. "You know this is ridiculous, right?"

He nods.

"I just want to make sure," I say. "Because it's seriously ridiculous." I point a finger at him. "This is where lying gets you."

I realize I'm scolding him as if I'm his mother, but Luke just nods, looking shamefaced. "I know," he mutters.

I try to remove my hurt feelings from the equation and think about Luke's offer logically. I look around my empty shop, in the peak of what should be the morning rush. I need help. I don't know if Luke can magically turn things around here, but I know that what I'm doing isn't working.

"Let me think about it," I say.

CHAPTER 8

Piper

I replay my conversation with Luke for the twentieth time today. I still haven't responded to his insane offer. I've been too stunned and confused. Once the shock had worn off, I'd been curious and yes, tempted. What does being a fake girlfriend entail? He'd said one dinner and maybe a few luncheons. Just long enough to get Arthur Mitchell to sign on with Wolfe Industries. How long does a business deal like that usually take to close? But then we're talking about a billionaire. The idea of having dinner with someone like that is intimidating. Add in lying to the man's face and I already feel like I might vomit.

What makes Luke think I'd be capable of pulling that off? I'm a terrible liar and a bad actress. When I'd tried out for my high school production of Grease, I'd been politely dismissed and had ended up relegated to set designs instead. I'd kicked ass at those set designs, but I'd also realized that I'm not meant for the stage. Behind the stage? Sure. In the limelight? Nope. I don't think Luke understands this. Not that I've told him any of it. I've just been obsessing over his offer for the last few hours instead of replying with a big, fat, resounding, 'Hell no'.

Why haven't I told him no yet? I know I should. This isn't something I'm confident I can pull off, no matter how badly I need his help with Piping Hot. Knowing me, I wouldn't make it five minutes into the dinner before spilling everything to Mr. Mitchell and begging him not to be mad. Deception is not my strong suit.

To his credit, Luke has left me alone with my thoughts after our conversation this morning. I'm not sure the time alone has helped or made things worse. It's been hours and I still haven't made a decision. But the time I close Piping Hot and lock up for the day, I'm mentally exhausted. My phone pings with a text from Harlow reminding me of our plans for this evening. I'd nearly forgotten.

When Harlow had invited me to hang out tonight, I'd been excited and a little nervous. The truth is, I haven't always had the easiest time making friends. In the corporate world, everyone is out for themselves. People aren't looking to make friends so much as they're looking to get ahead. It makes it hard to trust people enough to really get to know them. That's why Layna is probably the only friend I have. She's the only person I totally trust. But Peach Tree isn't Atlanta, I tell myself. People are different here. And Harlow doesn't seem like the type of person to stab someone in the back to get ahead. Besides, how would hurting me help her?

So, when 6pm rolls around, I find myself standing outside her shop, a bottle of wine in one hand. As nervous as I am about hanging out with someone new and trying to make friends in this town that hasn't exactly been warm and friendly to me, I can't get Luke's proposition out of my head. There's no way I can agree, right?

Harlow answers the door in a flurry of blonde and hot pink. She's all smiles and chattering a mile a minute as she ushers me inside and toward the back of the salon.

"I'm so glad we're getting a chance to hang out," she says. "There's never a lot of time during the day. What with my clients and your shop?"

"Ha!" I bark out a humorless laugh. "I don't think my shop is getting in the way at all. You're practically my only customer."

Harlow waves her hand dismissively as she leads me toward a hidden staircase beyond the shampoo bowls. "I doubt that's true. Your coffee is amazing."

"If no one knows how amazing the coffee is," I say as I follow her up the stairs, "It doesn't really matter."

"Give them time."

I bite back the urge to tell her that I'm running out of time. If I can't make this shop a success soon, I won't be able to afford to keep trying. When we reach the top of the stairs, I'm surprised to find a large, open living area with a couch and television. Beyond, there's a small kitchen. To our right is a short hallway. I take in the space with an appreciative gaze. It's light and open with little clutter, making the space feel larger than it is.

"Your place is great," I say with a smile.

"Thanks," Harlow says, leading the way to the kitchen.

I follow her, still carrying the bottle of wine. She motions toward the counter. "Just put it anywhere.

I have snacks. And I picked up a pizza earlier. Unfortunately, we don't have much in the way of food delivery in Peach Tree." She gives me a hopeful smile. "Hope you like pepperoni and extra cheese."

"That sounds amazing," I assure her.

I wander around the small living room while Harlow opens the wine and pours us each a glass. I study the framed photos on the walls, smiling at the younger versions of Harlow I see pictured. In one of them a teenaged Harlow stands next to a woman who looks a lot like the woman here with me now, but with hair a darker shade of blonde. She's also got a few more worry lines on her face. I take in the starched uniform and the instrument in Harlow's hand.

"You were in marching band?" I ask, a teasing note to my voice.

She rolls her eyes as she hands me a glass of wine. "Yes. As you can guess, it made me extremely popular." She nods toward the photo. "The uniform alone was enough to repel even the most desperate."

We both laugh and I turn to study the photo again. "I don't know," I say. "I think the blue wool really brought out your eyes."

"You're full of shit," she says, taking a sip of her wine. "But I'll take it."

I look around the room. "How long have you lived above the shop?"

She shrugs and takes a seat on the couch. "Since I bought the building. About 5 years ago."

"Did you always want to be a stylist?" I ask.

She looks wistful for a moment before shaking her head. "Not really. I didn't know what I wanted when I was younger. I just knew I wanted out of this town."

I make a show of looking around the room, then back to Harlow. "I hate to break it to you, but I'm not sure you pulled that one off."

She laughs. "Actually, I did," she says. "I got a full scholarship. Spent four years in Atlanta."

I give her an appraising nod. "That's amazing. What brought you back to Peach Tree?"

Her face loses some of its good humor. "It was just time to come home, that's all." I can't miss the sorrow in her voice. I think about the woman in the photo and her words from the day we first met. "I'm the only one left," she'd said. Her voice had held that same sadness. Part of me wants to ask her more. To reassure her that she can confide in me if she wants. But before I can, Harlow turns to face me, a bright smile fixed on her face.

"What's new with you?" she asks.

I'm about to tell her that absolutely nothing is new with me. Nothing has changed in my life since the last time we spoke. But that's not true. I think about my conversation with Luke. His offer.

"Well," I begin, taking a deep breath. "There is one thing."

Harlow's eyes sparkle. "Is it about that hottie from the coffee shop the other morning?"

I feel my face redden before I can stop it.

"Ha!" Harlow shouts, pointing a finger at me. "I knew there was something going on with you two. Spill it."

I roll my eyes and take another sip from my glass. "There's nothing going on between us," I say, annoyed that I sound almost defensive. "We're friends."

Harlow shoots me a look that says she doesn't buy my story.

I sigh. "Fine, I'll tell you everything."

She lets out an excited little squeal that almost makes me change my mind. But I need to confide in someone. I've considered Layna, but I know what she'd tell me. She'd say that guys are trouble and that I need to focus on the shop rather than getting involved in some fake girlfriend scheme. I'm not so sure Harlow won't give me the same advice, but at least she doesn't have the advantage of having known me all my life. She's more of a neutral advisor than Layna.

"A couple months ago, I signed up for a stupid dating app," I say. "One of my friends from Atlanta met her boyfriend on there, and they recently got engaged. Plus, she's convinced I'm going to die sad and alone. So, I signed up. I scoped out the guys on there."

Harlow waggles her eyebrows. "And hot coffee guy was on there?"

I nod. "Yeah. Luke. I got the notification that he liked my profile, so I checked his out. I liked what I saw, so I liked him back. We started messaging online, then texting. Just getting to know one another. We made plans to meet for coffee. Neutral location, in the city, daylight. I wasn't trying to get murdered. I've listened to plenty of true crime podcasts. I know better."

Harlow nods as if this makes perfect sense to her. "So, what happened?"

"As I'm trying on my fourth outfit of the day, trying to find the right thing to wear to meet this hot guy, he texts me to cancel."

Harlow's mouth drops open. "That dick."

"Right?" I say. "I was pissed. And a little hurt," I admit. "When I didn't hear from him for a few days, I deactivated my profile on the dating site and decided that I was better off focusing on work. I need the shop to make it and I don't have time for distractions." I shrug. "So, I ignored him when he started texting me again."

"What did he say?"

I roll my eyes. "Just that he was sorry, and he hoped we could reschedule when he got back into town."

She leans closer. "What did you say?"

I shrug. "Nothing. I didn't reply."

"Damn, girl!" Harlow says. "You ghosted him?"

I feel a twinge of guilt. I don't like the way that sounds. But it's true that I did, technically ghost him. I sigh. "I didn't set out to ghost him," I say, feeling defensive.

She holds her hand up, palm facing me. "You don't have to explain it to me. I'm on your side."

"Thanks," I say with a small smile.

"If you ghosted him," Harlow says. "Why was he in Piping Hot two days ago?"

I feel a flutter low in my belly at the memory of sitting across from Luke for those few minutes while he tried to work his charm on me.

"He came to apologize," I say.

"How did he know where you work?"

I point a finger at her. "Exactly! Weird, right?"

"Is your business listed online?" Harlow asks.

"Yes," I say on a sigh.

"And are you on social media?"

"Yes," I say again.

"Is your profile set to public?" Harlow asks pointedly.

"Okay, yes," I tell her, holding up a hand to stall her. "But only because I use it for publicity for the shop. I don't post any of my private stuff online."

"So, maybe he did a quick google search," Harlow says with a shrug. "That's not unheard of for people who are online dating. I'm sure you searched his name, right?"

I nod and Harlow's eyes light up.

"What did you find?"

I laugh and reach for my phone. I pull up one of the tabs I'd left open with Luke's info on it and hand it to her. "See for yourself," I say.

I watch Harlow as she reads the screen, scrolling down. At one point, she blinks, and her eyes grow wide, but she doesn't stop reading. I sip my wine, letting the pleasant warmth spread through me as I wait for her to finish.

"Holy shit," she says, handing me the phone.

"That's what I said," I mutter.

"His family is like rich, rich," Harlow says.

"Yep."

Then she voices the same question I'd had when I'd first read all about Luke. "What's he doing on a dating app in the first place?"

I shrug. "Beats me. He didn't tell me, and we didn't get much chance to get to know each other before he stood me up."

"Technically, he did cancel beforehand," Harlow says. When I shoot her a glare, she says, "But it was super last-minute. Which is extremely rude. I'm on your side."

I laugh and go to take another sip from my glass only to realize it's empty. I lcan forward and set it on the coffee table. "He's not a bad guy," I say. "He stood me up because his sister went into labor, and he was rushing to the airport to catch a flight to meet his niece."

I risk a glance at Harlow, though I know what I'll see on her face. I'm right. Her eyes are soft and dreamy and she's wearing a big smile.

"Aw," she gushes. "I think my ovaries just exploded. That is the sweetest thing!"

I force myself not to smile, because it really is the sweetest. And I can't deny that when Luke had confessed his reason for not making our coffee date, I'd felt a slight stirring in my own ovaries. Damned, stupid ovaries.

"It doesn't matter," I say. "We've decided to be friends."

Harlow's nose wrinkles like she just caught a whiff of something smelly. "Friends? Why?"

I sigh. "I'm not in a good place to date right now," I say, giving her the same line I'd given Luke. "I'm so busy trying to get the shop off the ground that I don't have time to invest in a relationship."

"Who said anything about a relationship?" Harlow says. "What about a good, old-fashioned booty call? Or a friends-with-benefits situation? That man was made for sex, and you know it."

I can't help but laugh at Harlow's blunt assessment. She's not wrong, though. Luke is sexy as hell. I can't pretend I hadn't noticed. Or that I hadn't gone home the other night and gotten off while I'd fantasized about him taking me in the booth at Piping Hot. But I'll never admit that out loud. Besides, it doesn't matter if Luke is hot or if I'd like to see what he's got under that fitted suit. We're just friends, and that's the way it's staying.

I tell Harlow exactly that, but she doesn't look convinced. "If you say so," she says skeptically.

I sigh, ignoring her disbelieving tone. "That's not the problem, anyway," I tell her.

"So, what is?"

I take a deep breath and tell Harlow everything I can remember from my conversation with Luke this morning. By the time I finish, she looks more shocked than she had earlier when she'd read about Luke's company. She picks up her wine and takes a long sip before speaking.

"Just so I understand," she says. "He wants you to pretend to be his girlfriend for a work dinner. In exchange, he'll give you a crash course in online marketing?"

I nod. "Pretty much."

Harlow seems to be thinking it over before she speaks again. She shifts on the couch, pulling her feet up so she's sitting cross-legged, facing me. "Is he good at what he does?"

I nod. "I looked into him and his company. His grandfather started the company. It was thriving for a long time, but he died when Luke was still a kid. Then, it looks like Wolfe Industries didn't do so hot for a lot of years. It was circling the drain. Ten years ago, things started to turn around. That's right around the time Luke stepped into his role. There are also a few articles online about him. They all say similar things about him. That he's changed the face of Wolfe Industries and without him, the company might have crumbled."

Harlow lets out a low whistle. "No pressure or anything, right?"

I don't say anything, but I'd had the same thought earlier when reading the article. Did one man really have so much influence over the future of a business as massive as Wolfe Industries? And if so, why would he be bothered with my little shop? Or me, for that matter? Luke is used to dealing with millionaires and billionaires. I used most of my savings for the coffee shop. I'm definitely not part of that crowd. What makes him think anyone would believe me as his girlfriend?

"What would this deal entail?" Harlow asks, pulling me out of my musings. "A couple dinners? Maybe some swanky lunch thing?"

I shrug. "He only mentioned the dinner tomorrow night, so far. I think he's hoping to close the deal this week."

Harlow nods. "That's not so bad," she says. "It's not like he's asking you to sleep with him."

I nearly choke on my wine. My face goes hot again, which Harlow picks up on immediately. Her eyes go wide, and her mouth drops open.

"Holy shit! Did he?"

I shake my head, choking back a laugh. "No! He didn't. I told you everything he said. Get your head out of the gutter."

She shrugs, unrepentant. "I can't help it if that's where it wants to live." She eyes me. "So, what are you going to tell him?"

I lift one shoulder in a half-hearted shrug. "I don't know, Harlow," I say. "What would you do?"

She watches me for a moment as if deciding what she wants to say. When she speaks, her voice is gentle. "How badly do you need his help?"

I feel a twist in my gut at what his help could mean for Piping Hot and what might happen if I do nothing and continue the way things are. I've done the math. I'm an accountant, for goodness' sake. Numbers don't lie.

"I've got six months," I say, not looking at her. "If things don't turn around, I'll have to shut down."

Harlow lets out a low curse. She reaches over and gives my hand a squeeze. "How badly do you want Piping Hot to succeed?"

I meet her gaze, knowing she can see the determination in mine. "More than anything."

She smiles. "Then you know what to do." She reaches for her wine glass. "And if you decide to sleep with him, that's just icing on the cake."

I can't hold back the laugh that escapes me. "I am not sleeping with him."

"I don't know why not," she says. "That man is delicious."

She's not wrong. Luke is gorgeous. If the timing or the circumstances were different, I might have taken him up on that date do-over. But I'd been telling him the truth when I'd said I don't have time to date right now. All my time and energy are tied up in Piping Hot and I can't afford to spare any for romance or dating. But I can't pretend I haven't noticed how hot the man is.

"I know," I sigh. "But I can't afford to take my eyes off the prize right now. I need to focus on making the shop a success. Then I'll worry about my sex life."

Harlow looks skeptical, but she doesn't argue the point. "Well, whatever you decide to do," she says, "I fully support you." She raises her glass and I touch mine to hers with a smile.

"Thank you," I tell her. "That means a lot to me. It's good to know I have one friend in this town."

"Of course," she says. "But just so you know, I'd also have your back if you slept with the hottie and told me all the dirty details."

I roll my eyes at her. "Mind. Gutter."

She just shrugs. "Guilty."

I narrow my eyes at her. "Okay," I say. "Since you want to discuss my sex life, let's hear about yours. Who are you dating?"

Harlow grimaces at me. "No one," she says. "And I'd like to keep it that way. I have terrible taste in men. My track record proves it."

"That bad?" I ask.

"Worse." She stands and walks toward the kitchen. "You want some pizza? I'm starving."

I shrug and follow her. "We can eat pizza while you tell me about your bad taste in men."

She pulls two plates out of the cabinet and opens the pizza box. "There's not much to tell. I like a guy. I date him. He turns out to be a loser, or a criminal or a cheater. Take your pick. I've dated them all."

She picks up her pizza and bites into it with more force than is probably necessary. She's still wearing a look of annoyance on her face as she chews.

"Seriously," she says after she swallows. "You'd think I could learn my lesson eventually. Nope. Not me. I just keep picking the worst possible men. It's a curse."

I shoot her a sympathetic smile as I pick a piece of pepperoni off my pizza and pop it into my mouth. "It happens to the best of us," I say. "Eventually the right one will show up and he won't be a loser or a cheater or a criminal. And he'll give you lots of orgasms and you'll have his six fat babies and live happily ever after."

She looks at me like I've just sprouted an extra head. "God, I hope not! There's no way I'm having six kids. Maybe one. Eventually. Far, far down the road."

I laugh at the sheer horror in her expression. "Calm down. No one said you have to get knocked up tomorrow. You still have plenty of time to find the right guy."

She sneers. "If he exists."

I sip my wine. "So cynical," I say. "Have a little faith."

"What makes you so optimistic?"

I shrug. "Just a hunch."

"I'll take your word for it," she says, not sounding the least bit convinced.

I take another bite of my pizza, but I don't have much of an appetite. I can't get Luke's offer out of my mind. I don't know what his plan is for a fake relationship with me. I don't know if I'll be able to pull off a ruse like this. What if we can't fool anyone? Luke and I barely know one another. What if we fail and Luke doesn't want to help me anymore? I wasn't lying to Harlow earlier. I don't have a lot of time to make Piping Hot a success. If this fails, I'm not sure what I'll do next.

"Earth to Piper!"

I blink, realizing that Harlow has been talking for the last few minutes and I've been completely zoned out, thinking about my own problems. I give her a sheepish smile.

"I'm so sorry," I say. "I spaced for a second."

"You okay?" she asks, concern in her tone.

I nod. "Yeah. I'm just in my own head a little too much tonight."

She looks at me for a moment before smiling. "You already know what you're going to do," she says. "Text him and tell him you're in."

I narrow my eyes at her. "How can you read me so well?"

She shrugs and pops a piece of pepperoni into her mouth. "It's my super power. Trust me, you'll feel better once you do it."

I take a breath, finish off the remainder of my wine and reach for my phone. I type out a quick message and hit send before I can chicken out.

Okay. I'll do it.

I realize that Harlow was right. As soon as the message is sent, I feel as if a weight has been lifted. I'm still nervous about what Luke expects of me and whether we'll be able to pull off this scheme, but I feel better knowing that I'm doing something to help the shop succeed. And I'm helping out my new friend. I ignore the little part of me that's clamoring with joy at the idea of spending more time with Luke. That's not what's important here.

My phone buzzes with an incoming text in less than a minute. It's Luke.

Really? You will?

I can almost hear the surprise and excitement in those three words as I read them. I tamp down the nerves threatening to rise into my throat and text back.

Yes. Can we talk details tomorrow?

When Luke responds in the affirmative, I shove my phone back into my pocket and turn my attention back to Harlow and our girls' night. I smile and push my wine glass toward her.

"Can I have a refill, please?"

Harlow grins and reaches for the bottle. We spend the rest of the night talking about everything except men and dating. It's the most fun I've had in a long time. If my thoughts occasionally stray to Luke and our new fake relationship, that's no one's business but mine.

CHAPTER 9

Luke

I can't believe Piper agreed. The relief I felt when I got her text last night hasn't worn off yet. This is going to work. I know it is. I don't know what finally convinced Piper to go along with my plan, but I know it's going to work. I can feel it. Piper and I will talk tonight and iron out the details of the upcoming dinner. We'll convince Art and his viper of a wife that we're an adorable, happy couple and Art will sign with Wolfe Industries. Piece of cake.

The work day passes with agonizing slowness, but at least I manage to avoid any interactions with my father. All in all, not a bad day. When I finally make it home, a bag of takeout in my hands, I'm exhausted and ready to relax. I quickly change out of my suit and tie and into loose gym shorts. I decide to skip the shirt and carry my dinner out onto the balcony with a beer. By the time I finish my beer and a healthy serving of fried rice, I'm feeling more relaxed than I have since I got back to Savannah.

Finally. I pick up my phone to call Piper. She answers after the second ring.

"Luke. Hi."

"Piper. How was your day?"

"Not bad. How was work?"

"Same as always," I say. "Dull."

"Hmm." I can feel an odd sort of tension between us that hadn't been there before. I don't like it. Rather than wonder if she feels it too, I decide to call it out.

I sigh. "This is awkward now, isn't it?"

To my relief, she laughs. I find that I like the sound of that laugh. "A little," she admits. "But I don't know why."

"We're still the same two people as before," I say. "We're just two friends helping one another out with work projects."

She laughs again and I feel my lips curve into a smile. "Is that all this is?"

"Yep," I say. "Nothing more or less. So, friend. Do you want to hear my ideas for Piping Hot before or after we discuss plans for tomorrow night?"

There's a moment of hesitation on Piper's end and I wonder what she's thinking. Probably that I'm crazy to believe this will work and that she should call the whole thing off. A hint of panic rises in me at the thought. If she backs out, I'll have to figure out some way to explain her absence tomorrow at dinner. It's not the end of the world, but I don't know how the Mitchells will react to me arriving solo. I'll just have to cross that bridge when I come to it.

"You've already started working on ideas for the shop?" she asks, surprising me with the direction of her thoughts.

Her surprised tone makes me smile. "It's more like I don't know how to turn it off," I say ruefully. "I tend to look at every business as a project, even if it's not a potential client. I'm always coming up with things in my head that I think might help, even if no one ever asks for my help. So, I've kind of been mapping out ideas for Piping Hot since the first time I stepped inside."

"I see," she says. "Just how bad is it?"

"Not bad, actually," I say, standing and leaning my elbows on the railing so I can look down at the city below. "From a business standpoint, I think you have great potential. If it was located somewhere with more traffic, I think you'd already be thriving. But Peach Tree is different. You have to approach business a little differently there."

She snorts. "I've noticed."

"So, I've come up with a few ideas that I think will increase the visibility of the shop," I say. "That means within the town and in the surrounding areas. Including Savannah. Believe it or not, there are some commuters who live near Peach Tree and drive to the city for work every day. And lots of them would probably rather shop local than the big city chain shops."

We talk for a while as I lay out my ideas for social media campaigns and for the shop's website. Piper doesn't just listen, though. She comments on my ideas, bouncing her own back at me. I can hear the excitement rising in her as we talk. Before, she had seemed nervous and a bit hesitant. Now, she sounds optimistic and excited. Before I know it, an hour has passed, and we still haven't talked about the dinner tomorrow night. I'm almost hesitant to bring it up. I've had so much fun talking to Piper that I don't want to bring the focus back to our fake relationship. It feels so deceptive after the genuine conversation we've been having. Before I can decide though, Piper beats me to it.

"About tomorrow night," she says in a low voice. There's a pause before she goes on. "We need to nail down a few details."

"Right," I say. I can hear the change in my tone as it shifts from casual and friendly to more business-like. I hate it, but I can't seem to stop it.

"I'll pick you up at 6," I say. "That will give us plenty of time to make it to the house the Mitchells have rented for their stay."

"Okay," she says. "What should I wear?"

"Something elegant, but not formal," I say. "A cocktail dress, maybe?" It occurs to me to wonder if she owns a cocktail dress. It's not something a small-town coffee shop owner might have in their wardrobe. Shit. I should have thought of this sooner.

"Do you need to go shopping?" I ask, scrambling. "I can take the day off tomorrow if I need to. I'm happy to buy you whatever you need for this dinner. This is my doing, after all."

Piper's voice is stiff when she speaks again. "No. That won't be necessary."

Shit. Now I've offended her. "I didn't mean—"

"It's fine," she says, cutting off my attempt at an apology. "What else?"

It takes me a second to understand that she's back to talking about the dinner "Oh, um. I can't imagine it will take more than a couple of hours. You should be home by 10, I think. I know that's late considering you have to wake up early for the shop. If we need to leave earlier, we can."

"That's fine," she says, still using that stiff tone that tells me I stuck my foot in my mouth. I want to find a way to get back to the laughing Piper from the beginning of this call. But that Piper hadn't been thinking of deception. I get the feeling she hates the idea of lying as much as I do.

"Piper, I'm sorry," I say.

"For what?" she asks.

I sigh and rake a hand through my hair. "For everything. Forcing you to lie for me, what I said about the cocktail dress. All of it. I know this isn't easy. You're a good person. Honest. I can tell."

The line is silent for a moment, and I almost wonder if she hung up on me. But then I hear a sigh.

"You're right, Luke," she says. "This is all new to me. I'm a shitty liar. I've never been able to pull it off for very long. So, I'm worried I'm going to screw the whole thing up. Then I'll ruin your business as well as mine."

"Whoa," I say. "Is that what's bothering you? I thought I said something to piss you off."

"Well," she says, her tone sharper. "You offering to buy me clothes did feel a little bit like prostitution, but I just assumed you were oblivious, and it wasn't an intentional implication."

My mouth drops open and I sputter, trying to find the right words to respond. I fail, though. What ends up coming from my mouth is, "Huh?" Smooth, Luke. Real smooth.

To my surprise, Piper laughs. The sound once again seeps into me, making me smile despite my unease.

"I didn't mean it that way," I finally say. "I'm sorry if it came across that way. Truly."

"Luke, I know you didn't," she says. "Which is why I'm not letting myself get offended over it. Don't worry about the dress. I'll come up with something suitable. But what about the rest of the night?"

"What do you mean?" I ask. "I'm not sure what they're serving. Do you have food allergies?"

She huffs out a laugh and I hear her mumbling something under her breath. I think I hear the word 'oblivious' again. Now, I'm getting irritated.

"What did I say wrong this time?" I ask.

Piper sighs. "We're pretending to be a couple," she says.

"Yes?"

"We're pretending to be madly in love, and we don't know shit about one another." I can hear the irritation in her voice. All at once, it dawns on me what she's saying. What if the Mitchells ask us about our past or how we met? These are questions that couples would easily be able to answer, but that we haven't discussed at all. I've been so caught up with everything else that I didn't think about the little details.

"Shit," I say.

"Mmhmm." She says in a smug voice.

I sigh. "You're right."

"This relationship is already going better than my last one if you can admit that," Piper says, pulling a laugh from me.

"I can admit when I'm wrong," I say. "Because it so rarely happens, it's not such a hardship."

Now, it's her turn to laugh. "If you say so."

"Okay," I say, walking inside for a pen and notebook. "What facts do we need to nail down before tomorrow night?"

We spend another half an hour discussing our fake past, creating a simple story that won't trip us up. By the time the conversation ends, I almost feel like we're in a real relationship. Piper can be a little bossy when she wants to. I grin at the list in my hand. Why does that make me smile?

CHAPTER 10

Piper

"Tell me again why you have so many cocktail dresses?" I ask Harlow as I stand in front of the mirror in her bedroom modeling a gorgeous sheath dress in a deep navy.

"Or any cocktail dresses at all," I mutter.

Peach Tree doesn't exactly scream cocktail parties. This town caters more to backyard barbeques and crawfish boils than to anything black-tie. When I'd texted Harlow to ask her to go shopping with me today for a dress for dinner, she'd refused right away and demanded that I come raid her closet. I hadn't been optimistic at first about finding something suitable. But then I'd found that her closet takes up the entire second bedroom of her apartment above the shop. I'd been overwhelmed, but she'd taken me directly to a rack in one corner that held nothing but dresses.

Harlow just shrugs as she hands me another dress to try on. "I'm a clothes whore," she says simply. "And I never throw anything out. You never know when you might need it again."

Something about her statement doesn't quite ring true, but I decide not to pry. If I've learned anything from Harlow, it's that as much as she talks, she doesn't give away any personal details unless she really wants to. Since I respect her privacy and value her friendship, I don't dig too hard into things she doesn't seem willing to discuss.

She gives me an appraising look. "That one is hot," she says. "But I think you need something that will dazzle a bit."

"It's dinner. Not the Grammy's," I say.

She shrugs. "You're trying to make an impression, right? Show Mrs. Barracuda that you've staked your claim on Luke and she needs to back off?"

I take the dress from her, ignoring the way the words 'staked your claim' make me feel. No matter what happens tonight or what lies we tell the Mitchells, Luke isn't mine. And I damned sure haven't staked my claim. If anything, this whole farce just drives home that fact. Before his offer, when we were friends, I could let my imagination wander. I could wonder if maybe, someday, something might change between us. Even though I told myself I didn't have time for dating—and I don't—I can't lie to myself and say I didn't wonder what it would be like if I did. But that all changed as soon as Luke made his offer. It's clear he only looked me up that day because he thought I'd be perfect for this ruse. And people don't pretend to be dating someone they actually want to date. That would be too complicated.

When the new dress is in place, I turn to face the mirror as Harlow zips me up. Holy shit. I stand there, stunned by my own reflection. Harlow had been right. This dress is the one.

"Damn, girl," she says from behind me.

I meet her gaze in the mirror. She's grinning at me. "He won't know what hit him."

I smooth my hands down the front of the dress, studying my reflection again. The dress hits just above my knees, hugging my body just right. It's a deep emerald color that I know will look great with my dark hair hanging loose around my shoulders. Harlow has already declared that she's styling it for the evening. I wasn't given much choice in the matter. She also wants to apply my makeup. I agreed only after she promised to keep it subtle. She hadn't looked happy about it, but she'd eventually conceded.

"You don't need a lot of makeup anyway," she'd said. I decide to take the compliment.

After spending 40 minutes in a chair while Harlow fusses over me, I almost wish I'd done my own hair and makeup. But she looks practically giddy to be doing it. There's no way I could have refused her. Besides, I've seen her clients leave with amazing hair that she'd been responsible for. I know I can trust her with my hair. And her own makeup isn't heavy-handed. By the time Harlow is finished with me, I have just enough time to drive home before Luke is due to pick me up.

I'm a bundle of nervous energy as she spins the chair around so I'm facing the large mirror.

"Ta-da!" she says with a flourish of her hands.

I blink at the woman staring back at me from the mirror.

"Wow," I say, turning my head from side to side to see how my hair moves.

Harlow shrugs. "You're already gorgeous. It wasn't hard."

I smile at her compliment, meeting her gaze in the mirror. "Thank you."

She waves away the thanks before motioning for me to stand. "Up, up," she says. "Let's get the full effect."

I follow her orders, rising to my feet on the low heels she'd all but forced me to wear. I walk the few steps over to the full-length mirror and check out my reflection. My hair is styled in loose waves that shimmer in the light. Harlow had put some kind of serum on my hair that smells amazing and has the added benefit of making my hair shiny and smooth. I wonder what Luke will think when he sees me in this dress.

As soon as the thought enters my head, I push it away. It doesn't matter what Luke thinks when he sees me. We're not a couple and this isn't a real date. All that matters is whether we can be convincing to the Mitchells at dinner tonight. Too much is riding on the outcome of this dinner. The future of my business is more important than whatever attraction I might feel for Luke Wolfe. I just need to keep my attention on what's most important and everything will work out.

CHAPTER 11

Luke

I arrive at Piper's house just before 6pm. I'm wearing a deep blue suit with matching tie. I don't know what to expect tonight. I'd been confident last night talking with Piper on the phone, but now that it's time to face the music, I'm feeling nervous. This might be the most important dinner of my career. So much is riding on the outcome of tonight. My brain tries to go to contingency plans for what I'll do if this fails, but I don't want to think about the option of failure. I make my way to Piper's front door and ring the bell, hoping she can't see the nerves just below the surface.

But it turns out I don't need to worry about that. Because when Piper opens the door and I see her standing there, every coherent thought leaves my mind at once. The only thought left is how gorgeous she is. Following quickly on the heels of that thought is another. I am so screwed.

I think I manage to say something complimentary about Piper's appearance before she joins me outside. She turns to lock her front door and I take the opportunity to let my eyes roam over her body. The dress she's wearing hugs her in all the right places and my eyes linger on her ass. She turns to smile at me just as I bring my gaze up to her face.

"Ready?" I ask, relieved when my voice comes out sounding normal.

She nods and gives me a smile that looks a little forced. "Ready," she says. I can see that she's nervous and the need to reassure her is overwhelming. I stand in front of her, stopping her.

"It's going to be fine," I say, injecting confidence into my words. I give her a smile that I hope is reassuring.

She nods and takes a deep breath before speaking. "You're right," she says. "This is going to work."

I wait to make sure she's okay before moving to the side to lead her toward my car. When she steps up beside me, I put a hand on her waist. I tell myself it's to guide her toward the car, but I know it's an excuse to walk close to her, to touch her. Piper stiffens slightly before relaxing. It isn't a big thing, but I'd noticed it. And I know she knows I did. Instead of pulling my hand away, I let it linger just a bit longer. When we reach the car, I hesitate before opening her door.

"Piper, couples touch one another," I say. "You can't flinch every time I put my hand on your waist."

"I wasn't," she says, not meeting my gaze. I wait until she looks over at me and sighs. "Okay, fine. I did flinch. But only because you caught me off-guard. I wasn't expecting it."

"If I do anything to make you uncomfortable, tell me," I say, not wanting there to me any misunderstanding about this. "I don't want you to feel like I'm forcing you to endure my touch when you don't want it."

Something flares in her eyes, but it's gone before I can understand what I'd just seen.

"Luke, you don't make me uncomfortable," she says, smiling. "I just didn't think about it. Now that I have, I won't flinch when you touch me. We want this to be convincing, right?"

I nod. "Right."

Before I realize her intent, she leans close and puts a hand on my chest. Then her lips brush my cheek in a chaste kiss that definitely shouldn't have my dick turning to stone. But that's just what happens.

"See?" she says with a smile. "Not a problem."

I swallow hard, trying to ignore the way her nearness seems to affect me.

"Good," I manage.

I turn and walk the rest of the way to the car, my hand still on her waist. Having my arm around Piper is enough to have me wanting to take her in my arms and kiss her right there in the driveway. Really kiss her. What I want to do is nothing like the gentle peck she'd planted on my cheek. I want to take her mouth with mine, taste her, feel her moan against me.

But that's impossible. Instead, I force myself to open her door and smile politely at her as she climbs inside. I take several deep breaths to clear my head as I make my way around to the driver's side. As soon as I sit down and close the door, it's obvious that it didn't work though. All I can see are Piper's legs disappearing under the hem of her dress. All I can smell is her subtle perfume. Her hair is down, falling in shiny waves to her shoulders. She's done something to her gold-brown eyes to make them stand out even more. But that dress. I can't understand how a garment that isn't the least bit indecent has me thinking all sorts of wicked things. If I'm not careful, we won't make it to dinner because I'll crash the car staring at Piper in the seat beside me.

CHAPTER 12

Piper

The best word I can use to describe dinner is awkward. The next best word I might use would be surreal. Arthur Mitchell and his wife have rented one of the old homes in Savannah that are normally used as a bed and breakfast. But they've rented the entire home for their stay. They've also hired a private army of servants to wait on them, cook for them, and clean for them while they're here. So, this is how billionaires live? I'm not quite sure how to feel about it.

When we arrive, a valet opens my door and drives off in Luke's car to park it while another man in a suit walks us to the front door and opens it for us. I don't know when I reached out to take Luke's hand in mine, but I'm now gripping it for dear life. I'm no longer nervous to touch him, it seems. Instead, it feels almost natural to hold his hand. Something about the connection makes me less nervous about the coming dinner and meeting one of the richest men in the world.

It turns out that Arthur Mitchell isn't the one I should have been worried about meeting. He's there to greet us as soon as we enter the foyer, a big smile on his face.

"Luke!" he calls out, his voice booming through the house. "Glad you could make it."

Luke smiles widely. "Thank you for having us, Art," he says, turning to me. I'm not prepared for the adoring look he gives me as he pulls my hand up to wrap it in both of his.

"I'd like you to meet Piper Brooks," he says, turning back to Art. "Piper, this is Arthur Mitchell."

I manage a smile though my heart is racing and I'm still wondering about that look from Luke. Had that been part of the act? It had to be, right? But if so, it had been far too convincing. It's a good thing this dinner is only a couple of hours long. If I had to resist looks like that for any longer, I'm not sure I'd be able to. Art comes over to greet me, pulling me out of my wandering thoughts of Luke and how handsome he is.

"Miss Brooks," he says, taking my hand. "It's lovely to meet you."

"Thank you," I say. "Please, call me Piper."

"Only if you'll call me Art," he says in response.

I nod, still smiling. "Of course."

I don't know what I'd expected from a billionaire, but he's certainly a pleasant host. He leads us into what he calls the parlor and offers us drinks. He explains that his wife is running late, but that she'll be down shortly. Luke keeps the pleasant smile on his face, but I detect a slight stiffening of his shoulders. Does this woman really bother him that much? I've yet to see Luke ruffled by anything. I'm curious to meet her now. Art makes our drinks himself, rather than relying on a servant. I take the glass from him and take a small sip, pleasantly surprised by how good it is.

The three of us make polite small talk for a few minutes. It's more comfortable than I'd expected to chat with a billionaire. I'd expected it to be awkward or uncomfortable, but Art is charming and kind. I feel myself relaxing as he asks me about my shop, and I tell him about the little town I moved to. I avoid mentioning dates as Luke and I didn't establish exactly when our fake relationship started. Which seems like a big oversight now that I think about it. We're nearly finished with our drinks when Art's attention goes to someone behind us and he stands, his face lighting up.

"Ah, there she is," he says. "The belle of the ball."

Luke and I turn to face the woman standing in the doorway. She's wearing a dress that's just a little too tight, with a neckline that's lower than anything I would wear. This must be Melody. By the way Luke's jaw tightens and he moves a few inches closer to me on the low couch, I'd say my guess is correct. She glides into the room in dramatic fashion.

"Sorry I'm late, darling," Melody says, making her way over to her husband to kiss his cheek. "I couldn't find a thing to wear."

Art gives her an indulgent look and they turn as one to face us. "Mel, you remember Luke?"

Mel's expression shifts from the childlike petulance of moments before to that of a hunter eyeing its prey when she looks at Luke.

"Of course." She all but purrs the words. "It's so wonderful to see you again."

Luke gives her a polite smile and dips his head in a nod. When it becomes clear that he's not going to stand to greet her, Mel leans down between us and kisses Luke's cheek, leaving a smear of red lipstick behind. I have to give props to whatever wardrobe tape she's using to hold in the girls. It's clearly fighting for its life to hold that dress on. I push back the urge to gag at her obvious flirting with Luke. She hasn't even looked my way, even though I'm sitting mere inches away from the man who's supposed to be my boyfriend. Ignoring the fact that her behavior is a blatant violation of girl code, it's also just plain rude to ignore a guest in your home. As soon as she stands and puts a little distance between herself and Luke, I use my napkin to wipe at his cheek.

"Can't have that, can we?" I say with a laugh. "That's why I buy lip stain. It's a little pricy, but it's worth it when it doesn't smudge." I look over at Mel with a smile. "Don't you hate when lipstick smudges? You start out looking classy and turn into the Joker by the end of the night!"

I muster up a laugh. Luke and Art join in, but Mel only smiles. I hold out a hand toward the other woman.

"I'm Piper," I say with, smiling. "Luke's other half."

Luke puts an arm around my shoulder. "My better half," he amends with a smile.

"Aw," I say, turning to wink at him.

I don't know when we decided to turn into the world's cheesiest couple, but it appears to be a unanimous decision. Mel releases my hand as quickly as possible and moves back to Art's side. Her fake smile falters just a bit.

"Charmed," she says, sounding anything but.

"It's so nice to meet you, Mrs. Mitchell," I say. "Your husband has told us such lovely things about you while we waited." I don't know why I think reminding her of her doting husband will make her suddenly stop flirting with Luke. She clearly doesn't care who sees her behavior. Art puts an arm around Mel, pulling her against his side. It would be sweet if I didn't see Mel's irritated expression.

"How about a drink before dinner, honey?" he asks. "I can make you something?"

"Oh, I'll get it," she says, deftly moving out of his embrace. "I don't want you to trouble yourself."

Art looks like he wants to say more, but he lets her go before turning back to me and Luke. "How about you two?" he asks, gesturing to our drinks.

We both raise our mostly full glasses and decline. The addition of Mel to our group has added a strange tension to the room that not even the drinks can dispel. By the time we make our way into the dining room to eat dinner, my face hurts from the fake smile I've had plastered on it for the last half hour. I can only hope dinner isn't an elaborate affair. I'm doing my best to be charming and win Art over, but Mel continues to talk over me or change the subject back to herself each time I speak. She's clearly the kind of woman who's used to being the center of attention.

She's maybe 10 years older than me, but it's clear she's had some work done to try and look younger. She's pretty, but would be more attractive if she weren't trying so hard to monopolize the conversation. At dinner, we sit at a table that's just a bit too large for four people. Which means that Luke is seated across from me, rather than beside me, with Art and Mel at either end of the rectangular table. When servants arrive with dishes of food, it becomes clear to me that this meal isn't going to be a quick one. I don't know how many courses are planned, but the dishes are all tiny and insubstantial. Some of them are unrecognizable.

Throughout the meal, Art and Luke talk business. I try to pay attention to their discussion, but some of it goes over my head. Mel seems content to eat her food and cast me judgmental looks from time to time. It's as if she's realized that she can't intrude on her husband's business dealings, so she's biding her time until she can once again point the spotlight at herself.

I pick at the food, taking small bites just to be polite even though I don't know what half of it is. At one point, a server places a dish before me that looks and smells as if it might still be alive. Nothing is moving, though. I peer over to catch Luke's gaze. He looks almost as skeptical as I feel. I glance at Mel and Art who are focused on their own meal before meeting Luke's gaze again.

"What is this?" I mouth the words to him.

"I don't know!" he mouths back.

"Try it!" I mouth, nodding toward his plate.

"You first!" he mouths back.

I shake my head quickly and point my fork at him.

"How is your meal?" Art asks, drawing both our attention.

I grin over at him. "So good," I say. "I'm getting full already."

Art gives Luke a knowing look. "She's not one of those women who refuses to eat, is she?"

I ignore my annoyance at him talking about me as if I'm not here and just smile.

"Not at all," Luke says. "She was just telling me today how much she was looking forward to tonight's meal. Weren't you, honey?"

He smiles over at me, and I swear if he was close enough, I'd kick his shin. "Absolutely, sweetie," I say with a matching smile.

I sigh and give Art a disappointed look. "But I think my eyes were bigger than my stomach today."

He laughs at the old line my mother used to use when I prepared a bigger meal than I could finish.

"Fair enough," Art says. "I'm guilty of that myself. Besides," he leans toward me conspiratorially. "I can't stand this fancy stuff. Give me a steak or a cheeseburger any day."

The smile that comes over me isn't forced. "Don't skip the French fries," I say.

"Wouldn't dream of it!"

"Is something wrong with the food?" Mel asks in a sharp voice that makes us all turn as one to look at her.

"Not at all, dear," Art says. "We were just saying that it's not what we're used to. That's all."

Mel raises a brow at me. "Some of us were raised with more taste than others, I suppose."

No one says anything for several seconds and I've just decided to let the implied insult pass when I hear Luke let out a low curse. I look over to see a dark red stain spreading across the white tablecloth.

"Oh gosh," he says. "How clumsy of me. This is so embarrassing. I'm so sorry." I almost believe him, but there's something in his expression when he meets my gaze that makes me wonder.

Mel snaps her fingers, and two members of the wait staff rush over and set about cleaning the mess as best they can, but it's clear that the tablecloth is a lost cause. Luke gets a fresh glass of wine in record time and the plates before us are taken away and replaced with tiny dessert plates. I'm glad, because if I'd had to look at that weird, gelatinous dish a moment longer, I might have added to the stain on the tablecloth.

Finally, blessedly, the dinner ends. There are no more courses to be served. Unfortunately, Art suggests we retire to the parlor for an after-dinner drink. Luke looks at me with a question in his eyes. I'm starving, my feet hurt, I wish I'd drank enough wine at dinner to account for my headache, and I think Mel is plotting my death. But, for some strange reason, I give Luke a nod. I know he and Art haven't had nearly enough time to discuss their business deal. With the little that I understood of their discussion, I could tell nothing had been settled yet. So, I'll keep doing my part to help him.

It doesn't take long for me to regret my agreement when Mel immediately takes Luke's arm to lead him into the parlor, leaving me behind with Art. Fortunately, Art doesn't insist on offering me his arm. He simply walks beside me, asking me questions about Piping Hot as we walk. I've decided that I could probably like Art as a person if he weren't attached to that woman. How he's so oblivious to her behavior is mind-boggling.

Speaking of Mel, she makes certain to seat herself on the small loveseat next to Luke, leaving barely an inch of space between them. I notice Art's gaze move over them before he makes his way over to the bar to play bartender.

"So, Luke," he calls out as he mixes drinks for the four of us. "What are your plans for the summer?"

Luke smiles ruefully. "I'm afraid I'll spend my summer working in Savannah," he says. "No fun summer plans these days."

Art shakes his head. "That's too bad. Mel and I rented a house for a few weeks. What's the island called, dear?"

"Tybee Island," Mel says. She's still sitting too close to Luke who looks like he'd like to be anywhere else.

He clears his throat. "That's great," he says. "I'm sure you two will have an amazing time. My family used to own a home there. We spent a lot of summers on the island when I was growing up."

I take note of the little bit of personal information. It's the first time he's mentioned his childhood. I got the feeling that his relationship with his father isn't exactly loving, but I wonder if it's always been that way.

Art grins as he hands Luke a glass. "I can't believe your old man would go for that," he says. "He seems like a workaholic."

Luke gives him a tight smile. "Oh, he is. It was usually just my mother and me. My father would come out on the weekends sometimes. But mostly, I spent those summers running wild across the island, trying to see what trouble I could get into."

I smile at Luke, wanting to ask more about his summers as a kid, but then I see Mel reach over and put her hand on his knee.

"That must have been so much fun," she says.

Luke shifts enough to dislodge her hand. To anyone else, it might have seemed incidental, but I know it was intentional.

"Oh, it was," he says, pouring on the charm. "To everyone but my mother, that is. I think I drove her crazy."

Art laughs and it's clear he likes Luke. If they were able to talk business, this deal might already be done. But Art keeps changing the subject to anything and everything other than what we came here to discuss. I'm starting to wonder if he really wants to make this deal at all.

"You two should come to the island," Art says suddenly, making me blink in surprise.

"Oh, yes!" Mel exclaims. "We'd love to have you."

Her hand is back on Luke's knee. Is it higher this time? It's hard to tell from here. Luke shoots me a look that begs for assistance, but I don't know what he expects me to do. Short of telling her to get her hands off my man, I don't know what I can do to diffuse the situation.

"That does sound like a nice time," Luke says. "It's been years since I went back to the island."

Mel's hand slides just a little higher.

"It would be so nice for us to get to know each other better," she says.

I bet she would like to get to know Luke better. I look over at Art who is busying himself with making another drink and doesn't seem to notice or care that Mel is two seconds away from groping my man. Well, he's not my man, but she doesn't know that. Which okay, kind of pisses me off.

"Mel," I call out loudly. "Can you show me to the powder room?"

"It's just down the hall on the left," she says, still without moving her hand from Luke's thigh.

"Oh, would you mind showing me?" I ask sweetly. "This house is so big! I don't want to get lost."

Art turns to look at her at the exact moment she removes her hand from Luke and stands. "Of course," she says.

Her words may sound agreeable, but her eyes are shooting daggers at me. She stalks toward the hallway, leaving me to follow her or be left behind. I don't really have to use the bathroom. It was the only excuse I could think of to remove her hand from Luke's thigh. I shake my head as I follow her the short distance to the bathroom.

"There it is," she says.

Her voice has turned infinitely colder now that the men aren't around. I ignore it and smile as sweetly as possible.

"Thank you so much, Mel," I say. I smile at her until she turns around and practically stomps back toward the parlor. "Bitch," I mutter under my breath as soon as she's out of earshot.

The parlor is still within sight of the bathroom door. There was no way I could have gotten lost on my way here. But it had been worth it to thwart that bitch's plans with Luke. I go into the bathroom and wash my hands, stalling for long enough that they believe I used the facilities. The more I think about Mel's behavior, the more irritated I get. As far as she knows, Luke is my boyfriend. He's practically my fiancé from what he's told them. But she feels comfortable flirting with him and touching him right in front of me. And in front of her own husband! Who does she think she is? And how many times has she done this before with other men? Art deserves better than her. At least, I think he does based on this one dinner.

After I feel like enough time has passed, I make my way back to the parlor. Now, Luke is standing between Art and the wall. There's no way for Mel to insinuate herself next to him. Good boy. If he'd been sitting next to her when I returned, I would have left him to fend for himself. There's only so much I can do for him. He meets my gaze and smiles.

"There you are," he says. "I was just telling Art that I might be able to make it to the island next week for a few days."

"Oh?" I ask, trying to hide the shock that Luke apparently accepted their offer in the 3 minutes I was gone.

He nods and walks over to put an arm around my shoulder. "But I told them you couldn't possibly make it. It's not a good time for you to leave the shop unattended, right?"

I smile up at him, grateful that he didn't try and include me in his impromptu vacation plans. "Summer is a busy season," I say.

Just then, I catch sight of Mel. She's got her eyes on Luke and it would be impossible to miss the calculating gleam there. It's obvious she's already thinking about when she can get Luke alone. It will be that much easier with him staying at their home. What was he thinking, accepting their offer? He must be desperate to close this deal.

"Oh, that's too bad," Mel says. Her words say one thing, but that look in her eyes says something different. She's downright thrilled at the idea of Luke going without me. What happens next feels like it's out of my control.

"You know," I say, taking a sip of my drink. "I'm sure I can rearrange some things and make it happen. Some time off might be just what I need. Right, honey? You're always saying I work too much. And we all know you do."

I laugh. After a second, Luke joins in, but it sounds forced.

"Right," he says, eyeing me warily. "Are you sure? What about the shop? Who will run it in your place?"

"Don't worry about that," I say. Both of us know the shop could close for a week and no one in Peach Tree besides Stevie would notice. But I don't say that. Instead, I say, "I'll take care of the details."

I loop my arms around Luke's waist and hug him close before giving Mel and wide, excited smile. "This is going to be so much fun!"

CHAPTER 13

Luke

I manage to keep a cordial smile on my face and uphold my side of the conversation until we're finally able to leave. Art and I make plans for tomorrow to discuss all the details for the upcoming trip. By the time Piper climbs into my car and I make my way around to the driver's side, I'm wound tighter than a spring. I work to unclench my jaw, feeling the ache there from swallowing back all the questions I have. I don't hold back for long, though.

"Why did you agree to go on this trip?" I ask as soon as I pull away from the curb. "I was giving you an out."

Piper slips her heels off and rubs her toes, wincing. "Because I saw that bitch eyeing you like you were prime rib, and she was starving. You know she'd make her move the second she got you alone in her house."

I shudder at the idea. I know Piper's right. But that doesn't explain why she volunteered. We hadn't discussed taking a vacation together. We'd agreed on dinner, maybe a lunch or drinks. But not a week on an island where we have to pretend to be madly in love 24 hours a day. How are we going to pull that off? More importantly, how the hell am I going to keep my hands off Piper for that long?

My eyes stray to where she's still rubbing her tired feet. If I weren't driving, I'd offer to rub them for her. I could start with her toes and work my way up to her ankles, her calves, those thighs. I realize that her dress has ridden up slightly, showing more of those thighs. I wonder what she's wearing under that dress. I picture my hands sliding up, pushing the fabric higher until she's exposed to my gaze. And now my dick is hard again. Shit. What is it about this woman?

"Hey," Piper says, her hand waving in my direction. I realize that my mind had completely wandered away from the topic.

"I gave you a way out," I say, my voice gruffer than I'd intended. "We didn't agree to a week away together. It's bad enough I have to endure that woman's presence."

Piper sucks in a startled breath. I glance over at her. I'm shocked to see a flash of hurt on her face that shifts quickly to anger. "Am I that difficult to *endure?*" she asks, crossing her arms over her chest and glaring at me.

Shock fills me and I don't know what to say. "That's not—I didn't mean you. I was talking about *her*. I don't want to force you to be around her. I'm stuck. But you're not."

"Oh," Piper says, clearly embarrassed by her initial reaction. "Sorry."

Her face immediately softens, and I can't help the smile that spreads over my own.

Then her lips curve into an amused smile and she shakes her head. "She really is horrible, isn't she?"

I laugh. "The worst."

She puts a hand on my upper arm, freezing as her hand meets my biceps. "We made a deal," she says softly. "I help you land this contract, and you help me make Piping Hot Brews a success. If that means I have to hang out with the scary lady for a week to keep her out of your pants, so be it."

The relief that comes over me at her words is overwhelming. I still can't believe she agreed to spend a week at a beach house with that awful woman, but I'm so grateful I won't have to face her alone. I'll have Piper on my side. I turn to smile at her.

"Thank you," I say. "Really."

She narrows her eyes at me, but I can see a teasing glint there. "Unless you don't want me there? Do you want her to get into your pants?"

"God, no!" I say, vehement. "I may have a reputation when it comes to women, but it's highly exaggerated. I do have some standards, you know."

Piper gives an approving nod. "Good to know not all men are so desperate that they'd sleep with anyone interested in them."

Something about the way she says it makes me wonder if she's speaking from experience. I want to ask, but I don't know her well enough to pry into her personal life. Do I? I mean, maybe I don't, but we're about to spend a week together pretending to be madly in love. Surely that means we can get to know one another a little better. Right?

I clear my throat. "Is there a particular guy you're referring to?" I ask.

Piper sighs and I see her toying nervously with the hem of her dress. That brings my gaze back to her thighs, and I force my attention back to the road before I do something crazy, like reach over and slide my hand over all that skin. My hands grip the wheel so tightly they hurt.

"No one important," Piper says in a low voice.

I can tell she's holding back, but I don't want to push her. It's not my place. But it's clearly a sore subject, which makes me wonder if some asshole cheated on her in the past. To my surprise, a flash of anger shoots through me at the idea. What kind of moron would cheat on Piper? She's gorgeous, funny, smart and sexy as hell. A man would have to be blind and stupid.

"I think we need to make a plan," Piper says, oblivious to my internal musings.

I blink, unsure of what she's talking about. "What kind of plan?"

"For the trip," she says, rolling her eyes. "Obviously."

The trip. Right. The one I'd agreed to, thinking it would be a perfect opportunity to get Art to sign with Wolfe. I hadn't expected Piper to agree to go as well. How the hell am I going to keep my hands to myself around her for an entire week? It's been difficult enough for just one evening. Why had I let her convince me we should be friends? Friends don't imagine fucking their friends until they can't walk straight. I try to discreetly adjust my pants to hide my growing erection. This is going to be a disaster.

"We did okay tonight," Piper says. She's digging through her tiny purse, oblivious to my own internal struggles. How she could possibly lose something in a purse that tiny is beyond me, but it takes her a full minute to find what she's looking for. "It's going to be a lot harder to convince them we're a couple for an entire week. Especially if we're in their home and it's just the four of us."

I feel my chest tighten. If Art finds out I lied about my relationship with Piper, I can kiss this contract goodbye. I'll also have to say goodbye to helping all those businesses I'd made promises to. Including Piper's. I glance over at her, noting the worried look in her eyes. I can't fail. We can't fail.

"We'll just have to make it convincing," I say.

"Right," she says, nodding. "We can do this."

She's fidgeting with the hem of her skirt again, worrying the fabric between her fingers. I glance over to see her brows drawn together in a little worried line. I reach over and take her hand in mine, smoothing my thumb over her knuckles. I don't miss the way she tenses in surprise. I don't know what made me do it. I'd just seen that she was worried, and I wanted to reassure her. Which is weird, right? We barely know one another. But, if we're going to do this fake relationship right, we need to at least become friends. And friends reassure one another when they're worried. I think.

"We're going to pull this off," I say, injecting more confidence into my voice than I feel. "Everything will work out."

Piper nods and blows out a breath. She's sitting there in the seat next to me, her back ramrod straight. Her hand is limp in mine, as if she's afraid to move. I stroke my fingers over the back of her hand and hear her suck in a sharp breath.

Making a quick decision, I turn off into a massive parking lot and pull to a stop under one of the lights. The big box store is still open, even at this time of night. But most of the cars are parked near the front of the lot, rather than the back where I've parked. Piper looks around at our surroundings then back to me, confusion evident in her gaze.

"What are you doing?" she asks.

I unbuckle my seatbelt and shift in the seat to face her more fully. "We need to talk, and I can't do that while I'm focusing on the road."

"Okay," she says, still clearly confused.

I take a breath and blow it out. "Piper, take a deep breath," I say. "You don't have to do anything you don't want to do. If you want to back out now, say the word. I'll come up with a believable reason for you to miss the trip. And I'll still do what I can to help your shop. You held up your end of the bargain already. I won't blame you if you want to bail now."

As I say the words, I know I mean them. If Piper wants out of this ridiculous arrangement, I truly won't fault her for it. But even though I know I mean the words, there's still a part of me that rebels against the idea of her ending it. There's a small part of me that wants to spend a week with Piper in a beach house, even if we do have to endure that woman. I realize that I just want to get to know Piper better. I want the chance to learn more about her. But I won't force her. I won't have her thinking this is the only way to save her business.

"It's your choice, Piper," I say.

I study her in the dim glow cast by the overhead lights. She looks nervous, thoughtful, and somehow still so gorgeous. All at once, it hits me. She's going to say no. She's going to tell me she can't do this. I'm hit with a mixture of disappointment, mild panic and something like relief. The disappointment and panic I understand. Everything I've worked for over the last ten years hinges on this deal going through. And now I've made her a part of it, even if I hadn't truly meant to. But the feeling of relief is confusing. Before I can evaluate that feeling further, Piper opens her mouth to speak.

"We made a deal," she says. "And I'm not backing out now. One week really isn't so long."

I can't stop the smile that spreads over my face. And I can't tamp down the excitement at the idea of spending a week with this woman. I have the ridiculous urge to lean over and kiss her. Which is a terrible idea. If we want this thing to work, we need to keep things between us friendly. Which means keeping our hands off one another until the contract is signed. I can do that. I can ignore this annoying attraction I feel for Piper for a week. One week. Seven days. Why does that suddenly sound like an incredibly long time?

She points to a fast-food restaurant on the other side of the parking lot. "Can we get drive-thru? I'm starving."

I sigh in relief. "That's the best idea I've heard all night. What the hell was that food?"

She shudders as I turn the car toward the bright lights of the restaurant. "I don't want to know. Just give me greasy fries and chicken nuggets, please."

I do as she commands. After going through the drive-through and getting the food, I park the car and we eat from paper bags as we laugh and joke about the ridiculousness of the evening. It feels normal and natural, being with Piper like this. It's almost enough to make me forget the reason we're here in the first place.

CHAPTER 14

Piper

"Repeat that, please," Harlow demands.

Harlow is standing in the doorway to her shop, blinking at me in confusion. Her hair is pulled up in a messy bun and she's wearing a pair of black-rimmed glasses. She's in a baggy shirt that says "Smut Slut" in swirling, hot pink font and blue pajama pants with llamas on them. I've clearly woken her with my early morning visit, but I needed someone to talk to. And I'm not quite ready to tell Layna about my latest predicament. I know she loves and supports me, no matter what. But I don't want to hear that worried tone she always gets when she hears I've done something rash and impulsive.

I take a deep breath. "I'm spending next week with Luke and the Mitchells at their house on Tybee Island." I say it as if it's no big deal, but I don't look at Harlow for several long seconds after I finish.

"That's what I thought I heard," she says.

"I need someone to tell me I'm not crazy for agreeing to this," I say.

Harlow blinks at me a few more times. "First of all, good morning," she grumbles. "Secondly, I'm going to need coffee to have any kind of coherent conversation this early."

I wince. "Sorry for waking you up. I didn't know who else I could talk to about this."

She sighs. "Wait here." Then she turns and walks toward the back of the shop. She's gone for less than five minutes before returning. This time she's holding a set of keys and her phone in her hand. She's also wearing a pair of lime green flip flops.

"Let's go," she says, gesturing toward the front door of the shop.

Confused, I don't move. "Where?"

She shoots me a glare. "I want coffee. You own a coffee shop. Let's go."

My eyes travel over her ensemble which hasn't changed since she disappeared upstairs moments ago. "You're wearing that?"

She glances down as if remembering that she's wearing pajamas. She shrugs. "I put a bra on." She looks back over at me. "Besides, we're not going to run into anyone this early."

I ignore the implication that there won't be anyone at my shop to run into either, even though she's not wrong. But that has nothing to do with the time of day. I stop arguing with Harlow and follow her out onto the sidewalk. We're silent as we make the short walk over to my shop. The sun is up, but only just. The streets of Peach Tree are empty and silent. It's not until I'm unlocking the front door of Piping Hot that I hear the rumble of an engine. Harlow and I both turn to see a pickup truck pass slowly by.

The vehicle slows even further as it passes us, and the driver makes no attempt to hide the fact that he's staring at us. Harlow and I watch as he passes. I don't think I've seen him in town before. I'd remember if I had. Even from several yards away, I can tell he's good looking. His dark hair is on the longer side, just brushing his shoulders and he's got a short beard that makes him look roguish. The truck has slowed to a crawl, and I can feel his intense gaze on us. Well, on one of us, anyway. I glance over at Harlow, who's suddenly preoccupied with her phone and pretending not to notice the big ass truck that's barely moving as it passes us. She's also very obviously not looking at the hot guy driving said truck. Interesting. I raise a brow, but say nothing. Instead, I paste on a polite smile and wave at the man. It takes him a second to notice me, but he does eventually return the wave before speeding up slightly and driving away.

I stand in front of the shop for a second, keys in hand, waiting for Harlow to look up from her phone. When she finally does, there's a flustered expression on her face that I know I've never seen there before. Her cheeks are faintly flushed, but she tries to adopt a casual expression Interesting, indeed.

"Who was that?" I ask brightly.

She shrugs. "No one." She's clearly trying for nonchalance, but I'm not fooled. Something about the man in the truck rattled Harlow. And I've never seen her rattled.

I narrow my eyes at her. "Don't think I'm letting this go," I say. "But first, coffee."

I turn and unlock the shop, letting her walk in ahead of me before re-locking the door. Not that anyone in Peach Tree is going to show up demanding coffee from me. I could keep the doors locked all day and it's not likely anyone would notice. Except Stevie. But she's got the day off today. Harlow follows me around as I turn on enough lights so I can see to work. Then she hops up on the counter to watch while I work.

I settle into the routine of grinding the beans and brewing the coffee. Harlow silently observes, making no move to help me. I'm glad she doesn't. It would take longer to show her how to work the machines than to just do it myself. Besides, there's something about the ritual that's soothing. My hands move almost without thought as I work and soon the pungent aroma of coffee fills the air. I love that smell almost as much as I love the taste.

When I finish making Harlow's coffee and hand it to her, she looks a little more awake than she had earlier. She smiles her thanks and takes a long sip. The moan she lets out after makes me laugh.

"You're a goddess among women," she says. "It's really too bad we're both into dudes. I'd marry you for this coffee alone."

I laugh again, shaking my head. "If only," I say, only half joking.

Harlow takes another sip before looking at me with raised brows. "So? Tell me. How was dinner?"

I think back over the events of the night before. Luke picking me up in his luxury car, meeting Arthur and Mel, the predatory way she'd looked at Luke during dinner and the surge of jealousy I'd felt. Then there had been the invitation to their island home. I still don't quite understand what had made me agree to go. I remember the way Luke had seemed angry at my agreement; how quiet he'd been until the drive home when he'd told me he didn't want me to have to endure that woman.

But I hadn't liked the way Mel had been eyeing Luke as if he were a piece of meat. There's more to him than that, not that she will ever find that out. And now I'm back to thinking of him as mine again, even though this whole thing is a lie. With a sigh, I launch into a recap of last night, ending with my conversation with Luke in that parking lot. Harlow listens intently as she sips her coffee, not commenting until I'm finished.

"We're supposed to talk today and make a plan for the trip," I say.

"Wow," Harlow says, eyes wide. "You're going to spend a week with people you barely know?"

I let out a sigh as I nod. Art doesn't seem like a bad sort, but the idea of hanging out with Mel for any length of time doesn't sit well. Then there's Luke. Spending a week in the same house with him makes me feel uncomfortable for a whole lot of reasons that have nothing to do with Mel or my business. Warmth spreads through me as I remember his proximity in the car last night. That had only been for half an hour. How many half-hours are in a week? How the hell am I going to be able to act natural around him for that long and not let on that I want to rip his clothes off.

"Will you and Luke share a room?" Harlow asks, a teasing tone in her voice.

My heart leaps into my throat at the idea. "Shit," I whisper. "I didn't think of that."

Harlow raises a brow. "You didn't consider that two adults who are supposed to be on the verge of engagement might share a room on a vacation? This isn't the 1940s, Piper."

"I know that," I say, defensive. "I just didn't think about it when I agreed to go. As soon as Luke told Mel I wouldn't be able to go, her freaking eyes lit up like a kid at Christmas. It was disgusting. The words just popped out. I wasn't really thinking about everything that would go along with it."

Harlow leans forward and speaks in a low voice. "You don't think Luke would take advantage of the situation, do you? If you two are sharing a room, or even a bed, I mean. You don't think he would push himself on you?"

I immediately shake my head. "He's not like that," I say.

"You're sure?" Harlow asks.

I nod. "He's been nothing but a gentleman so far. Plus, I don't think he'd risk this deal. It means a lot to him."

As I say it, I know it's true. Luke has made it clear that he needs this deal to go through if he hopes to keep taking small business clients. From everything he's told me, that's where his passion lies. I don't think he'll do anything to risk that. That includes blurring the lines with me. I push aside the pang of disappointment I feel at that thought. It doesn't matter if I'm attracted to Luke. That's not what this is about. I need to play my part and help him get Arthur Mitchell to sign on as his client so Luke will help make Piping Hot a success. I look around the empty shop and hope Luke can work a miracle.

Otherwise, my time as a small business owner is coming to an end sooner than I'd like.

CHAPTER 15

Piper

It's mid-morning when I hear the bell above the door ring. A swell of excitement surges through me. Finally, a customer. Maybe today is the day things start to turn around. People in town have probably seen Harlow in the shop or seen her drinking from the paper cup with the shop's logo and gotten curious. I put on a welcoming smile and turn toward the sound. When I get a good look at the person standing in the doorway, I freeze.

My older sister lets out a high-pitched squeal and skips over to where I'm standing, throwing her arms around me.

"Surprise!" she calls out in a sing-song voice. "I missed you!"

Surprised is right. Stunned might be more accurate. What is Layna doing here? She's supposed to be on the opposite end of the state. She never takes time off from work. And she definitely never shows up anywhere unannounced. She hates surprises and big displays. Her showing up here, out of the blue has me worried.

"Is everything okay?" I ask, trying not to let my worry show.

Layna rolls her eyes. "Can't I just come visit my baby sister for the weekend?"

I eye her warily. She certainly looks okay. She's dressed in what she would deem casual in a cream-colored, linen jumpsuit that I know from experience is as comfortable as it looks. Did she drive here? Or fly into Savannah?

"Of course, you can visit me," I say. "You just don't usually drop in for surprise visits. That's all."

Layna shrugs, not meeting my gaze. Instead, she's peering around at the shop's interior. "I missed you," she says again. "Besides, I wanted to see this town you've banished yourself to and check out your new shop."

"Right," I say, wondering if that really is the only reason she came to Peach Tree.

I love my sister. I do. She and I have always been close, even with a five-year age gap between us. After our mother died when I was thirteen, Layna took it upon herself to finish raising me. She'd only been 18 at the time, but that hadn't stopped her from stepping into the role. Almost overnight, it was as if she'd stopped being my cool big sister and had become the responsible mother figure she felt I needed. It took me a long time to realize what had changed, but by then, it was too late to change it back.

I know Layna had just been doing what she'd thought was best. We'd both been grieving. At the time, I'd needed someone to take charge and make sure I stayed on the right path. The trouble is, Layna had never stopped mothering me. It's been nearly 15 years since our mother died and she's still trying to protect me and make sure I'm happy. I love her for it. But I'd be lying if I said I don't miss my fun-loving older sister.

"I've missed you, too," I say, putting an arm around her shoulders and giving her a little squeeze.

I watch Layna as she peers around at the interior of the shop. I know what she's seeing. Or rather, not seeing. There isn't a single customer in Piping Hot Brews. Even at this time of the morning, someone should be here wanting coffee. But the place is empty. I know there's no way I'm going to be able to keep pretending things are going well here in Peach Tree.

"Slow day?" she asks, turning back to me.

I nod. "Seems like it," I say with a bright smile. I know I'm stalling, but I really don't want to talk about my failure as a business owner right now.

"When did you get in?" I ask, steering the topic away from the shop.

"Just now," Layna says. "I drove straight here. I figured you'd be working."

"Drove?" I ask. "You didn't fly?"

She shakes her head. "It was too last minute," she says. "There weren't any flights available. So, I figured I'd just make it a road trip."

I eye her warily. I wonder what time she left this morning.

"What time did you leave Atlanta?" I ask.

She shrugs. "Like 5 this morning."

"What about work?" I ask.

She shrugs again. "Called in sick."

Now I know something is going on with her. Layna never calls in sick unless she's on death's door.

"What's going on?" I ask. "Are you okay?"

Her expression shifts to one I recognize. Stubbornness. "I'm fine," she says brightly. "Nothing is going on. I just wanted to come see you, so I did. No big deal."

I know there's something she's not telling me. I also know her well enough to know I'm not going to pry it out of her until she's ready to talk about it. So, I let it go for now, opting instead to distract her from my own problems.

"How about you go back to my place and take a nap, then?" I steer her toward the front door. "You've been driving since before dawn and I know you've got to be tired. Even if you want to pretend otherwise."

She looks like she wants to argue with me, but I can see the exhaustion in her eyes. Instead, she just nods. "You're probably right," she says.

"Of course, I am," I say. "It's okay to let someone take care of you for once. Besides, this way you'll be all rested up by the time I close here so we can hang out tonight."

She smiles. "That sounds like a good plan," she says.

I return the smile. "I've been known to have a few of those."

I remove my house key from the ring in my pocket and give it to Layna before walking her out to her car. I'm still worried something's going on with her, but I know she'll tell me about it in her own time.

Piper

"You're coming out with me tonight," I say as soon as Harlow answers the phone.

"Hello, to you, too," she says dryly. "And why are we going out tonight?"

"Hello," I say. "And we're going out because my slightly over-protective sister showed up out of the blue today and I need to distract her from asking too many questions about the shop. Seeing that I have friends here and a social life might keep her from questioning why I don't have any customers."

There's a long pause while Harlow takes in everything I've said. "Why does it matter what your sister thinks of your business?" she finally asks.

I sigh. "It just does, okay. I don't want to disappoint her. Layna sacrificed a lot in her life for me and I don't want to let her down."

"Do you really think she'll be disappointed in you?" Harlow asks.

For some reason, the question makes my throat feel a little tight and I swallow hard against the lump there. "Okay, no," I say. "But I will be. And I'm just not ready to admit defeat yet. Can you help me?"

Harlow sighs. "Of course, I'll go out with you both tonight. That's not even a question. But I do think you should be honest with her. She's your sister and she loves you. She's not going to judge you. Besides, she's going to find out eventually."

"I know," I say. "And if this plan with Luke doesn't work, I'll have to come clean. She knows business hasn't been great, but she doesn't know how bad it really is. I'm going to tell her. But, for now, I want to keep it between us."

"Fine," she says. "But you're buying the first round."

I smile. "Deal. Be ready at 6. We're going to Peach Fuzz."

"Peach Fuzz?" Harlow's voice cracks on the last word and she clears her throat. "Why there?"

I shrug, though she can't see the action. "It looked like a cool place from the outside and it's got good reviews online. Besides, it's the only decent bar in town that also has actual food on the menu. Why? Is there something wrong with it?"

"No," Harlow says quickly. "No, I'm sure it's fine."

"Okay," I say, wondering at her quick response. "6 o'clock okay?"

"I might be a little late," she says. "I'll meet you guys there?"

"Don't stand me up," I say. "I'm counting on you."

She laughs. "I'll be there. I just have a late color for a client. Then I have to close up the shop. Have a margarita standing by."

I smile. "Rocks or frozen?"

"Rocks, obviously," Harlow says. "Plenty of salt."

"Done," I say.

After we say our goodbyes and end the call, I wander through the house toward the spare bedroom where Layna is still sleeping. It's been several hours since she left Piping Hot, and I wonder if I should wake her. I don't want her to sleep so much she's up all night again tonight. I'm also not sure I'm ready to answer the questions I know she'll have. Layna isn't blind or stupid. I won't be able to hide the truth of the shop's lack of success for long. I'm just putting off the inevitable. Before I can decide whether to wake Layna, the door to her room opens and my sister peers out.

She's wearing a t-shirt and a pair of cotton shorts, and her hair is loose around her shoulders. She looks so completely different from the elegant, put-together woman of this morning that I smile. This is the Layna I prefer. Casual, relaxed and herself.

"Did you sleep okay?" I ask.

She nods and reaches up to gather her wild hair up into a messy bun. "I guess I was more tired than I thought," she says.

That brings back my curiosity about why she'd decided to come visit me at the last minute without letting me know she was coming. I consider how to broach the subject without making Layna defensive, but she's talking again before I can come up with anything.

"You weren't exaggerating about the peaches," Layna says, leaning down to peer into the refrigerator. "This town is obsessed."

"Just wait until you see the water tower," I say. "A photo just doesn't do it justice."

She stands, holding a bottle of water. "I still don't understand why no one told the mayor what a peach means online."

"I think it's been painted that way since before emojis were a thing," I say with a shrug. "It grows on you."

Layna shakes her head, but she's smiling. "If you say so."

"So," I say. "You want to tell me why you're really here?"

Layna becomes suddenly interested in peeling the label from the bottle of water in her hand. "I missed you," she says, but her words don't hold as much conviction as they had earlier.

I reach over and put a hand over hers, stilling their movements. "Lay," I say softly. "What's wrong?"

She blows out a shaky breath and raises her gaze to mine. "Am I boring?"

I blink at her, taken aback by the question. Whatever I'd expected her to say, it's not that.

"What do you mean?" I ask.

Layna sighs. "I was at work yesterday, and everyone was talking about their plans for the long weekend. They were all asking one another where they were going and what they were doing. And they all seemed to have something to do." She pauses to take a sip from the bottle of water. "And then I realized that no one was asking me about my plans. They were all just talking around me, but no one was talking *to* me. And I realized they weren't asking me, because the answer is always the same. Nothing. I never *do* anything, even for long weekends. I bring work home or I sit in my apartment rearranging my closet or online shopping. I can't even remember the last time I went on a date."

She looks up at me and I can see a bright sheen in her brown eyes.

"How lame is that?" she says, her voice cracking on the words. "I'm 32 years old and I might as well be 80."

She swipes at her cheeks, and I feel my heart clench painfully. This is my fault. Layna gave up everything to be there for me after our mom died. She spent most of her 20s making sure I finished high school and got into a good college. She's been working her ass off since she turned 18 so that I would have a good life. And now that I've left her, she must feel like I've abandoned her. Like all that work was for nothing. Standing, I wrap my arms around my big sister and rub her back as she sniffles against my shoulder.

"I'm sorry," I say. "I miss you, too."

After a few minutes, Layna pulls away from me and wipes at her face. "I feel like an idiot," she mutters.

"You're not an idiot," I say, fiercely. "You're amazing. I'm sorry you had to give up so much of yourself for me."

Layna's startled gaze shoots to me and she shakes her head. "Oh, no," she says. "Don't ever think that."

"It's true," I argue. "You were too busy raising me to have a life of your own. You skipped out on going away to college after Mom died so you could take care of me. Your whole life could have been different if you hadn't been stuck raising your little sister."

"Piper, stop." Layna's voice has lost the softness of moments ago. She sounds almost angry now. "You're my sister and I love you. But you're being an idiot right now. I did what was best for both of us. Not just you. I couldn't go off to college after losing Mom that way. There was no way I would have been able to focus on school, even if I didn't have you to care for. I was a mess after Mom died. The only thing that kept me focused and moving forward was you. I knew I had to be an example for you. I needed to keep going so that you could see it was possible."

She shakes her head at me. "Don't ever feel like you were some sort of burden, holding me back. Because that's just not true."

My vision blurs and I have to fight back the tears that threaten to spill over. "I never knew," I say. "You were always so strong."

"I was faking it."

A watery laugh escapes me and Layna joins in. I sniff loudly and take a deep breath, then blow it out. "Okay," I say. "Back to you thinking you're boring. You aren't, by the way."

She rolls her eyes. "Whatever."

"You're not," I insist. "You're just in a rut. You need to try something new. Break out of your shell a little."

She sighs. "That's why I came here."

I look at her like she's crazy. "You came to Peach Tree for adventure? Because if that's the case, I hate to break it to you. You won't find it here."

She laughs and rolls her eyes. "No. I came here to prove to myself that I didn't have to stick to my usual, boring weekend routine of takeout and a face mask on the couch with Netflix."

"That sounds kind of nice," I say.

"It is. Very relaxing," she says. "But I needed to break out of the routine. So, I called in sick to work, packed a bag and started driving. I didn't really have a plan. But I knew I missed my sister, so I came here." She lifts one shoulder in a shrug. "Sorry to spring it on you."

"Are you kidding me?" I ask. "Having you here for the weekend is the best surprise. Don't apologize for coming to see me."

"Are you sure?" Layna still looks skeptical, so I roll my eyes.

"Yes, I'm sure," I insist. "I've already talked to Harlow and we're having a girls' night out tonight."

"Who's Harlow?"

I smile. "My new friend," I say. "You're going to love her. She owns the beauty shop in town and she's one of the only people in Peach Tree to give me half a chance. She also loves my coffee."

Layna smiles. "Then she's clearly smart with excellent taste."

CHAPTER 16

Piper

When we walk into Peach Fuzz later that night, I'm not sure what to expect. The place is well-lit, with plenty of tables spaced around the room. There's a low hum of chatter and I can hear music playing through the overhead speakers. Even though it's early, there are already a lot of tables filled with people eating and drinking. Over half the stools at the bar are occupied. A hostess wearing a deep green apron and a friendly smile leads us over to a booth and we sit. Layna looks around the room, assessing.

"This place is nice," she says, a hint of surprise in her tone.

"Try to hide your shock," I say, dryly.

She laughs. "That's not what I meant," she says.

"Sure, it is," I say. "And I get it. Peach Tree isn't Atlanta or Savannah. This isn't what you expected here, is it?"

She gives me a sheepish smile. "Maybe I was wrong," she admits.

I gasp, my mouth dropping open as I stare at my sister. She rolls her eyes.

"Did I just hear what I think I heard?" I ask, putting a hand to my ear. "Could you please repeat that? And maybe let me record it for future reference." I reach for my phone, but Layna smacks me with her menu before I can unlock the screen.

"Shut up," she says, but she's laughing. "I'm not that bad."

I eye her but say nothing.

"I'm not!" she insists. "I can admit when I'm wrong." She shrugs. "It's not my fault it doesn't happen often."

I just roll my eyes. "Whatever."

She turns her attention to the drink menu the hostess left for us just as someone approaches the table. We both look up to see our server standing there wearing a welcoming smile. I can't help but notice how attractive he is. His dark hair is nearly black and curls slightly over his ears. His eyes are hazel and crinkle at the corners when he smiles. It takes me a second to realize those hazel eyes are trained on my sister.

"Welcome to Peach Fuzz," he says. "Is this your first time here?"

He still hasn't looked away from Layna. When I glance over at her, I see something shocking. She's blushing. What the hell? Since when does my sister blush over a cute guy smiling at her?

"Yes," I say, since it's clear Layna isn't going to answer. "First time."

The server reluctantly drags his attention away from Layna and smiles at me, though with far less enthusiasm.

"Do you have any questions about the menu?" His voice is polite, but I can tell he'd rather be addressing Layna.

I shake my head. "I don't think so. I'll have a peach margarita."

He smiles again. "That's one of our most popular drinks."

I smile conspiratorially. "Can't imagine why." That gets a small laugh from the man before his eyes dart over to Layna.

"We have a friend joining us too," I say, pulling his attention briefly back to me. "Can we get a margarita on the rocks for her?"

He gives me a nod. "Absolutely." He turns back to Layna, his smile growing again. "And for you?"

If I wasn't so amused by how obvious he's being with his interest in Layna, I might have let his clear dismissal of me hurt my feelings. But, honestly, it's hilarious to watch.

"I'll have an old fashioned," Layna finally answers.

The server's smile widens. "A bourbon girl. Nice."

I hear someone call out from the bar, pulling his attention away from us for a moment. He holds up a hand toward whoever was shouting for him, then turns back to us.

"My name is Cole," he says with another flirty smile. "If you need anything at all, just let me know."

"Okay," Layna says with a shy smile of her own.

After Cole turns and walks back to the bar, I lean over the table and hiss, "What the hell was that?"

Layna's expression is all innocence. "What?"

"You know what," I say. "You let that waiter eye-fuck you."

Layna's mouth drops open in shock and she sputters before finding her voice. "That's not what he was doing. I was just ordering a drink."

"Yeah sure," I say, rolling my eyes before picking up the food menu. "It's a good thing I have an IUD. I could have gotten pregnant just now."

Layna snorts out a laugh, slapping a hand over her mouth. With her other hand she gives me a playful swat. "You're an asshole," she says.

I just grin at her and shrug. "You love me."

Layna rolls her eyes. "Lucky for you," she mutters.

I eye her for a moment. "He is cute, though," I say.

"Mm hmm," Layna says, her eyes glued to the menu in her hands. "I think I want a burger."

"You should get his number," I say, only half-teasing her.

She shoots me a look from under a raised brow. "No, thanks."

I sigh. "Why not? He's cute. You're cute. You're both clearly interested. What's the harm in flirting a little? Seeing what happens?"

"We both know I'm not a 'see what happens' kind of person," she says.

I sigh again, because she's right. Layna has always been a planner. She's never been spontaneous. Except for this unplanned trip to see me, I've never known her to do something without a plan and a back-up plan. Sometimes two back-up plans. But hadn't she said she wanted to have more fun? Loosen up a little? Not that

I'm telling her to hook up with a stranger or anything. But she could stand to let go of some of her obsession with planning. At least for one night. I open my mouth to tell her just that, but I realize our drinks are here.

I look up, expecting to see the cute server from before, but this time there's a petite redhead woman standing there. She smiles as she sets the drinks down. I glance over and see a sliver of disappointment in my sister's expression. She can say what she wants, but we both know she'd been interested in Cole. I wish she'd stop holding back so much and take a chance. But I know my sister. She's not going to change 32 years of ingrained behavior overnight. I decide to take the weekend to work on her. Maybe Harlow can help me. Speaking of Harlow, I've barely taken the first sip of my peach margarita when I see her across the bar. She waves enthusiastically as she hurries toward our booth. I slide over to give her room to sit next to me. When Harlow makes it to our booth, she plops down beside me with a weary sigh.

"Come to momma," she says, reaching for her margarita.

After taking a deep drink of the lime green concoction, she closes her eyes and smiles. "Ahh," she says. "I needed that." Her eyes pop open and she looks at Layna. Reaching a hand across the table she says, "Hi. I'm Harlow. It's nice to meet you."

Layna smiles and shakes her hand. "Layna," she says. "Likewise."

"Sorry I introduced myself to the drink first," Harlow says. "But it's been a really long day."

Layna laughs. "I get that." She raises her own glass in a toast. "Cheers."

Harlow and I lift our glasses and drink. The peach margarita was an excellent choice. I understand why it's so popular. It's sweet, without being overly so. I can barely taste the liquor. Before I realize it, I've downed half the drink and I'm feeling extremely relaxed. When the same server who'd delivered our drinks returns to take our food order, I see that hint of disappointment in Layna's expression return. After the redhead, whose nametag read Kylie, leaves again, I turn to my sister.

"I guess Cole isn't coming back," I say, almost casually.

Layna rolls her eyes but doesn't meet my gaze when she speaks. "I don't know why it matters."

"Cole?" Harlow asks. "Cole Prescott?"

I shrug. "He didn't give us his last name."

"Tall, dark hair, brown eyes, kinda hot?" Harlow asks.

"More than kind of hot," Layna mutters.

"Ha!" I say, pointing a finger in her direction. "I knew it!" Then, I turn to Harlow. "Wait, you know him?"

She rolls her eyes with a laugh. "Everyone knows everyone in this town, Piper," she reminds me. "But yes, I know him. He's the owner."

"The owner of what?" Layna asks, confused.

Harlow gestures at the room around us as she takes another sip of her drink.

"He owns this place?" I ask.

Harlow nods. "He started it a few years ago. He dropped out of business school and moved back to town. Then he bought this old building. He and his brother spent a couple of years renovating it. They did most of the work themselves, so it took a while. It was a real dump."

Harlow looks around the room with a soft smile. She looks almost proud. But why would she be proud of this place. Unless...

"Are you and Cole a thing?" I ask, figuring it's best to get it out in the open, especially for Layna's sake. I glance over at my sister to see that she's wearing a casual expression, as if she's not interested in the answer. But her eyes are glued to Harlow. But Harlow just laughs at my question.

"Definitely not," she says emphatically. "Cole is a couple of years younger than me. So, growing up, he was always more like a little kid to me. Then, when he started playing football, he got a little too cocky for my tastes. He dated most of the senior cheerleaders when he was still a freshman. He was even at my senior prom. With the prom queen!" She rolls her eyes, but the smile on her face is good-natured. "Cole Prescott was a bit of a legend around here, and he played up that legend as often as possible."

I can see Layna's disappointment and I can tell the exact moment it turns to disinterest. She's never liked the type of guy Harlow is describing. She's always gone for the quiet, studious men rather than the outspoken, cocky ones. It's too bad, though. Cole had seemed nice, even if he wasn't exactly subtle. It was obvious he'd been interested in Layna. But if he's anything like the man Harlow just described, he probably flirts with any woman who catches his eye. It's better that Layna found out about him now.

"How long has this place been open?" I ask, trying to change the subject. I think about The Peach Fuzz from a business standpoint. Judging by the way the tables are filling up and the friendly staff, it seems to be succeeding in this little town. I wonder what Cole's secret is.

"It's been about 3 years, I think," Harlow says. "Something like that."

I nod. "And it's been successful from the start? Cole being a local had to help, right?"

Harlow makes a noncommittal sound. "It didn't hurt, I guess," she says. "But I'm not sure why it took off the way it did. People come from neighboring towns to eat here or to have a drink. Somehow word got out about the peach margarita, and it was all anyone wanted when they walked in the doors." She shrugs. "It's a little sweet for my tastes, but people seem to love it."

I suck down the last bit of my own peach margarita, remembering the way Cole had said the drink was popular. Can one drink really put a business on the map like that? Interesting.

"Do you come here a lot, then?" Layna asks.

Harlow shakes her head. "Not really."

Layna looks at her with confusion. "Why not? It seems like a great place."

Harlow nods. "It is," she says, looking around the room, rather than at me. "The food is great. All the employees are really nice. There's live music on Saturday nights. Cole really—" she breaks off, her gaze locked on something or someone across the room. She sits frozen like that for a few seconds before dropping her gaze to the tabletop.

Layna meets my gaze, a question in her eyes. I shrug. I have no idea what just happened.

"Cole really, what?" I prompt, giving Harlow a little wave.

She shakes herself, blinking at me. "Huh?"

"You were talking about Cole and what he's done with this place," I say.

"Oh," she says. "Right. He's done a great job with it. You should have seen it before."

Harlow's voice is distracted, and her gaze keeps darting to a spot across the room. I watch her for a few seconds, wondering what's going on. I look over to see Layna is watching my interaction with Harlow. She looks just as confused as I feel.

"What do you keep looking at?" I finally ask, turning to follow Harlow's gaze. Before I can get a good look at whatever has her so worked up, she grabs my arm.

"Don't," she hisses, her eyes wide with alarm.

I freeze, giving her a concerned look. "Are you okay?" I ask. "You're being weird."

"Fine," she squeaks. She looks around again and her eyes widen before she turns her focus to her drink.

Before I can ask her what the hell is going on, I hear a familiar voice from behind me.

"Piper?"

A warm feeling starts low in my belly, then spreads throughout my body. My heart jumps into overdrive as I turn and see the last face I'd expect to see in a bar in Peach Tree on a Friday night. Luke stands there beside our booth, looking down at me with a smile that absolutely does not make my insides quiver. I've never seen him dressed casually like this in jeans and a t-shirt.

I know I just saw him last night, but I'm struck by how *good* he looks right now.

"Luke!" His name comes out as a choked squeak, and I clear my throat. "Um, hi. What are you doing here?"

I ignore my sister's confused expression and the way Harlow seems to be trying to melt into the seat under her. Is this why she'd been acting weird? Because she'd seen Luke? That doesn't make any sense. As for Luke, he doesn't look bothered by my less-than-enthusiastic greeting. Instead, he looks amused, and pleased to see me.

"I'm friends with the owners," he says. "I try to make it out here to hang out once a month or so."

I nod, only just noticing that Luke isn't alone. There are two tall, dark-haired men standing on either side of him. One is Cole, whom I've already met. But the other is someone I don't recognize right away. He's the tallest of the three men, and his hair is long. It's pulled back at his neck, but the longer strands in front have pulled free. I watch as he reaches up to tuck them behind one ear.

Luke gestures to Cole first. "This is Cole Prescott," he says. Then, pointing to the other man, he says, "And his brother Lincoln."

Both men smile politely at me. "I'm Piper," I say. I point to Layna. "This is my sister, Layna. She's in town visiting me for the weekend." I look over at Harlow. "You probably know Harlow already?"

Cole smiles politely and dips his head in a nod. Lincoln's gaze lingers a little longer on Harlow before he follows his brother's lead.

"Harlow," he says. "Good to see you again."

"Hey, Linc," she says, her voice giving off a breathless quality. I resist the urge to turn and ask her if she's okay.

"No llamas tonight?" Lincoln—no, Linc—asks, looking at Harlow.

For a second, there's a beat of silence as Harlow gives him a questioning look. Linc grins and okay, I can see why Harlow looks so flustered now. His smile is devastating.

"This morning?" he prompts.

It dawns on me right away. He's the guy who was staring at us from his pickup truck this morning when Harlow and I had walked to Piping Hot. He's teasing her about the llama pajama pants she'd been wearing during our early morning excursion. Harlow's cheeks redden slightly, but her eyes narrow in annoyance.

"A true gentleman wouldn't have mentioned that," she says. "Besides, anyone who sees me before 8am is stuck with whatever I give them. I won't apologize for it."

Linc's smile widens. "I'll remember that," he says.

From the corner of my eye, I see my sister lift her glass and polish off the last of her drink. I turn and eye her. That's not like her. She usually nurses one drink for an hour, especially since her drink of choice tonight is practically straight bourbon. I raise a brow at her, but she ignores me, turning to Cole.

"You guys should join us," she says, drawing the attention of Harlow as well as all three men.

My gaze goes to Luke who's watching me for my reaction. It's almost as if he's waiting for my agreement before acting. I remember his words from last night. *You don't have to do anything you don't want to do.* He's still holding to his words. I feel my lips curve into a little smile as I nod. I slide closer to Harlow, making room for another person beside me. The booth is large enough to seat 6 adults, but without much room to spare. Luke moves to sit next to me, but Cole remains standing.

"I'll go get us another round of drinks," he says.

To my shock, Layna slides out of the booth and stands. "I'll go with you," she says, smiling up at Cole.

What the hell? Since when does my quiet, shy sister throw herself in front of cute boys? Hadn't she just denied interest in him and argued about getting his number? Now, she's inviting him to join us and running off to the bar with him? Is she having some sort of midlife crisis? Before I can open my mouth to question her behavior, Cole smiles down at her and gestures toward the bar.

"After you," he says politely.

I watch them go, still confused by my sister's behavior tonight. Then again, she's been acting a little weird since she got here this morning. I tell myself she's a responsible adult and capable of making her own decisions. I'll try to have a heart-to-heart with her tomorrow. I want to make sure she's really okay before she goes back home to Atlanta. Bringing my attention back to the table, I see that Lincoln has slid into the booth across from Harlow and is picking at the label on his bottle of beer. Harlow is toying with the corner of her napkin. The awkward silence feels heavy enough to choke me.

"Well, this is fun," I say brightly.

I feel, more than hear Luke's soft chuckle beside me. It reminds me of his nearness in the booth. I can feel the heat of his body next to mine. Looking down, I see his jean-clad thigh inches from mine, and I suck in a breath. I instantly wish I hadn't because my nose fills with the scent of him. I feel something inside me clench with sudden wanting. Why does he have this affect on me? I wish I could pinpoint it so I could find a way to counteract it.

"Fun," Harlow echoes in what I can tell is false enthusiasm.

I know I've only known her for a week, but I've gotten used to her sarcasm and her wit. Right now, she's uncomfortable but pretending not to be. I want to know why. But I know it's not the right time to address it. My guess is it has something to do with Lincoln. I haven't missed the way she seems to be avoiding looking at him.

"So, Linc," I say. "What do you do?"

He turns to look at me and I can almost understand why Harlow is avoiding his gaze. Those hazel eyes look so much like Cole's, but there's something about Linc's gaze that's more intense. Which might explain why Harlow seems so bothered by his nearness.

"Linc is a contractor," Luke says, answering before Linc can.

Linc rolls his eyes, but he's smiling. "That's an exaggeration," he says. "I do a lot of odd jobs around town. Everything from plumbing to roofing and carpentry. But I never had any formal training in any of it. So, I can't really call myself a plumber or a roofer or a carpenter. I guess I'm a glorified handy man."

"That's not true," Harlow says, speaking unprompted for the first time since Linc appeared. We all turn questioning gazes on her.

"What do you mean?" Linc asks.

Harlow's mouth twitches into a smile. "Wood shop," she says. "Junior year. Your lamp was the best one in the class."

Linc narrows his eyes in thought before recognition dawns and he starts laughing. Then he shakes his head. "I forgot you were in that class with me," he says. "That was one of my favorite classes."

"Well, you were good at it," Harlow says.

"So, you do know each other," I say.

She shrugs. "I told you. Everyone knows everyone in this town."

Cole and Layna return with a round of drinks for everyone. After handing them out, they slide into the booth across from us.

"How do you all know each other?" I ask Luke.

He smiles. "College. Linc was a big football star."

Linc shakes his head. "He's full of it," he says. "I was a decent enough player in high school to get a scholarship. In college, I was second string the entire time I played. Good enough for the team, but not good enough to be a starter."

"Bull," Cole says. "You would have started after Dawson left for the NFL."

Linc just shrugs. "I guess we'll never know now."

"The real question," Layna says, narrowing her eyes at me. "Is how do you two know each other?" She points at me and Luke.

I open my mouth to speak, but Luke beats me to it.

"We're dating," he says with a grin.

My mouth falls open and I stare at him in shock. He laughs at my reaction, which causes a very different reaction somewhere in the vicinity of my lady parts. Seriously. What the hell?

"Fake dating, anyway," he says with a sexy grin.

When I continue to stare at him with a horrified expression, he turns to me, all innocence.

"What?" he asks. He gestures to Layna. "Were you going to lie to your sister?"

"No," I sputter.

Luke points to Cole and Linc. "These two already know everything." He peers around me at Harlow. "I assume you know, too?"

She smiles. "Yep."

Luke turns back to me. "So, that just leaves your sister. And you just said you weren't planning to lie to her." He shrugs and lifts his beer. "So, I told her for you. You're welcome."

He brings the beer to his lips and takes a deep drink. My unruly eyes can't seem to stop staring at him, so of course, I watch his throat move as he swallows. I have an insane urge to run my tongue over the exposed skin there, but I blink away the image as soon as it enters my brain. Pulling my gaze away from Luke and his kissable neck, I look over to see that Layna is studying me with a mixture of amusement and confusion. I sigh and shoot a glare at Luke.

"Yes, I was planning to tell her," I say through gritted teeth. "But I wanted to wait until after we had a few more drinks."

Cole grins. "I have a solution for that." He waves toward the bar then gestures to the six of us seated at the booth. When we all just stare at him questioningly, he says, "Shots are on the way."

I look at him in horror. I haven't taken a shot in nearly a year. The last time had been the night I'd quit my corporate job. The mood that night had been part celebration, part panic. Considering I'm about to explain to my extremely sensible, overprotective sister that I've agreed to spend a week on an island pretending to be the doting girlfriend of the man who's currently starring in all my sexual fantasies, maybe Cole's idea isn't a bad one. There's definitely some panic rising up in me right now.

A server appears with a tray of shots far faster than I'd have thought possible and I wonder if Cole had this planned. But he's all innocence as he thanks the server and begins passing out the glasses filled with amber liquid. Linc puts up a slight objection but takes his in the end. I expect Layna to balk, but she takes hers with something that almost looks like excitement. I don't know what's gotten into her tonight. I can't remember the last time she took a shot. Harlow takes her glass with a smile of thanks. Luke just shrugs and shoots me a wink that does nothing to dispel that lingering urge to kiss him. I sigh. Maybe the liquor will help me get control of those baser urges.

"Fuck it," I say with a shrug. Then I reach over and take the offered glass.

"There's the spirit," Cole says with a grin.

Linc leans over and peers at Cole. "Dad joke?"

Cole shakes his head with a chuckle. "I'll leave that to you, big bro."

"What are we drinking to?" Layna asks.

To my surprise, it's Luke who answers. "To my new girlfriend," he says, shooting me a grin.

"Fake girlfriend," I say, putting emphasis on the first word.

But I raise my glass along with the others and knock it back. I don't know why I'm surprised to taste the peachy flavor of the whiskey, but I fight the urge to laugh as I swallow down the liquor. Of course, it's peach. I don't know why I expected anything else. I'm surprised that there's not much of a burn accompanying the sweetness of the peach. I give the empty glass an appraising look.

"Mm," I say, looking at Cole. "That's delicious."

"And dangerous," he says with a smile. "Don't let the taste fool you. It's stronger than you think."

"So," Layna says, narrowing her eyes at me. "What's this about fake dating?"

I sigh. "Luke and I are friends," I say, deciding to leave out the part about the dating app for now. "He works for a marketing firm and he's trying to get a big-time client to sign on with the company."

"Not just any client," Luke says. "Arthur Mitchell."

Layna's eyes widen. "Wow." She looks at me. "What does that have to do with you?"

Luke answers before I can. "Mitchell's clearly in love with his wife. To the point of being blinded to her shortcomings."

He's being tactful, I know. He doesn't want to seem rude in front of my sister.

"She's a cheating skank," I say, not sharing Luke's compunction for polite euphemisms. "And she's had her sights set on Luke since they met. He doesn't return the sentiment."

Luke gives me a grateful smile. "So, when they insisted that I come to dinner at their house, I had a feeling it would be a bad idea. I made up a story about having dinner plans with my girlfriend that night. I was hoping the wife would get the hint that I wasn't available for whatever plans she had in mind."

"Let me guess," Layna says. "It didn't work?"

Luke shakes his head. "Nope. If anything, she got more insistent. She also seemed pretty dismissive of my girlfriend. So, I played it up. Told them both how in love we are and how I'm on the verge of proposing.

"It didn't make a difference," Luke says. "Then Arthur insisted I bring my girlfriend to dinner. That he'd love to meet the amazing woman who has me thinking of settling down." He shakes his head. "So, I made an offer to your sister. If she pretends to be my girlfriend for this dinner, I'll help her turn things around at the coffee shop."

Layna's eyes shoot to me, and I know she's wondering what Luke means by 'turn things around'. She knows business hasn't exactly been booming at the shop, but I haven't been completely forthcoming with how dire things have gotten. I give her what I hope is an apologetic smile, but she still looks disappointed in me. I can't tell if it's because of the lie I've concocted with Luke or my withholding information from her about my business. It's probably some of both.

"She agreed," Luke says. "We went to dinner at the Mitchell house last night."

I make a face. "It was just as awkward as you can imagine."

Luke gives a theatrical shudder. "Worse," he says. He turns to me. "Did I tell you that while you were in the bathroom, she slipped me a note?"

My mouth drops open and my eyes go wide. I'm equal parts horrified and amused. "What did it say?"

"It was a hotel room number in the city," Luke says. "And a date and time to meet her."

"Ew!" I shout. "Has she ever heard of subtlety?"

Luke shakes his head. "I don't think that word is in her vocabulary."

We both laugh over the ridiculousness of the situation. "So," I say, leaning close. "You going to take her up on that offer?"

Luke's mouth drops open. "I'm shocked, Miss Brooks," he says. "I'll have you know that I have a girlfriend that I am one hundred percent faithful to. I would never dream of betraying her that way."

I know he's just going along with my joke and playing up the fake relationship thing. But some small part of me imagines he's saying the words about me for real. As soon as the idea enters my head, I'm hit with a sharp stab of longing followed by immediate denial. I do not want this man. I can't.

Layna clears her throat loudly to get our attention. When I look her way, I can see she still has questions. Not that I can blame her.

"This doesn't explain why you're still pretending," she says. "What aren't you telling me?"

I see Cole gesture to the bar for another round of shots, and I don't object. Neither does anyone else at the table. The liquid courage seems to be working. I finish off the rest of my margarita and go over all the details from last night's dinner. During my long explanation, we down the second round of shots and a plate of loaded fries appears in the center of the table. Thank goodness for the food, because I'm starting to feel the effects of the alcohol by the time I get to Art's invitation to Tybee Island. I explain how Luke had tried to let me off the hook, but that I'm the one who agreed to go along. I don't want Layna thinking he pressured me into something I'm not comfortable with.

By the time I finish talking, the plate of fries is nearly demolished, and Layna looks far less irritated with Luke than before. She still doesn't look exactly happy with the situation, but she's not scowling at him anymore.

"Does the shop need the help that bad?" she asks, surprising me with the direction of her thoughts. I'd assumed she would be full of questions about the trip and the arrangements, but instead she's just worried about me. I open my mouth to answer her but remember all the other people seated at the table. I feel my face redden in embarrassment, but I nod.

"I think so," I say. "Yes. It does."

I wonder if Layna is angry with me, but she looks more hurt than anything. "Why didn't you tell me?"

I lift one shoulder in a helpless shrug. "I thought I could turn it around myself."

To my surprise, I feel a hand grip mine where it rests on the bench beside my leg. I look down to see Luke's hand on mine. The comfort I feel is immediate. Twisting my hand slightly, I squeeze his in return, a silent thank you for his support.

"Piping Hot is a great shop," Luke says, looking at Layna. "It's easy to see that as soon as you walk inside. Plus, the coffee is amazing. The trick is visibility. We just need people to show up. This town can be hard on outsiders. But it's not impossible to make a business work here. We just need to find the right angle."

"Luke's a genius with marketing," Cole says, speaking up for the first time in several minutes. "It's his vision that made this place so popular."

Luke shakes his head. "I just got the word out there. You did the hard part."

"He's being modest," Linc says. "Before Luke worked his magic, this place wasn't even breaking even most nights. Now, Cole can afford to expand."

"Are you planning to?" Harlow asks, leaning forward to look at Cole.

Cole grins. "I just bought the empty lot next door. I want to add a patio, outdoor seating and maybe a spot to hold outdoor events."

"There's nothing like that in Peach Tree," Harlow says.

"That's why it's going to work," Linc says.

The pride Linc feels is evident when he looks at his brother. It's the same way I've seen Layna look at me. If I can do with Piping Hot what Cole has done with Peach Fuzz, maybe I can see that look again. I'm not stupid. I know my sister loves me and would be proud of me, no matter what I did. But I can't help feeling like I need to succeed for her. She poured so much of her energy into making sure I turned out okay. She put her own dreams on hold for mine. I don't want to let her down. But I can't say any of that right now.

It isn't until I notice Luke's gaze on me that I remember I'm still gripping his hand. Only now, I'm squeezing tighter than before. I'm probably cutting off circulation to his fingers. But he makes no move to extricate himself from my grip. Instead, I feel his thumb stroking lightly across the back of my hand as if he's trying to comfort me. I force my fingers to loosen their death grip on his and give him a small, grateful smile. Luke returns the smile, making my heart trip in my chest. I take a deep breath and remember that all of this is fake. If I'm not careful, I could get used to this man's hand holding mine.

CHAPTER 17

Luke

I don't know what made me reach over and take Piper's hand. I'd been watching her talk and I could sense the tension building in her as she explained our predicament to her sister. It's clear she's close with her sister and looks up to her. Admitting to her that the business isn't doing well must be hard for Piper. I'd been hit with an overwhelming urge to comfort her. Taking her hand had felt like the right thing to do. But when she'd turned her hand over and squeezed my hand back? That had just felt right.

The feel of her palm pressing against mine seemed like the most natural thing in the world. I hadn't wanted to let go. So, when she'd kept hold of my hand longer, I didn't pull away. That's why I'm still holding her hand, I tell myself. Because Piper clearly needs my support. But the truth is, I just like touching her. And that's a dangerous avenue to explore. Because it makes me want more than just friendship and the innocence of holding hands.

"So, you're going on a week-long vacation with people you barely know, while pretending to be in a relationship with a guy you also barely know?" Layna says. "Did I get that right?" There's a sharp bite to her words.

I open my mouth to assure Layna that her sister will be perfectly safe with me, but Piper beats me to it.

"Luke is a good guy," she says, emphatically. "I trust him. He's been a total gentleman. I know he won't make me do anything I'm uncomfortable with."

I'm oddly touched by her defense of me. But Piper's not finished yet. Before I can thank her for her kind words, she goes on.

"And besides," she says, "I'm 28, not 14. It's not like I haven't thought everything through."

Layna sighs. "I know you're an adult, Piper. But it doesn't stop me from worrying about you."

Piper doesn't seem to have a response for this, but I do. "She's right," I say, looking at Piper. "Just because someone is an adult doesn't mean the people who love them stop worrying. I had a similar discussion with my sister not all that long ago."

I shake my head with a smile. "She wasn't too happy with me barging into her life and interrogating her future husband."

Piper rolls her eyes. "Don't take her side," she mutters.

I smile at her. "I'm not taking sides," I say gently. "I don't think there are sides, anyway. We all want the same thing here."

"We do?" Layna asks, eyes narrowed.

"We do?" Piper asks, clearly skeptical.

I nod. "Yes. We do. We all want Piping Hot Brews to be a success. And I think I can make that happen. Now, I've already told Piper this, but I'm repeating it for you. She does not have to go through with this. She already upheld her end of our arrangement. Our agreement was for dinner and maybe a few appearances. Not for a full-on vacation by my side. If she changes her mind at any time, I'll still do everything I can to keep my end of our bargain. No hard feelings and no repercussions."

Layna looks surprised and still a bit skeptical. "Can we get that in writing?" she asks.

Before I can nod my agreement, Piper lets out a sound of disgust. "Seriously?" she asks. "We don't need to bring ink and paper into this. We have a verbal agreement and I trust Luke."

"Humor me," Layna says, ignoring Piper's outburst and keeping her gaze trained on me.

I give her a confident smile. "Anyone have a pen?"

Cole pulls a pen from his shirt pocket and holds it out to me. I reluctantly release Piper's hand and take it from him. Piper is rolling her eyes and shaking her head. She's also muttering something under her breath, but I can't quite make out the words. It's kind of cute, the way she's outraged on my behalf. I can't remember the last time someone stood up for me like this. I think I like it. I reach for one of the napkins and turn it over so the Peach Fuzz logo isn't visible. Then, I write out the most ridiculous contract I've ever written.

When I'm satisfied that the wording is sufficient, I pass it over to Piper for her approval. She begrudgingly reads what I've written. I can tell she's still annoyed, but there's a hint of a smile curving her lips. Like me, she's recognized the ridiculousness of this whole situation. But she's going along with it for the sake of her sister. She gives a nod and passes the napkin over to Layna for her inspection. Like the rest of us, Layna has been drinking. But that doesn't stop her from reading every word as if inspecting it for loopholes. But she won't find any.

I meant everything I said earlier. If Piper changes her mind tonight and decides not to go through with this, I'll still help her. The more I'm around Piper, the more I find that I like her company. I want her to succeed. Plus, I think this town needs more people like her. If the shop fails, I know she'll go back to Atlanta. I'd probably never see her again. That thought bothers me more than I want to analyze tonight.

Layna finally finishes with the napkin contract and passes it back to me. "Looks sufficient," she says, all business.

I give her a nod, deciding to match her no-nonsense energy, even though this whole situation feels nonsensical. I just wrote a contract for a fake relationship on a bar napkin after downing two shots of peach whiskey while a group of drunk women shake their asses to Lizzo on the dance floor twenty feet away. My life has certainly gotten more interesting since I met Piper.

I sign and date the contract before passing it over to Piper so she can do the same. She rolls her eyes again, but signs it before sliding it back across the table. She holds the pen out to Cole who takes it. There are a few seconds of awkward silence where it seems like no one knows quite what to say. Then Cole sits up straighter and claps his hands together once.

"Well," he says brightly. "I don't know about the rest of you, but business always makes me thirsty. Another round?"

The ladies all look around at one another. Harlow is the first to shrug. "Why not?"

When I see the delighted grin on Cole's face, I wonder if I'm going to regret letting him talk me into coming out tonight. The last time I drank shots was when I met my sister's new family. The next morning hadn't been fun.

"Last one for me," I say. "I eventually have to drive home."

"You can crash on the couch if you want," Linc offers.

I consider it for a second before I remember the last time I took him up on a similar offer. I'd woken up just after sunrise, after far too little sleep to find a pair of dark eyes peering at me under a mop of even darker curls. Linc's daughter Ella is an early riser. And she has no qualms about waking up her 'Uncle Luke' and making him watch Brave with her. For the hundredth time.

"Thanks," I say. "But I'd rather sleep in my own bed."

Linc just nods. "Offer stands," he says with a grin. "Ella's always down for pancakes."

I shake my head. "I still don't know how I got roped into that one."

Cole laughs. "She's wily," he says with a wink. "Gets it from her uncle."

I notice Piper watching the conversation with some confusion. "Ella is Linc's daughter," I say. "She's the cutest kid ever, and she knows how to get grown men to do her bidding."

Piper smiles. "Cuter than your adorable niece?"

"No, because Millie is the cutest baby ever," I say. "She's not a kid yet."

"Whoa, whoa," Cole says. "I'll have you know that Ella was absolutely the cutest baby ever."

"Are two grown men really arguing over who has the cutest niece?" Layna asks to no one.

Piper laughs as Cole pulls out his phone and searches for baby pictures of his niece to prove his point. We each take turns showing off photos of the two babies to the three women. They all gush over every photo and declare that it's a tie for which baby is cutest. Cole and I accept the verdict, but secretly I still think Millie wins by a hair.

The conversation flows around me. Sometimes I join in, but mostly I observe the others as they discuss the town, their businesses and the weather. It's the most relaxed I've felt in a group in a long time. I've never been the type of person who makes friends easily. After growing up with my father, I learned to keep my guard up most of the time. It's not always easy to let people in.

If Linc and I hadn't been assigned to the same dorm room in college, I don't know if we'd have become friends the way we did. Now, I'm grateful for whatever twist of fate threw us together. He's the closest thing to a brother I have. Even after he left college in our junior year, we remained friends. With that friendship, I got Cole in the bargain. I always say that Cole doesn't meet people. He just makes new friends immediately. It's just the kind of person he is. Which means that I now have two men I think of as brothers.

The three of us have spent many nights drinking and talking and laughing together. But this is the first time since college that we've been in a group setting like this. Linc has been busy being an amazing father to Ella while Cole spent years getting this place up and running. I notice that tonight, the dynamic seems to have shifted a bit. It might just be the fact that Piper is sitting so close to me that I can smell the subtle scent of her perfume, but I think I like this better. At least, I'm smiling and laughing a lot more. I'm not worrying about tomorrow or next week. I'm not thinking about my father or Wolfe Industries. I'm happy just being present in the moment with these people. It's a new experience for me, and I'm not sure who or what to credit for the change.

"Can we talk?"

I'm surprised to hear Piper's voice, low and unsure in my ear. I turn to look at her and see that she looks nervous. She glances around at the others as if worried they'll overhear. I wonder if she wants to go someplace private where we can talk, but she surprises me by nodding toward the dance floor. I'd all but forgotten about the music until now. But now that she's called my attention to it, I can hear the slow melody of an old country song I haven't heard since I was a kid. Without hesitation, I stand and hold out a hand to her. She takes it and I pull her to her feet and lead her out onto the floor.

Her free hand moves to my shoulder while mine goes to her hip, gripping lightly. I can feel my heart thundering in my chest, and I wonder at my reaction to her nearness. It's not like I'm some young kid who's never touched a woman. I've slept with more women than I'd like to admit, if I'm being honest. I've never had trouble getting attention from women. I've also never really felt nervous around them. But something about dancing with Piper tonight has me all tangled up. She says something in a low voice that I can't quite make out. I lean down and pull her closer.

"What?"

Piper leans up and I feel her breath on my neck.

"I'm glad you're here," she says.

Her voice is low and husky, sending a shot of lust through me.

"So am I," I say, pulling her closer.

I can feel her breasts brushing against my chest as we move slowly to the music. Her hand slides up my shoulder to the back of my neck and I feel her thumb brush against my skin. Something about that light, innocent touch sends a thrill through me that I can't explain. She's drunk, or close to it. Which means she's not in full control of what she's saying or doing. I should steer her back toward the table and her friends. But all I want to do is pull her even closer to me and feel her curves against me. But I'd be the worst sort of man if I did that. So, I ease back just a little, putting enough space between us that her body is no longer touching mine.

Piper looks up at me, a small frown on her face. "What is it?"

"You've been drinking," I say.

She laughs. "We've all been drinking."

When I don't return the laugh, her eyes narrow and her expression turns serious. "Are you worried I'll think you took advantage of me? With one dance?"

"I don't want you to think I'm that kind of guy," I say.

She shakes her head, but the amused smile is back. "Luke, if I thought you were that kind of guy, I wouldn't be here with you right now. I damned sure wouldn't be taking this trip with you. For the record, I'm not drunk. I'm just pleasantly buzzed."

She smiles up at me and I have to fight the urge to kiss that full mouth.

"This is going to be harder than I thought," she says, surprising me with the sudden softness to her voice.

"What is?" I ask.

"Pretending."

She doesn't elaborate, and I don't ask for an explanation. Besides, I think I know what she's saying. Or rather, what she isn't saying. Being here with Piper, holding her in my arms? That's easy. That feels natural. It won't be difficult to pretend that I want her, because I do. I think I've wanted her since the first moment I saw her. Maybe even before, when I'd seen that smiling photo on my phone. No, pretending I want her won't be hard. Remembering this is all fake will be the hard part.

Piper lets out a small sigh. "We need to make a plan for next week," she says.

I know she's right. We need to talk about how we're going to make this work. We're going to have to be extra careful around Art and Mel. Especially since we'll be spending so much time around them. It would be easy to slip up and get found out. Then this ruse will be for nothing. Neither of us wants that.

But I find that I don't want to think about that right now. Not while I'm holding Piper in my arms, dancing to a song about falling in love. I just want to be here, in this moment. I want to pretend she's here because she wants to be. I want to pretend this isn't fake, if only for a few more minutes.

"Tomorrow," I say. "We'll talk about it tomorrow."

Piper doesn't question my reasons or make a comment. She just nods. And she doesn't resist when I pull her just a little closer to me. Our bodies aren't quite touching. I don't trust myself enough for that. Besides, we just went to great lengths to convince her sister that we're just friends faking a relationship. I know Layna is probably watching us right now, wondering what I'm up to. But when I glance over to the table, I only see Harlow and Linc sitting there. I wonder if Cole and Layna are dancing too. The dance floor is crowded now, and I can't make out the faces of every couple. So, I don't try. Instead, I focus on the woman in my arms and how right it feels to hold her.

CHAPTER 18

Piper

What the hell was that?

I lie awake later that night with that question repeating in my head like a giant, flashing neon sign. The events of the night play on a loop along with it. What the hell *was* that? Why had I asked Luke to dance with me? What had I thought was going to happen? Of course, I'd almost kissed him. I've spent the last week thinking about kissing him. And more. So much more. My panties had been damp just from his proximity. But I don't let those thoughts enter my brain tonight. I refuse to have another session with my vibrator where Luke is the star of all my orgasmic fantasies. Nope. Not going there again.

We'd been dancing and he'd made a comment about how he wasn't the kind of guy to take advantage of a drunk woman. Or someone had. I can't remember, exactly. I'd been looking up at him. For just a second, I'd leaned toward him. It was as if I'd been pulled by some invisible force. I could imagine exactly what his lips would feel like on mine. How he would taste. And I'd been just buzzed enough to forget it was a bad idea. Then I'd caught a glimpse of Layna from the corner of my eye. She hadn't been watching us, but just seeing her there had pulled me back to reality. I remembered all the reasons I shouldn't kiss Luke. That brief moment of hesitation had been enough to stop me. But it didn't stop my imagination from playing through a dozen scenarios in which I hadn't stopped myself from kissing Luke on the dance floor.

I sigh as I stare up at the dark ceiling above my bed. How am I going to make it an entire week without begging him to rip my clothes off? There's no way. I'd been crazy to think this would work. But what other choice do I have? We're supposed to leave on this trip in less than 48 hours. I can't back out now. I'll just have to be more careful. I'll keep my distance as much as possible. And absolutely no dancing. Being that close to Luke Wolfe is just too tempting.

When I talk to him again, I'll just have to reiterate the ground rules. No matter what happens, we'll keep things strictly platonic. I can't afford to let a sexy grin and pretty eyes distract me from what's important. Business first. Then, maybe we can explore whatever this thing is between us. That sounds perfectly reasonable and responsible, right? I'm sure Luke will agree. Eventually I drift off to sleep, but my dreams are filled with ocean eyes and strong arms holding me against a firm body. I wake up exhausted, but more determined than ever to keep things platonic between me and Luke. He's a distraction I cant afford right now. He's got just as much riding on this as I do. I'm sure he'll see reason.

I spend the morning with Layna who looks like she got even less sleep than I did. I don't think she drank more than I did, so I'm not sure why she's so subdued this morning. Maybe her lack of sleep from the night before is finally catching up with her. I make us some coffee and a breakfast of scrambled eggs and toast, and we lie on the couch watching The Food Network until the early afternoon. It's nice. Comfortable. It reminds me of Sunday mornings before I left for college, when it had just been me and Layna against the world. I realize how much I've missed having my sister close by.

"I'm glad you're here," I tell her.

"Me, too," she says with a smile. "I think this trip was just what I needed. It helped me figure out some things."

She doesn't elaborate, but I think she looks happier than she had when she'd arrived, so I don't push her to open up to me. I know my sister. She doesn't respond well to prying. She'll eventually talk to me in her own time.

"I love you, you know?" I tell her.

Layna looks at me with amused suspicion. "What did you break?" she asks, making me laugh.

It used to be a running joke that I'd only tell her I loved her if I'd done something wrong. Especially when I was younger. I'd sneak into her room to play with her things or try on her clothes or jewelry. When I was seven, I'd gone into her room after school one day when she'd been at volleyball practice and played in her makeup. I don't know why I'd assumed she wouldn't notice my face covered in makeup and her new lipstick snapped in half. Layna had been pissed off as only a 12-year-old girl can be. She hadn't spoken to me for 3 days. Not until our mother made her accept my apology and made me promise to respect my sister's privacy and stay out of her room without permission.

I don't know why that memory comes to me now, but I can see it so clearly in my mind. As always, thinking of my mom brings up mixed emotions. The strongest emotion is happiness. I know I'm lucky to have those memories of her. But there's also the overwhelming sense of loss. Not just of my mom, but of the person I'd been before I knew true grief. There's a before and an after, and I know I'll never be able to go back to who I was. What I mourn most are the people my sister and I might have been if our mom hadn't been taken from us. I do my best to shake off the sudden melancholy and focus on spending time with Layna. She'll head back to Atlanta tomorrow and it could be months before I see her again. The last thing I need to be doing is moping about a past I can't change.

"I didn't break anything," I say, rolling my eyes. "I'm trying to be nice."

Layna's face softens into a smile. "I love you, too."

We spend another hour watching television, both of us giving a running commentary on the various dishes we see. We speculate on whether we could make them and how they'd taste. Eventually, the clock on the wall tells me I need to get off my ass and start packing for my upcoming trip. When I mention it to Layna, she doesn't comment, but her eyes narrow slightly. I can tell she still disapproves, despite the napkin contract that's now stuck to my refrigerator with a magnet in the shape of a banana.

It catches my eye every time I walk into the kitchen, making me smile at the absurdity of the thing. Luke hadn't batted an eye, though. He'd written out the contract on a bar napkin as if it was something he did daily. He'd wanted to reassure my sister, I know. The whole scene had annoyed me at the time, but now it just seems funny. Thinking about last night brings me back to that dance and what I'd nearly done. I need to talk to Luke about that.

I need to make sure he knows it can't happen again. As much as we need to keep up appearances in front of Art and Mel, we should keep our distance when it's just us. I don't want to confuse my already muddled brain and body. I toy with the right way to approach the subject, but in the end, I decide directness is best. He and I aren't the type to hide from the truth.

"What about the shop?" Layna asks. "Who's going to run it while you're gone?"

"I talked to Stevie," I say. "She's going to open it for half the day each day while I'm gone and close in the afternoons."

"Won't you lose business?" she asks.

I sigh, unable to keep the despondence out of my voice. "Unfortunately, I doubt anyone will notice."

Layna puts an arm around my shoulders and gives me a little squeeze. "You really think Luke can work some kind of magic with the shop?"

"I don't know," I say. "I hope so. I have to believe something will change. Otherwise, I'm just giving up. And I can't do that. Not yet."

She nods. "I get that. Giving up isn't an option for you. It never has been."

"Is that a nice way of calling me stubborn?" I ask, voice wry.

She laughs. "Not stubborn. Determined. It's a good thing."

"If you say so."

"I do," she says. "This is going to work."

I give her a look. "Where's this coming from?"

"What?"

"This positivity?" I say. "I know you don't approve of this scheme. So, why the sudden cheerleader routine?"

Layna shrugs. "I've given it some thought," she says. "Plus, I researched your new fake boyfriend. He's good at what he does. Plus, you saw Peach Fuzz last night. You heard what Linc said about it before Luke got involved. The evidence speaks for itself." She takes a deep breath and blows it out. "So, while I may not approve of you taking a vacation with this man you barely know, I do believe he has what it takes to help your shop succeed."

We spend the rest of the afternoon deciding what I need to bring on the trip and packing my bag. It's hard to know exactly what I'll need for a vacation at a billionaire's beach house, but I do my best to cover all the options. I've packed a little bit of everything. Now, I've just got to remember to keep my hands to myself for the next week. No matter how hot Luke Wolfe is.

CHAPTER 19

Piper

The Mitchell's beach house isn't at all what I expect. For one thing, it's smaller than what I'd expect the typical billionaire's vacation home to be. But it's still far larger than any place I've ever lived. It's raised up off the dunes and painted a soft gray with white shutters and porch railings. The large porch wraps around the house to the back. I'm sure there's a stunning view of the beach and the ocean, especially at sunrise. Maybe I'll have a chance to watch it while I'm here.

I'm surprised again when no servants come out to greet us. After our reception in Savannah, I'd expected an army of servants to be here as well. Instead, Art greets us. He smiles and waves at us from the top of the stairs as we climb out of the car. He's dressed casually in khaki shorts and a white t-shirt. It's the most relaxed I've ever seen him, including in the photos of him online. He looks friendly, approachable and happy.

"Welcome to the beach cottage!" he shouts as he walks down the stairs to meet us.

Cottage isn't the word I'd use to describe the large house, but I suppose to someone like Art, it's considered small. Art and Luke pull our bags from the trunk while I'm left to carry only my purse. I'm not complaining, especially not when I remember how much I managed to cram into that one suitcase. Luke isn't exactly struggling to carry it up the stairs, but I don't miss the slight grimace on his face.

Art chatters the entire way up the steps to the wide porch about the house and when it was built, how long ago he bought it. I'm only half-listening, too busy taking in the house and the scenery. It's gorgeous here. I can see why they like to stay here. I make it a point to say the same to Art.

"Oh, yes," he says, beaming. "We love it here."

We. That one word is enough to remind me of the other person staying here for the week. Mel. I dread seeing her again, though I know I won't be able to avoid her. I might as well get it over with.

"Where's Mel?" I ask.

Art waves a hand as he opens the front door. "Oh, she went into town to do some shopping. She's not one to sit around the house all day."

I share a look with Luke. Does this mean we won't have to spend much time with her while we're here? Somehow, I doubt she'll stay away now that Luke is here. Unfortunately for both of us, we won't be able to avoid her altogether.

"I'll show you to your room and let you get settled in before dinner," Art says as we follow him through the entryway. He points toward the back of the house. "Through there is the kitchen and dining room. To the left is the living room and my office. I'll give you a proper tour once you're settled."

We both nod and follow him up the stairs. He turns left at the top of the stairs and stops in front of the last door on the right. Smiling, he pushes open the door.

"This is it," he says. "You have your own bathroom." He gestures down the hall behind us. "Mel and I are on the opposite end of the house. So, you have your, uh, privacy."

It takes me a second to realize what Art is hinting at. When I do, I feel my face heat. I want to speak up, assure him that we won't be doing anything that requires a need for privacy. Before I can, Art sets the suitcase inside the door and backs out of the room.

"I'll leave you to it," he says. Before turning to go, he looks at each of us in turn. "I'm really glad you decided to come." His voice is low and kind.

"We're happy to be here," I say, injecting as much warmth into my voice as possible.

Art smiles and gives us a nod before turning back down the hall. Luke gestures for me to enter the room and I get my first good look at the space that will be ours for the next week. The room is large and bright. The wall of windows accounts for the sunlight streaming in. It's tastefully decorated with furniture made of dark wood. The walls are painted a pale blue and gauzy, white curtains hang in front of the windows. I wander around the room, taking everything in. The bedding on the massive bed is white like the curtains, but I try not to let my gaze linger on that piece of furniture. It feels too intimate with Luke standing beside me. There's a small couch opposite the bed. I point to it.

"I'll take the couch," I say.

Luke shakes his head. "No. You can have the bed."

"No way," I say. "You're like a foot taller than me. You won't fit on the couch."

He shrugs. "That's my problem."

"You're being ridiculous," I say.

"Some would say I'm being a gentleman," he says.

I eye the bed. It really is massive. It could probably fit three or four adults. It's possible we could both sleep in it without ever touching. I feel my face go hot at the thought of lying in bed next to Luke. Nope. Bad idea. In the history of bad ideas, that one's of the worst. I may be playing with fire by sharing a room with him, but there's no scenario in which I could lie next to Luke in bed and not have sex with him.

I shrug. "Suit yourself," I say, busying myself with opening my suitcase.

Maybe if I focus on unpacking, I can forget how small this room suddenly feels with Luke and me in here together. Luke doesn't say anything. He grabs his own suitcase and hauls it over to the corner of the room. He clearly has no intention of unpacking right now. Instead, he lounges on the couch. I can feel his eyes on me as I remove clothes and shoes from my suitcase. It sends a little shiver of awareness through me, and I'm reminded of the dance we shared the other night, the way I'd almost kissed him. I can almost feel his hands on my hips as we'd swayed to the music. I don't know why I say it, but something about his nearness and the memory of what I'd almost done means I need to set boundaries.

And I need to state them aloud, so I won't cross them myself.

"About the other night," I say, turning to look at Luke.

When he doesn't seem to know what I'm talking about, I clarify.

"At Peach Fuzz?"

"I had a good time," Luke says with a smile.

Damn it. That smile is lethal. I manage a nod. "I did too. But we can't do that again."

He looks confused for a moment before his expression clears. "You mean the dance." It's not a question, but a statement. But I nod anyway.

"We need to be more careful," I say, unable to meet his gaze. Instead, I focus on unpacking my suitcase and hanging clothes in the closet. I talk as I work. "If we want to keep our friendship intact after this is all over, we can't let whatever this is get in the way."

I can hear the amusement in Luke's voice when he responds. "Whatever this is?" he repeats slowly. "The attraction, you mean?"

I feel my face go hot. I hadn't expected him to come right out and say it. But then, I'd been the one to bring it up. This is on me. I nod again, though I don't stop what I'm doing. It's easier to say it if I'm not looking at him. If I don't focus on how hot he is.

"Yes," I say, pretending to search for something in my now empty suitcase.

Luke is quiet for a moment, thinking. When he finally speaks, I'm surprised by his words.

"Look at me, Huff," he says.

When I meet his gaze, I almost wish I hadn't. The heat in his eyes is unmistakable and it makes my breath catch in my throat. I know, without doubt that he's never looked at me like that before.

"I won't lie to you," he says slowly. "I am attracted to you. I have been since I saw your profile on that app. It's why I came to see you after our failed date. I wanted to know you. It had nothing to do with needing a fake girlfriend. But I was willing to be your friend if that's what you wanted. I still am. This arrangement doesn't have to change that."

I nod, wondering why the idea of friendship doesn't sound quite so appealing anymore.

"But that doesn't mean I don't still want you," he says, his blue-green eyes locked on mine. "That didn't change because we agreed to just be friends. But I won't push you to do anything you don't want. Ever. Got it?"

I nod, no longer trusting my voice.

"Good."

Luke steps toward me. He's close enough that I can smell the spicy, earthy scent of him. It's too much. With the large bed only a few feet away, having him this close to me puts too many dirty thoughts into my head. I force myself not to lean in closer and suck in a deep breath, not to bury my face against his chest and commit his scent to memory. He leans even closer, and I feel like those ocean eyes can see directly into my thoughts. Does he know what affect he has on me? Can he see it on my face?

"One more thing." He's close enough that I can feel his words as much as hear the low, husky tone. It sends a shocking rush of moisture to my core, and I resist the urge to squirm. Luke's mouth quirks up in a lazy half-grin as if he knows how turned-on I am just by his nearness.

"Pretending I can't keep my hands off you?" he says. "That won't be difficult."

He straightens and his face takes on a casual, almost indifferent expression. "I'll see you at dinner?"

I still don't trust my voice not to shake, so I just nod. Luke gives me what seems like a genuine smile before turning to go. I watch him walk out the door, fighting against the urge to call him back here and make him show me just what he meant by not keeping his hands off me. Instead, I force my feet to stay planted right where they are while I count to 50. Then I go into the bathroom and take a cold shower.

CHAPTER 20

Luke

After leaving Piper in our room, I find my way out onto the large deck overlooking the beach and the Atlantic Ocean. Luckily, I don't encounter anyone along the way and the deck is empty. I need the time alone to pull myself together. Why had I told her I want her? What the hell had I been thinking? I hadn't been. That's the truth. I'd spoken without thinking of the consequences. And now I've gone and told her that I want her. What's going to happen now?

I get my answer later at dinner. Nothing. That's what's happening. Whatever Piper thought of my little confession, she's not letting on. She's not acting any differently around me than she has all the other times we've been around Art and Mel. Which is a little annoying, if I'm being honest. I don't know what I wanted, but I'd hoped for some reaction.

I could tell she wasn't unaffected by my nearness in the room earlier. But now she's laughing and chatting with Art and Mel, seemingly without a care in the world. She's even been casually affectionate toward me, putting a hand on my arm as we ate dinner and shooting me a teasing wink for Art's benefit when he'd made a joke about me being a workaholic. After dinner though, she sits on the opposite end of the small loveseat, putting distance between us. I don't know what to make of her behavior tonight. Luckily, there's not enough space for Mel to insinuate herself between us. Instead, Mel and Art sit across from us in separate chairs.

We sip our drinks and make small talk. Once again, Art steers the conversation away from business. It's frustrating. This trip is supposed to be about closing this deal with his company and mine, but so far, he isn't talking business. Maybe once we get settled in more, I can get things back on track. We've planned a fishing trip for tomorrow on his boat. It might be a good opportunity to try and gage his interest in Wolfe Industries.

"You two don't have to be so proper on our account," Art says, pulling my attention back to the present.

"What's that?" I say, wondering what he means.

He lifts a hand and motions back and forth between Piper and me. "You don't have to sit so far apart," he clarifies. "Being so careful not to touch each other."

He laughs. "Young people in love shouldn't have to hide their feelings. Hell, it wasn't so long ago that Mel and I couldn't keep our hands off each other. Right, honey?"

Mel gives him a smile that doesn't quite reach her eyes. "That's right sweetie," she says, her voice sickeningly sweet.

Piper slides a little closer to me, but she's still just out of reach. I realize that to everyone else, she and I aren't acting like a couple at all right now. This ruse isn't going to be believable if we keep acting like we're afraid to touch each other. Making a quick decision, I slide over until the length of Piper's thigh is touching mine. My heartbeat ratchets up a notch, but I ignore it, putting an arm around her shoulders and pulling her to me. Luckily, she's too stunned to resist, but I can tell she's nervous by the way her body stiffens against me. Under my arm, I can feel the muscles tense in her shoulders and back. This won't work.

Turning, I brush my lips across her temple and whisper one word low enough that only she can hear me. "Relax."

I'm close enough to breathe in the subtle scent of her. Citrus and lavender. It's intoxicating. I have to restrain myself from leaning in even closer and filling my nose with the scent. I stroke my fingers over the bare skin of her upper arm, feeling goosebumps break out in their wake. As the seconds tick by, I can feel the slow relaxation of Piper's muscles. She's far from pliant in my arms, but she's not quite as rigid.

"How did you two meet?" Mel asks, her voice a little too harsh to be genuine curiosity. Instead, it sounds almost suspicious.

I pull my attention back to the couple seated across from us and paste a wide smile on my face. Piper and I hadn't discussed this. We'd only come up with a vague backstory. I don't know why. I'm usually much more thorough than this. I should have known the subject of our supposed past would come up. I scramble to think of a believable story, but before I can come up with something, Piper speaks.

"It's kind of a funny story," Piper says, smiling up at me. "The first time we were supposed to meet, he stood me up."

She laughs and I shoot her a questioning look before smiling sheepishly at Art and Mel. They chuckle before turning back to Piper for the rest of the story. I'd like to hear it myself. Is she really going to tell them we met through an online dating app?

"My sister's college boyfriend was in the same fraternity with Luke. She badgered her boyfriend to convince Luke to meet me." Piper shakes her head. "But Luke had a bit of a reputation in college, and honestly, I didn't want anything to do with him. No way did I want to date some man-whore."

Piper laughs and I narrow my eyes at her. She's ignoring me though, totally caught up in her story. Art laughs with Piper, but I notice that Mel is watching me as though assessing whether I'm still a man-whore. I suppress a shudder at the look in her eyes.

"Anyway," Piper says. "Eventually, my sister convinced me that Luke was a great guy. I just needed to give him a chance. So, I agreed to meet him for coffee."

She shoots me a glare, but it's clear she's fighting a smile. "Only he canceled at the last minute."

I open my mouth to defend myself, but I don't even know what story she's telling. I don't want to contradict her, so I stay quiet. Art takes my silence for guilt and laughs.

Pointing a finger at me, he says, "Women never forget, son!"

I laugh with him. "Don't I know it!"

"Anyway," Piper says, clearly caught up in her story. "I was a little irritated and hurt, so I decided to cut my losses and move on."

"But he won you back?" Art asks, shooting me a sly grin.

Piper turns and looks at me. Her gaze softens and a smile plays at the corner of her mouth. It's almost enough to make me believe this thing between us is real.

"Then he just walked into my coffee shop one day," she says softly. "Caught me by total surprise."

"Swept you off your feet?" I ask with a wink.

She smiles. "Something like that."

She turns back to Art and Mel who are both waiting for the rest of the story. "He apologized for standing me up."

"Hey!" I say. "I called and canceled."

"At the last minute," she says.

"Still counts," I mutter.

"He asked me to dinner," she says. "I should have said no. I had so much going on and a business to run."

"But she was dazzled by my charm," I say.

She shrugs. "Well, you are cute."

Something about that little compliment from Piper makes my smile even wider. "Thank you," I say. "You're not so bad yourself."

"Aren't you charming?" she teases.

"I have my moments."

My gaze goes to her mouth, and I lean closer.

"Then what happened?"

Mel's harsh tone pulls me out of my trance. Piper blinks and looks back over at Art who still looks enraptured by our story. One glance at Mel shows that she has the opposite opinion. Her face is pinched into an angry glare, and she looks like she'd rather be anywhere else. I'd almost forgotten the two of them were sitting across from us. I'd been so caught up in the flirty banter with Piper that I'd almost started believing the tale we were weaving. I'd been seconds away from kissing her. If Mel hadn't spoken, I don't know how far I might have taken things.

Piper smiles. "I agreed." She shrugs. "The rest is history."

"She couldn't resist me," I say with a grin.

The conversation shifts to tomorrow's fishing trip. Art and I discuss different bait and tackle options. It's been years since I've been fishing, but I used to love going when I'd come here for the summers. Before I'd gone to work with my father, that is. Thinking of him pulls me back to reality and I remember why I'm here in the first place. I need to focus. I can't afford to lose sight of the purpose of this trip. Which means I can't let my attraction to Piper distract me.

So, when we go back to our room for the night, and Piper goes into the bathroom, I find the spare linens in the closet and make myself comfortable on the small couch. Piper had been right earlier. It's not large enough for me. But there's no way I'm making her sleep on the couch. This trip is all because of me. At least one of us should have a decent night's sleep. I'd rather it be her. That's why I pretend to be sound asleep when she comes out of the bathroom. I can hear her hesitate for just a second before she lets out a little sigh and climbs into bed. The room goes dark. I lie there for a long time before sleep finally claims me.

CHAPTER 21

Piper

I wake up just after sunrise, my gaze straying to the couch to find it empty. Luke must have already left for his fishing trip with Art. That leaves me here alone with Mel all day. I grimace at the idea, wondering how long I can avoid her without making it obvious.

I make my way down to the kitchen without encountering anyone else. After pouring myself a cup of coffee, I carry it out onto the porch to watch the sun come up over the waves. I don't know how long Luke and Art plan to be gone on this fishing trip, but I assume they won't be back for several hours. Which means I need to find some way to pass the time. I'd prefer not to hang out with Mel, if possible. Maybe she'll go shopping again today and not return until dinner. But I doubt my luck would hold out for that long.

I spot some lounge chairs on the beach and an idea forms. What better way to spend a beach vacation than reading a book on the beach? Thankfully, I brought my e-reader with me on this trip. By the time I finish my coffee, the sun is higher and it's already warm. The breeze off the water is still a little cool, but I know that won't do much to combat the heat later. The morning might be the best time to spend on the beach. Decision made, I head back to my room to change into a swimsuit and slather on sunscreen.

I spend most of the morning alternating between reading and lazing in the sun and walking along the shore looking for shells. I even get brave and wade into the waves when it gets too hot in the sun. The water is cool and inviting, but I don't stay in too long. I still haven't seen any sign of Mel. Maybe she's not a fan of the beach? If not, it seems strange to vacation here. But I'm not upset at her absence. I find that I'm enjoying the time alone.

In Peach Tree, it was easy to feel lonely. But here, under the expanse of blue sky with the ocean stretching out before me, I feel more at peace than ever. And to think, this trip wouldn't have happened if I hadn't agreed to be Luke's fake girlfriend. Thinking of Luke makes me wonder if he and Art are back yet. I check the time on my phone and see that I've been out here longer than I thought. I should probably go inside before I burn. I gather up the few items I carried with me, wrap my towel around my waist and head back toward the house.

I don't see anyone in the kitchen, but I can hear someone walking around upstairs. Maybe Mel is finally awake and moving around. She must be a late sleeper. I make my way upstairs and head left toward the bedroom. My phone buzzes with an incoming text and I smile when I see Harlow's name on the screen. I open the door, my attention focused on reading Harlow's text. That's why it takes me a second to notice the naked man in the room. It's also why I stand there, staring for several seconds before my startled gasp squeaks out, alerting Luke to my presence.

My eyes grow wide, and I turn and flee, closing the door behind me. I don't remember the mad dash down the stairs and out onto the porch. All I can see is Luke and what he'd been doing before he'd noticed me standing there. I don't know that I'll ever be able to forget it. Luke, totally naked, his body in profile. His eyes had been closed, his mouth slightly open. And he'd clearly been in the middle of a solo pleasure session. And I'd just stood there and watched him. Like a pervert. But holy hell, it was hot.

I can't bring myself to regret watching him for those few seconds. The idea of being able to watch him until he came flits through my head, sending a rush of heat through me. Why is that idea so hot? Before today, I would have said that watching a man jerk off is weird or awkward. But seeing Luke as he'd gripped his thick shaft and worked his hand up and down, his body tense with the anticipation of release? It's nearly enough to make me shove my hand into my bathing suit and seek out my own release. But I'm standing on the porch, in full view of anyone who might look over. I wave my hand at my face in a futile gesture to try and cool my heated skin, then I try my best not to picture Luke as I'd just seen him.

He must have come home and thought I was gone for the day. He clearly hadn't expected me to walk in on him. Why hadn't he locked the door? Should

I find him and apologize? Or would that make things more awkward for both of us? I can't imagine how he feels right now. Maybe I'll just wait and see how he responds and take my cue from that. If he brings it up, I'll apologize and suggest he lock the door next time he needs privacy. If he doesn't bring it up, I'll assume he never wants to speak of it again.

I stay outside for another half an hour, hoping that's enough time for Luke to finish whatever he's doing in our room. The idea of him finishing sends that vision of him back to the forefront of my thoughts. Damn it. I'm never going to be able to un-see that, am I? Eventually, I go back into the house. Luke walks into the kitchen as I'm closing the back door, his hair still damp from his shower.

He meets my gaze. I'm about to open my mouth to apologize, despite my earlier decision when Art walks in behind Luke. He gives me a big grin.

"Did he tell you about our trip?" Art asks, clearly in a great mood.

I shake my head and return the smile. "I was just about to ask how it went," I lie.

"Best fishing trip in years!" Art says. "We caught more fish than we could eat. Had to start tossing them back after a while."

Art's happiness is contagious, and I find my smile growing wider. "That's amazing! I'm glad it was a good trip."

I don't risk a glance at Luke. The air between us still feels charged, even with the buffer of Art in the room. Something between us shifted in those few seconds upstairs, and I'm not sure how to shift back to the way it was before. I'm not even sure I want to.

"I had a great day, too," I say. "I spent the morning on the beach with a good book."

Art grins. "Good thing you did. It's supposed to storm later in the week."

I nod, barely hearing his words. "I'm going to go get cleaned up," I say as I rush past the two men.

When I make it to the room, I do what Luke didn't. I lock the door before I strip off my swimsuit and climb into the shower. Only then do I give into my need. Standing under the hot spray, I slide a hand between my legs and find my clit. It takes mere seconds for me to come, my pussy squeezing around nothing as the image of Luke stroking himself plays on a loop in my head.

CHAPTER 22

Piper

The next two days pass with agonizing slowness. I'm acutely aware of Luke each time I'm near him. I do my best to avoid being alone with him, even going so far as to retire to bed early so I can pretend to be asleep before he joins me in our room. I'm doing everything I can to avoid being tempted by his nearness. But I can't stop my brain from conjuring up that image of him with his dick in his hand.

Mel tends to leave the beach house during the day to go shopping. She joins us for dinner each night, but she spends most of that time complaining about the house, the food, the heat and the lack of servants. Honestly, the woman is exhausting. She also makes sure to tell Luke how handsome he is with his face "kissed by the sun". While she's not wrong, her obvious flirting is enough to make me want to slap her. Somehow, I manage to restrain myself until we finish eating and I can excuse myself for another early bedtime.

But sleep usually eludes me. I end up lying awake until long after Luke comes in and quietly makes his way to the bathroom to change before climbing under the blankets on the too-small couch. On the third night, I can't take it anymore. The two of us have barely spoken since I walked in on him that day. Anytime we're around the others, we put on our little act, convincing them we're in love. But as soon as we're alone, it's like we turn into strangers. It's exhausting and I want to go back to the way things were before. But I don't know how. I need to talk to him, I know. But what do I say?

"Luke?"

My whisper sounds loud in the dark silence of the room. I freeze, waiting for his response. He's probably asleep already. I'm the only idiot still awake in this house. I let out a quiet sigh as the seconds tick by. It's just as well. I don't know what I'd even say to Luke if he were awake. I'm just tired of tossing and turning with nothing but my own thoughts to keep me company. I'm just about to roll over and give in to counting imaginary sheep when I hear him blow out a breath.

"Yes?" His voice is low, but I can hear the almost annoyed tone. I don't know why the sound of that one exasperated word makes me smile, but it does. Only Luke Wolfe can say so much with just a single word.

"I can't sleep," I say, my voice just above a whisper.

He sighs again. "Me either." He sounds resigned. My smile grows wider. It's not that I'm happy that he can't sleep. I'm just relieved not to be alone in the dark tonight.

"What's your favorite color?" I ask, throwing out the random question.

When he answers, there's a hint of amusement in his voice. "Green, I guess. What's yours?"

I smile, happy that he's going along with my question-and-answer session rather than telling me not to interrupt his attempt at sleeping. All hint of his earlier annoyance is gone.

"Purple," I say.

He chuckles. "That's such a girly answer, Huff."

"Purple is the color of royalty," I say, pretending to be offended. "It's not girly."

"It may be the color of royalty," he concedes. "But it's still girly."

I know he's trying to push my buttons. But I don't mind. It feels more like the way things were before.

I shrug. "So? I'm a girl."

"I noticed," he says, his tone dry.

I speak without thinking, the words flying out of my mouth before I have a chance to call them back. "What's that supposed to mean?" I realize immediately that my tone is teasing, almost flirty.

Luke is quiet for a moment, and I worry that I've just changed the dynamic between us. After what happened the other day, and our unspoken agreement to pretend it never happened, I'd hate for one silly comment to be the thing that ruins our friendship.

"It means," he says slowly, "that I'd have to be blind and deaf not to notice that you're a woman." He mutters the next part under his breath, but it sounds like he says, "Not even then."

I feel my face heat and I'm glad Luke can't see my blush or my pleased smile. The silence stretches between us for several seconds and I wonder if maybe Luke fell asleep after all. But then he speaks.

"Favorite time of year?" Luke asks.

I smile, happy he's keeping up this game of questions with me. "Autumn," I say. "I love that part of the year when you've made it through another sweltering summer and the air starts to turn just a little cooler. The mosquitos start to die off, and it's actually bearable to be outside again. It's the best. What about you?"

"Spring," he says quietly. "For the opposite reason. I hate the cold weather. I know winters here are nothing like they are up north, but I still hate the dreary skies and the short days. It's dark when I go to work and dark when I come home. I hate it. I love when the weather starts changing and the days get longer. I love the view outside my office window when the leaves come back to the trees and the flowers start blooming."

I've never heard him talk this way. There's a soft, almost dreamy quality to his voice. Maybe it's because it's just the two of us here in this room. Maybe it's the fact that we can't see one another across the darkened room. But it's easy to talk to Luke tonight. It's like we're in our own little bubble of solitude in here.

"Okay," I concede in a soft voice. "Spring is pretty great too, I guess."

"Damn right, it is."

I laugh. Trying to lighten the mood, I consider my next question for a few seconds before asking.

"Favorite form of potato?"

"What?" Luke's confused response has me giggling.

"Favorite form of potato," I repeat, trying to inject seriousness into my voice. "The potato is a very versatile food. It comes in many forms. And I need to know what your favorite is."

"Why, exactly, is this an important question?" he asks, skeptical.

"Because," I say, "If you say you don't have a favorite, then we can't be friends. I take potatoes very seriously."

"I see," Luke says. I can hear the laughter he's trying to hold back. "I've never put much thought into my favorite potato. There are so many options to choose from."

"See?" I say. "I'm over here asking the tough questions."

Luke lets out a low laugh that does something to make my insides turn to jelly. I don't hate the feeling. All at once, the scene I'd walked in on the other day flashes into my brain. I immediately push it away as I've done the other hundred or so times it's happened since I saw...what I saw. I feel my face heat again and I'm glad for the darkness between us.

"Curly fries," Luke says, finally, breaking into my filthy thoughts. It takes me a second to remember what we're even talking about. Potatoes. Right. I clear my throat, banishing the images in my mind.

"That's a respectable choice," I say, glad my voice comes out steady.

"What about you?" Luke asks, oblivious to my internal struggle.

"Hashbrowns," I say in a rush. "Breakfast is my favorite."

Is my voice to high-pitched? Why am I talking so fast?

"I'll keep that in mind," Luke says.

The silence goes on for several seconds before I speak. I don't know what makes me say it. Things are finally back to normal between us. But I can't seem to stop myself.

"I'm sorry," I say.

His reply is immediate. "For what?"

I close my eyes and try to summon the courage to say the words. Taking a deep breath, I decide to just do it. "Walking in on you that day. I should have knocked. I should have called out. Something. I'm sorry."

I blurt the words out quickly, even as the image of Luke's naked body flashes into my mind again. That memory is burned into my brain forever. When I'm an old woman on my deathbed, I'm going to remember exactly what Luke looked like in that moment. For once, I don't push away the memory. Instead, I savor it, remembering every detail of the way he'd looked. Eyes tightly closed, tendons straining, one hand braced on the side of the dresser, the muscles in his back flexing as his hand moved up and down, stroking what might be the biggest dick I've ever seen. Heat flows through me at the memory and I want to toss the blankets off me to get some relief. I feel myself growing wet and I clench my thighs tightly together against the familiar ache in my core.

"Don't worry about it," Luke says, as if that's something I'm capable of doing. "Let's just pretend it never happened."

Right. Like that's even possible. But, if he'd walked in on me touching myself, I know I'd be mortified. So, even though I know I'll never be able to forget the sight, I decide I'll follow his wishes and put it behind us. Only now, I'm thinking about Luke walking in on me touching myself. Would he stand there, watching me? Or would he quickly avert his gaze? What does it say about me that the idea of him watching me sends a fresh rush of moisture to my already damp panties? I take a deep breath and banish those thoughts, trying to focus on the present conversation.

"Next time put a sock on the door or something," I say, trying to inject a teasing tone into my words.

But Luke doesn't laugh. His voice is tight when he speaks again, as if he's being careful with his words. "If I put a sock on the door every time I get turned on, Huff, you'll never be able to come back into the room."

My heart beats faster at his words and their implications. What is he saying? I know I'm treading on dangerous ground here. I should drop the subject and return to simpler topics. But I can't help myself. I want to know if he's as affected by me as I am by him.

"What's that mean?" I ask, my voice cautious.

I hear Luke sigh in the dark. "Nothing."

His tone implies that it's the opposite of 'nothing'. "Not nothing," I say. "Tell me."

I hear a rustle of blankets as Luke sits up on the tiny chaise. I can't quite make out his features in the darkness, but I know he's looking in my direction.

"You really want to know?" His voice is harder now. The rational part of me thinks I should say no. I shouldn't open this particular Pandora's box. Once I do, I know I won't be able to shut it. Too bad the rational part of me isn't running the show right now.

I nod, my gaze pinned to his darkened silhouette. Then, realizing he probably can't see me, I say, "Yes." I'd meant to sound confident and sure, but the single word comes out as little more than a whisper.

Luke is silent for several long heartbeats. I almost think he's not going to answer, but then he speaks. "It means that I haven't stopped wanting you since I saw you in that dress the night of the dinner party."

I suck in a breath, shocked by the words and the low, gravelly tone of his voice. But mostly I'm shocked by the sharp stab of desire I feel low in my belly. But Luke isn't finished talking.

"There hasn't been a single day where I haven't fantasized about all the things I'd do to you if this thing between us was real. If we weren't just pretending to be a couple."

Holy shit. I'm in trouble. My heart pounds in my chest. That spike of desire in my belly? It's traveled a bit lower. I clench my thighs together against the ache his words bring.

"Like what?" I whisper.

"Piper."

I can hear the warning when he says my name. That single word tells me more than anything else he's said tonight.

"I'm trying to be the good guy here," he says, his voice strained. "I'm trying to be honorable."

There's a small part of me that wants to keep pushing him. That wants to see how far I can push him before he snaps, breaking the tight leash on his control. But I'm not that kind of woman. I never have been. I've always played it safe. Tonight is no different. So, instead of begging Luke to come join me in this bed, I pull the blankets tighter around my chin and ignore the way my pulse seems to be pounding hard enough for me to feel it in my clit.

"Goodnight, Luke," I say softly.

There's a beat of silence before Luke replies. "Goodnight, Piper."

I tell myself this is for the best. Nothing about me and Luke makes sense. We wouldn't be good together. We're friends. No matter how hot he is, we can't complicate this thing by adding sex to the mix. It's better this way. But no matter what I tell myself, I can't seem to make my traitorous pussy listen to reason. It's a long time before I fall asleep.

CHAPTER 23

Luke

The morning dawns gray and stormy, much like my own mood after last night's talk with Piper. Why had she brought up walking in on me? All it had done was remind me of why I'd been jerking off in the first place. Seeing her in that damned skimpy bikini when I'd come back from fishing with Art was more than I'd been able to handle, apparently. And that thought turns my cock to stone all over again. What the hell is wrong with me? I'm not some teenager who can't control himself around a pretty girl. So, why am I walking around with a tent in my pants every time I so much as think of Piper?

Hell, that's the reason I'd decided to jerk off that day. I thought that a quick release would help ease some of the tension inside me. It's been months since I had sex with a woman. Of course, there's some pent-up sexual frustration. It probably has nothing to do with Piper at all. She's an attractive woman, certainly. Attractive? Shit, she's fucking gorgeous. Those golden brown eyes that seem to be able to see into my soul, the long fall of her dark hair, the single dimple to the left of her mouth that comes out when she smiles just right? All of it combines to turn me into a raging ball of hormones with a perpetual hard-on.

It's for that reason that I slip quietly from the room without waking her. I do my best not to look in the direction of the bed. I don't know what it will do to my fragile restraint if I see her lying there, tangled in the bed covers, hair spread across the pillow. No. It's best if I avoid her until I can get control of my libido. It's quiet in the house as I make my way down to the kitchen. Luckily, I've come to realize over the past few days that Mel isn't an early riser. So, I should be safe from her clutches for the morning. Thunder rumbles outside, making me glance toward the wall of windows that looks out over the Atlantic. I guess this puts a damper on Art's plans to go boating today. I check the weather on my phone and see that the forecast shows the possibility for random thunderstorms for the next several hours.

Sighing, I pocket the phone and pour myself a cup of coffee. I guess we're going to be stuck inside for a while. I sip my coffee and watch the storm rage outside. Eventually, Art and then Piper join me. We drink coffee and talk about our plans for the last half of the week. Art wants all of us to go out on his boat before we leave, and Piper wants to explore more of the island.

The day passes with agonizing slowness, the weather making everyone a little stir crazy. Art suggests a board game to pass the time, but after an hour of playing, he announces that the rain is making him sleepy and declares he's taking a nap. I stand along with him.

"Actually, that sounds like a great idea," I say. "I didn't sleep great last night. Maybe I'll head up and take a nap too."

Piper doesn't say anything. She just gives us both a tight smile. Now that I think about it, she hasn't said much all day. She's been unusually reserved. I wonder if what I said last night took things too far. I wonder if I've made her uncomfortable. I sigh as I walk up the stairs. I need to apologize. More, I need to keep my thoughts and desires to myself. Piper hasn't done or said anything to indicate that she's interested in being more than friends. As a matter of fact, the day we arrived, she specifically said we needed to keep our distance if we wanted to maintain our friendship. And I'm the jackass who can't stop thinking about having sex with her.

I close the bedroom door behind me as I enter, raking a hand through my hair. I need to get ahold of myself before I royally fuck this up. Piper is amazing. I've come to value her friendship in the short time I've known her. I don't want to lose that just because I'm a horny bastard. I'll apologize to her later this evening and make sure she knows I never want to make her uncomfortable. As I'm about to head toward the couch, the door opens and I turn to see Piper standing there. Her expression is wary, but something else is mixed with it. Something a little wild.

"What are you doing, Piper?" My voice comes out harsher than I'd intended. She looks cautious, but she doesn't seem deterred by my tone or my words. She holds my gaze for a moment before answering.

"What does it look like?" she finally says. "I want to take a nap, too."

Her voice is low and if I didn't know better, I'd say there's a teasing quality to it. My eyes follow the movement of her hands as she toys with the hem of her shirt. The dim light coming from the window behind me is enough that I can see her clearly, though she's cast in shadows. A bright flash of lightning from outside illuminates the room for several seconds as we stand there, watching one another. My heart races as I wait for the boom of thunder to follow behind it. When it comes, I can see the tiniest flinch from Piper at the sound, but there's something else in her eyes. Excitement. Exhilaration.

"Piper?"

I watch as she seems to deflate. Her shoulders slump, and she closes her eyes on a sigh.

"I can't do this anymore." The words are low, just above a whisper, but I hear them clearly.

When she opens her eyes to meet my gaze, her expression is one I haven't seen there before. She looks wild, almost panicked. Is this it? Is this where she tells me she wants out of our arrangement? Is she going home to Peach Tree? The realization is like a punch in the gut. The idea of her leaving, ending things now, causes an almost physical ache in my chest. I want to talk her out of it. Beg her to reconsider. Promise her anything if it means she'll stay here with me. For the first time, I don't try to lie to myself about why. It has nothing to do with this deal or deflecting Mel or advancing my career. It's her. It's Piper. I don't want her to leave me. But I promised her it would be her decision. I can't go back on that promise now, just because it's not the decision I want her to make. I open my mouth to tell her that it's okay. To reassure her that it doesn't change the terms of our deal. But she speaks before I can.

"I can't keep touching you out there," she says softly, taking a step toward me. "Kissing you. Putting on a show for them." Another step closer. "Then coming into this room and pretending I don't want you in that bed with me every night."

Her eyes drift to the bed, then back to me. I feel myself go completely still. The only sounds are the rain against the window, our rapid breathing and the pounding of my own heart in my ears.

"I don't want to pretend anymore," she whispers. "I don't think I can."

I'm stunned. I want to say something articulate and meaningful, but what comes out just sounds desperate and needy. "Thank god."

The words are barely out of my mouth before Piper closes the distance between us and her lips are on mine. The last tiny thread of control holding me back snaps. Her arms lock around my neck as mine circle her waist, pulling her tightly against me. I groan at the feel of her lips pressed against mine, her soft curves molded to me. There's none of the tentative awkwardness of a first kiss. This kiss isn't gentle or sweet either. It's nothing like the tentative displays we've put on in front of the others. It's wild and hungry like the storm raging outside. When her lips part, my tongue sweeps inside to taste her. She tastes like the strawberries I'd watched her eat earlier and I let out another needy groan.

This Piper is different from the one I've come to know over the last couple of weeks. She's not gentle or teasing. She's fierce and full of barely leashed passion. It's clear she wants me just as much as I want her. It would be clear even if she hadn't just told me. That knowledge has me growing impossibly hard in seconds. My mouth leaves hers to trail kisses across her jaw, down to her neck. She sucks in a gasp when I deliver a soft bite to the spot where her shoulder meets her neck. I make a mental note to revisit that spot later, when I can take my time with her. But now, I just need her naked.

As if she can hear my thoughts, Piper pulls away from me long enough to pull her shirt off and drop it to the floor. I do the same, tugging off my own shirt and tossing it somewhere off to the side. Her hands skim up over my chest as her eyes track their movement. I watch a little smile curve her lips before she grips the back of my neck and pulls me down for another kiss. Kissing Piper is addictive. It's as if now that I've given in to temptation, I can't seem to get enough of her lips, her tongue, her taste. I pull her against me again, letting her feel how hard I am, how much I want her. The little gasp she lets out is unbelievably sexy. My hands skim up the smooth skin of her back as I trail more kisses down her neck to her collar bone.

"I want you."

"I want you, too," she says in a breathless voice as she reaches for the button at the front of my pants.

I straighten and grin down at her. "Glad we're on the same page."

"I don't have condoms," I say, kissing her again. "I didn't think I'd need them."

"I have an IUD," she says, breathless. "I got tested after my last boyfriend cheated on me." She kisses my neck. "I'm clean."

The anger and disbelief at the idea of someone cheating on her wars with the more pressing realization that I'm going to be inside her soon. With no barrier between us. That's a first for me.

"I get tested twice a year," I say. "I'm clean."

"Good," she says. "Because I'm tired of waiting."

I reach behind her and find the clasp of her bra. With a quick flick of my fingers, it's open and I'm sliding the straps off her shoulders, watching as the hot pink lace lowers to reveal a pair of mouth-watering breasts tipped with the prettiest pink nipples I've ever seen. I bring my hands around to cup them, teasing my thumbs over her nipples. Piper sucks in a breath and I feel her push forward, leaning into my touch.

I lower my head and do what I've been longing to do since I saw her in that tiny bikini the other day. I wrap my lips around her nipple and suck lightly, swirling my tongue over the tender flesh until I feel it stiffen in my mouth. Piper sucks in a shocked gasp that sends a bolt of lust straight to my cock. I release her nipple and turn my attention to the other, giving it the same treatment. She squirms in my arms, her fingers digging into my hair as she holds my face to her chest. When both her nipples have turned into hard, rosy little peaks, I move lower, kissing my way down her stomach to her hip.

I curl my fingers into the waistband of her shorts, popping open the button at her waist. The zipper gives way next, and I push the shorts down her legs, along with her underwear. Normally, I'd prefer to use a little more finesse and take my time with a woman, especially when it's our first time together. But I can't do that with Piper. I want her too much. This thing between us is too explosive. It's been building up for days and I can't contain my need for her anymore. My movements are hurried and jerky, but so are hers. She quickly steps out of the shorts and underwear and kicks them away, leaving her standing there beautifully, gloriously naked.

I take half a second to admire Piper's naked body before wrapping my arms around her, lifting her and tossing her onto the bed. She lets out a breathless little cry when she lands and laughs. Her lower legs dangle over the edge of the bed and I move to stand between them. I let my eyes roam over her body again, taking in every curve, every peak and valley. Piper leans up on her elbows and watches me watching her. She gives my pants a pointed look.

"You going to take those off?" she asks in a teasing tone.

I shake my head. "Not just yet."

Reaching down, I place a hand on each of her thighs. My hands skim over the smooth skin, gripping lightly. Before Piper can understand my intent, I use my grip on her legs to yank her closer to the edge of the bed until her ass is right on the edge. Ignoring her startled gasp, I sink to my knees between her thighs. I need to taste her. I have to know how she feels against my tongue, what sounds she makes as she comes apart under me, around me. Piper doesn't resist as I spread her legs wide and bury my face between them.

My first taste of Piper's pussy is better than I imagined. She's wet already, and so responsive. The feel of my tongue on her sensitive flesh must have shocked her, even though she'd known it was coming. She gasps and her hips buck against my face. I tighten my grip around her thighs, holding her in place as I lick her again. This time, the sound that escapes her is closer to a low moan and her legs fall open wider, inviting me to taste her as much as I want.

I start off slow at first with short, teasing licks, learning her responses. I follow with long, lazy strokes of my tongue down to her opening and back up to swirl around her clit. It doesn't take long for me to discover what she likes, though. When I hit on a certain rhythm, her breathing quickens, and her hips start to move as if they have a mind of their own. I focus my attentions on that spot, just to the left of her clit, brushing my tongue against it over and over, not changing my pace. I look up to see Piper's eyes are tightly closed and she's gripping the bed covers in both fists. Her entire body is tense with anticipation, and I know she's getting close. Her breaths come faster, and little gasps escape her with every swipe of my tongue against her clit. She's almost there. I want to see her when she finally lets go. I want to feel her come against my mouth, knowing I'm the one who got her there.

Releasing one of her thighs, I reach down to tease my fingers against her opening. I don't change my rhythm on her clit as I coat my fingers with her juices until they're slick. Her breathing is even faster now and she's writhing against me. I bring my free hand and up and pin her hips with my forearm, holding her still for me. That's all the warning I give her before I push two fingers inside her.

"Oh," Piper moans. "Yes!"

Encouraged, I begin to pump my fingers in and out, fucking her slowly with my hand while my tongue continues to work on her clit. The addition of my fingers inside her seems to have whipped Piper into a frenzy. She's bucking against my hold on her, her gasps turning to little whimpers. Curling my fingers slightly upward, I begin to move faster. Piper raises up, her body bowed toward me as her shoulders lift off the bed. Her pussy clamps down on my fingers and she lets out a loud cry before clapping a hand over her mouth. I can feel the rhythmic pulsing of her around my fingers as she comes. I don't let up, holding her down as I continue to lick her and finger fuck her through her orgasm. Her cries are muffled by her hand, but I can still hear the sexy sounds she's making. I watch her from my vantage point between her legs. I'd been right. Seeing Piper come is one of the sexiest things I've ever witnessed.

When her keening moans turn to gasps and she starts to shake her head, I ease my movements. I keep my fingers inside her though, wanting to feel every fluttering spasm of her climax. But I lick and kiss my way over to her inner thigh, loving the feel of the smooth skin against my face. I'd be content to keep licking her to orgasms all day, but after a few moments, Piper leans up on her elbows and looks at me. She's gorgeous like this, flushed and relaxed from her orgasm. Her eyes are soft and languid. The edge of her need has been tempered, but it's still there.

"Pants," she says. "Off. Now."

I smile at her demanding tone. Holding her gaze, I slide my fingers in and out of her once more with agonizing slowness. Her mouth opens, just a bit and she sucks in a breath. I feel another faint flutter of her inner walls around my fingers as I do it again.

"Luke..."

The way she says my name is almost a plea, almost as if she's begging me for something. I'd love to take some time exploring that, but my cock is painfully hard and straining against the confines of my pants. I don't have it in me to tease her further. I need to be inside her when she comes again. In this moment, I need it like I need my next breath.

I stand, letting my fingers slide out of her. Piper watches me as I bring them to my mouth and lick them clean. Then, I quickly strip off my pants and boxer briefs and stand nude before her. Her gaze tracks down my body until landing on my cock with a look of anticipation. I look down at her, stunned by how gorgeous she is right now.

"You're so beautiful."

I hadn't planned to say it. The words had just come out in a ragged whisper as I'd looked down at her. Her golden skin is tanned from the sun and her dark hair spills across the white sheets beneath her. She's looking at me with a hunger that I know matches my own. Her mouth quirks up in a smile.

"Funny," she says. "I was thinking the same thing about you."

When I huff out a laugh, she raises one eyebrow in challenge and glances down at my dick. "Are you going to use that thing, or what?"

I didn't know about this playful, teasing side to Piper, but I like it. Bracing myself over her, I lean down and capture her mouth with mine, letting my tongue plunge inside almost roughly. Piper matches my intensity, telling me with her kiss just how needy she is for me. When I break off the kiss and stand, her face has a slightly dazed expression. I don't give her long to contemplate the kiss though. Instead, I position myself between her legs, line up my cock at her opening and slide inside in one swift motion.

The sound Piper makes is so incredibly sexy. It's somewhere between a gasp and a moan, and I think I could almost come from that sound alone. Her legs go around my back and I grip her hips, holding her in place as I begin to move. She feels incredible, better than anything my feeble imagination had concocted. The lack of a condom makes everything more intense. She's hot and wet and feels like she was made for me. I pull back slowly until just the head of my cock is inside her before thrusting deep inside her body again. I do it again, watching the way Piper's eyes close every time I thrust home. When those brown eyes shift their attention to the place where we're joined, I follow her gaze. We both watch my cock disappear swiftly inside her, then remerge slowly, glistening with the evidence of her arousal each time. I slow my thrusts, wanting to savor the visual of her body taking every inch of me. It's the hottest fucking thing I've ever seen.

Gradually, I pick up speed, sliding in and out faster while keeping my hold on her hips. Piper grips my forearms, fingernails digging into my skin. The slight sting of pain somehow excites me more. Piper's eyes fall closed as I thrust into her over and over. My breaths come in pants, and I know I'm dangerously close to losing control and pounding into Piper until we both break. I know I should draw this out, savor it. There's no guarantee that Piper won't come to her senses soon and decide we need to go back to being friends. But knowing what I should do and making myself do it are two very different things. When I hear Piper gasp my name, I know I can't hold back any longer.

I hook my arms behind her knees and shift the angle between us. I pull her against me with each pounding thrust inside her. Her mouth drops open and I feel her pussy tighten around my cock with the telltale flutters that let me know she's about to come. A primal satisfaction spreads through me at the knowledge that I did that. I made her come.

"That's it, Piper," I say through gritted teeth. "Come for me. Come on my cock."

Her eyes open and her gaze locks on mine as a moan escapes her. It's as if my words spur her on, pushing her over the edge. I can feel her pulsing around my cock over and over as she comes. Our bodies make wet, slapping noises that compete with the sexy little gasps she's making with each thrust of me inside her. There's no way I can hold off my own orgasm. Not with those sounds and the feel of her squeezing my length over and over. I give myself over to sensation and need. Something like a roar is ripped from my throat as the orgasm slams through me, shocking in its intensity. Waves of pleasure slam through me with each pulse of my release inside her. My thrusts slow and eventually stop, though I don't pull out of Piper just yet. My dick twitches inside her with the aftershocks of my release and I want us to stay joined like this for as long as possible.

When I finally ease my cock from her, Piper lets out a shaky breath. She looks magnificent like this. Naked, sprawled out with her legs still open, flushed and exhausted from fucking me. Her chest heaves as she tries to slow her breathing, making her breasts move up and down. Eventually, I tear my eyes off her and go to the bathroom to find a washcloth. I dampen it with warm water and return to the bed. Piper hasn't moved a muscle and I can't help but smile at the sight of her.

I don't know how I resisted her for this long. It's crystal clear to me as I look down at her that we were always going to end up here. There was no way we were ever going to keep things between us platonic. And now that I know what it's like to be with her, to hold her, to watch her unravel around me; I don't know if I'll be able to go back to being her friend.

CHAPTER 24

Piper

Luke returns from the bathroom with a wet cloth and stares down at me for a few seconds. I finally make myself move enough to reach out a hand for the cloth. But Luke shakes his head and reaches between my legs to gently clean me. The move is unexpected, and I know I should feel embarrassed by the intimacy of the moment, but it's somehow endearing. Luke taking care of me isn't something I'd anticipated, but I'd be lying if I said I didn't like it. The storm outside seems to have moved on, finally. The rain is still coming down, but the lightning has stopped. I can hear the faint rumble of thunder in the distance.

Luke tosses the cloth into the dirty clothes hamper and leans down to kiss me lightly on the lips.

"That," he says, "Did not feel fake to me."

I can't help it. I laugh. After a few seconds, I sober and put on a serious face. "Speak for yourself," I say with a careless shrug.

Luke leans back and glares down at me through narrowed eyes. "Not that I'm bragging or anything," he says. "But those sounds you made were very real."

I decide to keep messing with him. Keeping my tone casual and unbothered, I ask, "How do you know?"

Instead of becoming indignant or annoyed, Luke's gaze turns thoughtful as his eyes trail over my naked body. "Maybe you're right," he says, his voice dropping an octave. "Maybe I need to try again."

Despite the orgasms I just had, I can feel some part of me stirring in excitement at his words. That fact alone is shocking to me. I've never been obsessed with sex. But then, I've never had sex that good before. I know I should be exhausted after what we just did. I am, but I'm also strangely energized. Part of me still can't believe what just happened, even though I'd been the one to instigate it. But I can't find it in me to regret having sex with Luke. Not when the sex was so incredible.

Luke reaches out a hand and trails a finger down the center of my chest, between my breasts. He keeps his touch light, barely skimming over the surface of my skin. Though my skin is still covered in a light sheen of sweat, I feel goosebumps sprout in the wake of his touch. Looking down, my eyes follow the path of his fingers, watching to see what he does next. I can feel my pulse quicken with excitement and anticipation. Instead of continuing lower, his hands move to the side, to my ribs. Before I have a chance to wonder what he's doing, he starts to tickle me. A shout escapes me as I laugh and try to squirm away from his hands. But Luke is relentless, and he follows me. I roll over in an attempt to avoid his deft fingers.

"Stop, stop," I shout, using my arms to deflect his tickling. "Luke, please!"

Through my laughter, I can hear him say, "Admit you weren't faking."

"Ah!" I shout as another round of tickling assaults my ribs. "Okay, okay," I say. "I admit it."

Luke stops tickling me and hauls me up against him. My back is against his chest and his arms are locked around me. When he speaks, his voice is right next to my ear.

"Admit what?" he asks.

I go still at the feel of his hard body pressed against me. I can't understand the affect this man has on me. He just fucked my brains out and I'm already wondering when we can do it again.

"I admit," I say in a voice I almost don't recognize as my own, "that I was absolutely not faking things with you."

"Good," Luke says, making no move to release me.

I let my head rest back against his shoulder. "I admit that you made me come so hard I saw stars." Luke's grip tightens on me as he sucks in a breath.

"That even though I just came twice, I'm already thinking about fucking you again," I add, pushing back against him.

I feel, more than hear his laugh. "You're dangerous to my health."

"Worth it, though," I whisper, turning my head to kiss his neck.

Instead of taking what I'm offering, Luke sighs and plants a kiss on my temple. "You're definitely worth it," he says. "But I'm not a machine. I think I need a few minutes to recover."

I wiggle my ass against his cock which is already semi-hard again. "Feels like you're on your way." Sighing, I turn in his arms. "But if you insist." I kiss his cheek and climb off the bed to head for the bathroom.

When I emerge from the bathroom, I find Luke on the bed with the covers pulled up just above his hips. He's sitting back against the headboard, one arm propped behind his head looking far sexier than he has a right to. He also looks damned good in my bed. Like that's where he should have been all along. I stand naked in the doorway, looking at him until he gives me a crooked grin. When he pulls back the covers and pats the bed beside him, I cross the room in a few quick steps and climb in, tucking myself against his side as if it's the most natural thing in the world. Luke's arm comes around me and my head finds his shoulder.

It feels good to be held by Luke this way. It feels right. As quickly as the thought forms in my head, I push it out. That's not what this is. Luke and I are friends. We're doing a reasonably good job faking a relationship, but that's all this is. We're not in a real relationship just because things are physical between us now. Right?

"I can hear those wheels turning, Huff," Luke says. "What is it?"

The ridiculous nickname makes me smile despite my rambling thoughts. "Nothing," I say.

"Do I have to tickle you again to get a straight answer?" he asks. "Because I'll do it."

"No," I say with a sigh. I take a deep breath and decide to just say it. "I was just wondering what this means for us now. Where we go from here."

Luke goes still for several seconds. When he speaks, it's clear he's choosing his words carefully. "What do you want it to mean?" he asks.

"I'm not sure," I say, honestly. After a moment of hesitation, I say, "I like you. More than I planned to."

"I get that a lot," he says, making me laugh. His hold on me tightens briefly before he speaks again. "Piper, I like you too. Hell, I don't think 'like' is a strong enough word. But whatever it is, I want to see where it goes. We don't have to rush anything or label it."

I nod my agreement, but part of me is disappointed that he doesn't want to label things. Which is ridiculous since this thing between us is barely an hour old. There I go, trying to rush into a relationship again. Why can't I ever just relax and go with the flow? Why am I always in a hurry to make things official? I should know by now that it will only lead to disappointment. I need to let this thing with Luke play out and just see what happens. I can do that, right?

"Piper?"

"Yeah?"

"Even if we don't label it," he says, "I just want you to know that for as long as this thing lasts, I won't be with anyone else. It's just you."

A warm feeling spreads through me at his words. I'd wondered if Luke would have any other women warming his bed while he and I acted out this fake romance, but I'd been too chicken to ask him. Now that we've had sex, the idea of him hooking up with someone else makes me feel a little sick to my stomach. I don't think too hard about why. Instead, I snuggle closer to him.

"Good," I say, injecting a light tone into my voice that I don't necessarily feel. "Because I'm terrible at sharing."

Luke's laugh rumbles under my ear. "So, am I," he says, though it sounds almost like a question.

Surprised, I lean up and look at him. "Is that your way of asking me if I'm going to be sleeping with random men in Peach Tree?"

Luke shrugs as if it's no big deal, but his gaze is trained on mine. "I wouldn't phrase it that way, but yeah. Maybe."

I shake my head before relaxing back into his embrace. "You don't have to worry about that," I say, yawning. "I'm not a cheater. I'm always the one cheated on. If I'm with you, then I'm *only* with you."

I let my eyes close, feeling suddenly exhausted after the afternoon's activities. My arms and legs feel heavy and all I want to do is lie here for the next couple of hours. Luke's warm arms around me combined with the gentle rain outside have me more relaxed than I've felt in months. I feel Luke kiss the top of my head.

"That guy was an idiot," he whispers.

"Mm hmm," I mumble, my eyes drifting closed again.

I fall asleep to the feel of Luke gently stroking my hair.

Piper

When I wake, the rain is gone, and the evening sunlight casts a dim glow around the room. Luke is still lying beside me, but we've shifted during our nap. Instead of me lying on his chest, I'm on my side with Luke curled around me, his front to my back. I can hear his slow, even breathing telling me that he's still sound asleep. I think about the past few nights and how awful his sleep must have been on that tiny couch. The poor man is probably exhausted. I should let him sleep a little longer.

Carefully, I try to extricate myself from his embrace, but as soon as I move, Luke's arms tighten around me, pulling me back against him. My lips quirk into a smile. Luke's arm around my waist is heavy and curled tight around me. I relax back into his embrace, loving the feel of him holding me far more than I care to admit. When did I become this desperate person so in need of affection? I've slept alone for the last year without an issue. Before that, I was in a relationship with a man whose idea of affection was a few kisses before he tried to get into my pants. It's not like I'm used to being cuddled. But I'm honest enough to admit that I like the feel of Luke's big body pressed against me, his arms around me. Before I can tell myself all the reasons I shouldn't, I push my hips back against him. When I do, I feel something hard press against my ass. Just the knowledge that Luke is aroused, even in his sleep, is enough to make my pulse quicken. I ease my hips back some more, pressing against that hard bulge.

In his sleep, Luke moves against me, grinding his hard cock against my ass. The shiver of desire that rolls through me catches me off-guard. I remember the way he made me come earlier and I can feel myself grow wet all over again. I wiggle my hips more, trying to wake him up now. Forget stealth and letting him sleep longer. I want him inside me. I want to break that tight grip he has on his control. I wonder what it would take.

Reaching down, I take Luke's hand and gently ease it upward until his hand cups my breast. He doesn't resist or make a move to pull away. His hand opens to cup my breast and he makes an appreciative noise in his throat.

"You have permission to always wake me up with your tits in my hand," he says, squeezing lightly. "Or in my face. Or my mouth."

His voice is rough with sleep, making him sound so unlike the carefully put-together man I've come to know. I like him this way. He's not pretending or putting on a fake smile. He's not hiding. His fingers pluck at my nipple making me suck in a breath as it sends a lightning bolt of sensation straight down to my core. I arch back against him again, feeling him grow even larger against me.

"I'll be sure and do it more often," I say, earning me a growl of approval when I press my breast into his hand again.

Luke's mouth finds my shoulder. His kiss is gentle at first, teasing my skin and making me want more. Then, I feel his teeth graze a sensitive spot where my shoulder and neck meet, pulling a startled gasp out of me. He'd done that earlier and I'd been shocked by how much I liked it. It's as if he's found an erogenous zone I never knew I had. Clearly pleased by his discovery, Luke repeats the action. My entire body comes alive at the feel of his tongue and teeth against my skin.

"Oh!" I can't hold back the moan.

Luke makes an appreciative noise before continuing his assault. His hand trails down between my legs and I open them to give him access. When he finds me already wet, he repeats that little hum of appreciation. His fingers slide over me, grazing my clit on the way down to my opening. He dips a finger inside me before bringing it back up, swirling the wetness across my clit.

"You're so wet, Piper," he murmurs against my skin. "Is this all for me?"

I'm nearly beyond words, but I nod and manage to gasp something that sounds like an agreement.

"I can't wait to slide into this tight little pussy, feel you come around me while I pound into you."

God, I love that he says delicious, dirty things while touching me. Luke strokes my clit almost leisurely, as if he's got all the time in the world. My plan to make him lose control seems to have backfired. I'm the one who's a writhing mess right now while Luke is totally composed. I reach back between us to grip his cock, marveling at how hard he is. Luke sucks in a breath when I lightly squeeze his shaft, stroking his length.

"Is this all for me?" I say, my teasing words mimicking his.

Luke answers me by pushing two fingers deep inside me. I gasp, but give his cock another long, slow stroke. It feels as if we're locked in a battle now, both of us seeing just how far we can push the other before someone gives in. I add in a twisting motion to each stroke of his cock, lightly squeezing the tip each time. He hisses in a breath and works his fingers deeper into my pussy. Our movements grow more hurried as we push each other closer to the edge. I can hear the little whimpers I'm making, but I can't seem to stop them. Luke brushes his thumb lightly against my clit. It's just a tease, but it's enough to remind me that he's holding back.

"Just say the word and I'll stop teasing you," he says, as if reading my mind. "All you have to do is ask me and I'll be inside you in a heartbeat."

His arrogance would annoy me if I weren't so turned on right now. Instead, some part of me finds it sexy. I know he could easily make me come. He's somehow already learned my body's responses in a single afternoon. And the dirty talking? Fuck, it's hot. It's not something I realized I liked, but clearly, I do. Each time he says something filthy in that low, growly voice it sends a new rush of arousal through me. It just adds another layer of eroticism to what we're doing.

"Piper." His fingers slide inside me again.

"Hm?" I brush my thumb along the sensitive underside of his dick.

"Ask me." I suck in a breath as Luke rubs my clit.

"Ask what?" My voice is a breathless whisper. I want so badly to come. For Luke to fuck me. Something. Anything to end this delicious torture. But I can't say I'm not enjoying every second. And besides, I don't want to give in just yet. I'm having too much fun.

"Ask me to fuck you," Luke says. I can't hold back the little whimper of need his words draw from me. His mouth is brushing my shoulder as he speaks, the slight stubble there sending goosebumps across my skin.

"Tell me to fill you up and make you come on this hard cock you're holding right now. Or, better yet, open your legs and push it inside yourself. Use it the way you know you want to."

My breath is coming in rapid pants now. I'm on the verge of begging Luke to fuck me. The idea of using his body the way he's telling me has merit, but right now that's not what I need. Right now, I want him to use me. I want to see him lose control and take me rough. But I don't know how to ask for it. I've never been the type to speak up and ask for what I want in bed. Besides, the guys I've been with in the past haven't been receptive to suggestion. Something tells me Luke might be different, though. As if sensing my thoughts have wandered, Luke's free hand comes up to cup my jaw, pulling my head back against his shoulder.

"Come back to me, Piper," he says, his grip on my jaw commanding. His fingers thrust deep inside me and go still, holding me impaled on them. "When we're together like this, I want all of you here with me. Got it?"

I nod, unable to stop my hips from rolling, pressing up against his hand. My hand on his cock has gone still.

"Say it, Piper. Say you understand."

Gone is the lazy, leisurely tone of before. Luke's voice is hard and unyielding. And it's so fucking hot.

"I understand," I whisper.

"Good girl." Luke's hand resumes its lazy movements between my legs. "Now, *tell me* what you want."

I feel a fresh rush of moisture between my legs at his words. My thighs are trembling. My entire body feels like a tightly strung bow, ready to snap at the slightest provocation.

"Luke," I whimper. "Please."

"Please, what?"

His voice is harsh, demanding. But his movements on my clit are still light and teasing, hinting at what I know he can give me. I've given up all pretense of teasing him. It's clear he's won. But he won't give in until I ask. I'm on the verge of doing just that when I feel Luke's teeth graze my shoulder lightly. It's a little thing, considering what he's doing to my pussy right now, but I'm wound tightly enough that just that small touch has my body jerking. I thrust my hips against his hand, trying to make him move faster. His free arm bands tightly around my chest, holding me still.

"Say. It." He demands.

I whimper in his arms, my frustration an almost physical pain. I can't take it anymore. I give in.

"Fuck me," I beg. "Hard."

Before I can finish the last word, Luke flips me facedown onto the bed and is kneeling between my thighs. He uses his knees to push my legs further apart, spreading me open for him. Then, he's fitting the head of his cock to my entrance. I rise up onto my elbows, pushing my ass higher into the air as he slams into me.

"Fuuuck!" Luke's shout echoes in the room as he fills me.

The cry is ripped from me as the force of his thrust sets off a chain reaction in my body. The orgasm that slams into me is shocking in its intensity. I can do nothing but clutch at the blankets as I spasm around Luke's dick. I make no effort to stifle my moans. I can't think beyond the pleasure spreading through my body. I'm dimly aware that Luke is talking, telling me in a hoarse voice how good I feel. He's gripping my ass in both hands, fingers digging into my soft flesh.

"Is this what you wanted?"

"Mhhmph." My answer is muffled by the fact that my face is buried in the pillow. I manage to turn just enough to shout, "Yes!"

"Good girl," he says, pounding into me so hard I can hear the slapping sounds our bodies make.

Why those two words have such a staggering effect on me, I'll never know. But I can already feel another orgasm building inside me.

"You're so close," Luke says. "I can feel it. Touch your clit. Play with it for me."

I don't think. I just obey his command, reaching down to touch myself. The addition of the pressure to my clit has me coming in seconds.

"That's it. Come for me, Piper."

This orgasm is less intense than the first one, but no less devastating. I feel myself tightening around Luke's dick, squeezing him in time with the pulses of pleasure radiating through me. He doesn't stop, fucking me through this orgasm as he had the last one. When my clit becomes too sensitive for stimulation, I let my hand fall away and grip the pillow instead. Luke finally comes with a long groan, thrusting deep inside me as his release pours out. He goes still, the only sound our harsh breathing and my pounding heartbeat in my ears.

Luke strokes a hand up my spine to my shoulder and back down to my ass before smoothing it over the spot where he'd just been gripping me so tightly. I collapse face-down onto the bed in a boneless heap when he releases me. I feel Luke's weight settle beside me a moment before he tenderly gathers me into his arms and pulls me against his sweat-slicked body. His hand strokes my hair gently.

"Are you okay? I didn't hurt you, did I?"

I almost laugh at the absurdity of the question. Am I okay? I don't know how to answer that question. I just had the most amazing sex of my entire life and I'm not sure how to go on living now. Because surely, it will never be that good again. There's no way I'd survive it. But words are hard, so I just smile up at him.

"That. Was. Incredible."

Concern still lingers in those ocean eyes that seem to see so much of me. I reach up a hand and cup his cheek.

"You didn't hurt me," I assure him. "I'd tell you if anything we did was painful or uncomfortable."

This doesn't reassure him. If anything, he looks even more upset. Almost angry.

"That's not okay," he says. "It should never go that far. Ever. I shouldn't have pushed you like that without discussing it first. I got carried away and broke my own rules."

"What rules?" I ask, confused.

Luke breathes in deeply and exhales before answering me. "I was too rough with you. I'd be surprised if you don't have bruises on your ass from my fingers."

He looks genuinely upset by his behavior, which I might find endearing if it wasn't ruining my post-orgasm glow. I take his face in both hands and force him to look at me.

"Lucas Wolfe," I say in a stern voice. "Listen to me and listen well. Because I'm not going to say this again. What we just did was amazing. It was also entirely consensual. I wanted you to take me rough. I asked for it, remember?"

He still looks conflicted. "Yeah, but—"

I put a hand over his mouth to silence him. "No. No buts. I asked you—no, I begged you—to do what you just did. And I loved every second of it. Am I going to want that every time we have sex? No. Not every time. But when I do, I don't want you to look at me like you did something wrong. And I promise to tell you if you do something I don't want. Okay?"

Luke looks like he might want to say more, but instead he nods. "Okay," he says.

Lowering his head, he kisses me with a tenderness I don't expect. Something inside me shifts and seems to settle as I kiss him back. I have the sudden thought that I'd like to lie here with this man forever.

Oh, no, I think. *That can't be good.*

It's probably just the orgasms. Yeah. That's it. Good sex can make people think crazy thoughts. Shaking off those insane notions, I give Luke a playful smile and lean up onto my elbow.

"Want to help me wash my back?" I ask with a wink.

Luke's grin is instant. To my dismay, I feel that same strange flutter inside me at the sight. *Shit.* But I do my best to ignore it as we climb out of bed and make our way to the bathroom.

It takes far longer than my usual shower, but together, Luke and I manage. Between soap-slicked embraces, teasing touches and playful kisses, we eventually emerge from the shower clean and relaxed. Wrapped in towels, we each go about getting ready for dinner. Though I'd love nothing more than to stay in this room with Luke for the rest of this trip, we came here for a reason. And we've only got a few more days to convince Art that he needs to sign with Wolfe Industries.

CHAPTER 25

Piper

When Luke passed up the opportunity to go fishing again with Art today and offered to give me a tour of the island instead, I'd been shocked. The whole point of this trip is for him to convince Art to sign with his company. He can't do that if he chooses to spend time with me instead of Art. But there's another part of me that's happy I get to spend the day with him. Since yesterday when I followed him to the bedroom and admitted that I wanted him, he's barely left my side. I'd be lying if I said I didn't like the attention. Not to mention the affection.

If Art and Mel notice anything different about our behavior, they haven't said anything. Maybe it's less noticeable to them. But I can't help but notice every touch, every kiss, every casual embrace. I didn't know about this affectionate side of Luke, but if I'm not careful I could become addicted to it.

Luke and I leave the beach house early. He barely let me drink my coffee before ushering me out the door and into his car. He's like a kid today, barely containing his excitement. I love this side of him. I hadn't known it existed until coming on this trip. I hope it doesn't go away when we get back to the real world.

The first stop on our excursion is a small café just off the main street. It's a small, glass-fronted building with a brightly colored interior. I give Luke a questioning look.

"Is this why you wouldn't let me eat breakfast?"

He just smiles. "You'll be happy I stopped you," he says, taking my hand. "Trust me."

"I do," I say, realizing as I say it, how true it is.

Once we're seated, I study the menu, and something occurs to me. I look up to find Luke smiling at me.

"This place is known for their hash-browns," he says. "They make any way you can think of, and they'll add whatever you want."

I don't even try to stop the silly grin that spreads across my face. "You remembered."

He lifts one shoulder in a shrug, but he looks pleased. "I would never underestimate the importance of potatoes."

I go back to studying my menu, trying to ignore the warm feeling spreading through me. This sweet, thoughtful Luke is one I'm not sure I'm prepared for.

We spend nearly an hour at the restaurant, eating, talking and laughing. Luke was right. The food is amazing. I'm glad I didn't eat breakfast at the beach house. The hash-browns are some of the best I've ever eaten. I try to get Luke to tell me his plans for the rest of the day, but he's being tight-lipped. I know he came here during the summers when he was a kid, so he knows the island better than I do. Or he did when he was younger.

I'm sure a lot has changed over the years. Even so, he navigates the streets with ease on our way to the next destination. Instead of going back to the car, we walk down the main street to a building with lots of brightly colored sculptures out front.

"This place is run by local artists," Luke says, holding open the door for me to enter. "They take turns manning the storefront. Each piece is one of a kind."

"You know a lot about this island, don't you?" I ask, eyeing a sculpture of a frog smoking a cigar.

Luke shrugs. "I told you. I spent a lot of summers here before I went to work for the company."

"How old were you when you started working for Wolfe Industries?" I ask as we meander slowly through the shop. There's so much to look at that it's hard for my eyes to take it all in.

"The summer I turned 16, my dad made me start shadowing him at the office instead of coming here with my mom." He says it casually, but there's something about his demeanor that shifted at the mention of his father.

I think about what he's saying. He's basically been working for his family's company since he was 16 years old. He'd been thrust into responsibility at a time when most teenagers are just trying to hang out with their friends or trying to get dates. Instead, he'd been forced to follow his father around in a suit and tie. I think about the man that Luke is today. It's clear that he takes his work seriously. He's also turned Wolfe Industries into the kind of high caliber corporation worthy of catching the attention of someone like Art. Still, that's a lot of pressure to put on one person's shoulders. I don't say any of that though. I know Luke wouldn't want to feel like he's being pitied. Not that I pity him, but I'm sure that's how he would interpret it.

"Do you like working for Wolfe Industries?" I ask.

Luke seems to consider my question for a long moment before answering.

"Sort of," he says. "I like what I do. I like helping businesses become what they're meant to be. I like seeing them go from struggling to thriving after I work with them. Especially the small businesses. Those are my favorite accounts."

Something occurs to me and I smile. "Like Peach Fuzz?"

Luke nods, smiling. "Cole's was the first small business I worked with. Peach Fuzz wasn't struggling, exactly. But it wasn't living up to its potential. He asked me for some pointers, so I helped him out. He did most of the work."

I narrow my eyes at him. "Why are you being so modest?"

Luke laughs. "I'm not. That's what happened."

"Hmm."

He rolls his eyes. "Anyway, I found that I liked small business accounts better. With big companies, it's hard to see the impact from one of my marketing campaigns. With Peach Fuzz, I could see exactly what my work was doing. It made me want to do more of that."

"So, why don't you?" I ask.

"Charles Wolfe doesn't feel that small business accounts are lucrative enough to justify the drain on resources," he says. There's an edge to his voice that tells me exactly what he thinks of that.

I roll my eyes. "Maybe they're not making billions or even millions, but those accounts do make the company money. And you're making a difference."

"My father doesn't see it that way," Luke says. "He shut down the small business department while I was gone visiting my sister. Canceled all the accounts."

My mouth drops open. "What a dick!" I clap a hand over my mouth, shocked that I just called Luke's dad a dick. But Luke doesn't look mad. Instead, he seems to be trying to hold in a laugh.

"I'm sorry," I say.

He shakes his head. "Don't be. He is a dick."

"So, what happens to those accounts now?" I ask.

"I made him a deal," he says. "If I can get Arthur Mitchell to sign with Wolfe Industries, he'll let me reopen the small business department and run it the way I see fit."

I think over everything I just learned about Luke and his father and their company. It's clear there's no love lost between the two men. There's also a fair amount of resentment and anger there. Not that I can blame Luke for that. His father doesn't sound like the nicest man.

"That's why you're so set on making sure this works."

Luke nods. "There's a lot riding on this deal. Not just for Wolfe Industries, but for a lot of small companies that just need that push in the right direction. I don't want to give up on them."

I think about today and how he'd skipped out on fishing with Art to give me this tour of the island. This deal means so much to him and he'd missed an opportunity to work on convincing Art just to spend time with me. I don't want to read too much into the gesture, but I've got to work hard to suppress the goofy grin that threatens to take over my face.

Instead, I ask, "When is the last time you were on the island?"

His brows furrow. "This is the first time since before I went to work at Wolfe. First time in 13 years."

Again, he says this casually, but I can tell it bothers him. He has such a clear love for this island and this town. I reach down and twine my fingers through his, then pull him toward me for a kiss. It's just a light peck. It's quick and sweet.

"What's that for?" he asks.

I shrug. "For today. Showing me the island. I can tell this place means a lot to you."

He smiles. "Yeah. It does. I didn't realize how much I missed it until I came back."

"You should come back every summer," I say. "There's nothing stopping you."

Luke smiles, but it doesn't quite reach his eyes. I wonder what he's thinking, but before I can ask, he ushers me into the next room. We spend the next hour wandering through the building. Each room seems to be devoted to a different local artist. I find a small sculpture of a llama wearing a fedora that I think Harlow will like and buy it for her. Luke looks like he wants to question the purchase, but he just shakes his head.

After the gallery, he takes me to the lighthouse. We walk the grounds and I take tons of pictures of the old building. Luke explains interesting historical facts to me as we walk. We stop for a late lunch at a local seafood restaurant and gorge ourselves on fresh-caught crab legs and drink ice-cold beer. We walk along the pier where there's live music playing and kids running around with beleaguered parents begging them to calm down.

Luke lets me see a side of him I hadn't known existed. He's happy and carefree. He hasn't checked his phone once today. Normally, he's compulsively checking emails or texting someone or calling his assistant. But today, he's totally present. With me. I try not to read too much into his behavior. It would be easy to convince myself that being with me changed him. But I've made that mistake with men before. They don't change overnight, and they never change unless they want to. He's just making an allowance for today. I'm sure things will go back to normal soon enough. I ignore the pang in my chest at the thought. I'd much rather keep things this way for as long as we can.

We stay at the pier until the sun sets, spreading its brilliant purples, pinks and oranges across the sky. When we get back to the beach house, it's long after dinnertime and Art and Mel aren't downstairs. It's just as well. I don't want to make small talk tonight. I just want to take Luke upstairs and let him have his way with me. He seems to have the same idea because he shoots me a wink and tugs me toward the stairs.

CHAPTER 26

Luke

The last half of the trip goes by faster than I would have thought possible. I spend my days and evenings trying to talk business with Art and avoiding Mel. I spend my nights wrapped up in Piper's arms having the best sex of my life. I still don't know what pushed her to come to me that day, but I've loved every minute of our time on the island. She's incredible. Being with her makes me feel lighter, somehow. Like I don't have the heavy weight on my shoulders I've carried for so long. I like who I am when I'm with her.

I dread going back to the real world. I don't want things between us to change. I know they will, though. It's inevitable. She has to go back to her shop in Peach Tree and I have to go back to work in Savannah. We won't be able to spend every night tangled up in each other's arms. I won't get to wake up to her teasing smile and sexy body pressed to mine. I'm shocked at how much the idea bothers me. I've never lived with a woman or been in a relationship serious enough to consider that step. So, why does the idea that I want Piper in my bed every night not scare me? It should, right? But it doesn't.

We still haven't discussed what happens when we go back home. Like a coward, I've been too afraid to bring it up. I don't want to think about it. But we leave tomorrow, so it's happening whether we discuss it or not. I keep wondering if she'll bring it up, but she hasn't so far. I know I should just man up and ask her what she wants, but I'm not quite ready for that conversation.

I'd had to force myself to climb out of bed this morning to meet Art for one last day out on the water. Piper had grumbled sleepily and pulled me back for a kiss before letting me go. Now, Art and I are on his boat a few miles off the coast, trying to catch fish, but nothing is biting today. We could use the fish finder and search for another spot, but I don't think either of us is particularly motivated to catch anything. I decide to bring up the whole reason I came on this trip. It's now or never.

"Have you given any more thought to my proposal, Art?" I ask.

Art looks out at the horizon for a few seconds before he answers.

"I'll be honest with you, Luke," Art says, eyeing me shrewdly. "I did some digging around before we met. I looked into your company. You. And I've got some talented investigators who get paid an obscene amount of money to find information."

I smile, not surprised that he had me investigated. "I hope I didn't disappoint?"

He grins and shakes his head. "Actually, no. The opposite, in fact. It doesn't take an overpriced investigator to see what you did with that company. It was dying before you came along. Which makes me think two things. One: You're very good at what you do." He eyes me for a moment. "And two: That company needs you more than you need it."

I don't know what to say to that. It's nothing I haven't thought before, but it's the first time anyone has said it aloud. My father certainly never has. Not that he's capable of admitting that he needs anyone or anything. He'd never acknowledge the ways I helped the company when it was floundering.

"Thank you," I say. "That means a lot."

"It's just the truth. No need to thank me for saying it." He looks thoughtful for a minute before turning to shoot me a direct stare. "Why haven't you left Wolfe Industries yet? Is it loyalty to your father?"

I bark out a laugh. "Hell no! I don't owe him any loyalty."

"Then why?" he asks. "You could start your own firm and make it what you wanted."

I nod, feeling that hint of excitement and fear that always wells up whenever I consider leaving Wolfe Industries. "I know," I say. "But without the capital, I'm stuck. At least for now."

Art just nods thoughtfully. "I can understand that," he says. "Give me a few days to get back to the real world and really look over your proposal and we'll have a meeting. Fair?"

I nod. "Sounds good. Thanks, Art."

He eyes me. "For what?"

"This week," I say, turning back to the water. "This trip. I didn't realize how much I needed some time off."

He nods. "It's good to take a step back sometimes and remember what's important." He gives me a meaningful look. "Like that girl of yours."

Piper. The mere mention of her brings her image to my mind and I smile. "She's pretty great," I say.

"Of course, she is," Art says. "So, why haven't you married her yet?"

My mind goes blank for a moment, confused as to why Art would be mentioning marriage. Then I remember how I'd told him I was on the verge of proposing to Piper. That seems like such a long time ago. Was it really only two weeks ago? So much as happened since then. I realize Art is still waiting for an answer.

I flash him a smile. "Just waiting for the right time to ask her."

Art smiles, but it doesn't quite reach his eyes. "You'll spend your life waiting for the right time if you're not careful. Sometimes you just have to go for it."

I nod. "You're right," I say. "But it's not easy to take the chance sometimes."

Art gives me a smile. "I'm glad the rumors about you aren't true."

"What rumors?" I ask, confused.

"That you're just like your old man," he says. "Cold, calculating, obsessed with business, only out for yourself. I'm happy to know they weren't true."

I feel a surge of anger at the idea of being compared to Charles Wolfe. "I'm nothing like him," I say through gritted teeth.

Art waves a hand dismissively. "Oh, you're a little bit like him. You've got his drive and determination. Dedication to your work. But there's more to you than your career. I can see it in the way you look at Piper. It's a good thing. Work won't keep you warm at night," He leans in with a smile. "But it will buy you a really comfortable mattress."

I manage a weak smile, but I'm shaken by the idea of people comparing me to my father. I've worked so hard to make sure I'm nothing like him. I never wanted to be in his shadow, but it seems that no matter where I go, he follows me.

CHAPTER 27

Piper

Settling back into life in Peach Tree is harder than I thought. I find that I miss the island and the days of lazing on the beach with Luke. The nights spent in his arms. I miss Luke. Which can't be a good sign, right? I'm growing too attached to having him around. Being back home, in my own space, without him constantly around should be a good thing. It will give me some perspective. Which is why I don't call him the day after our return home. I need time to get him out of my system. Instead, I spend my first night back hanging out with Harlow.

It takes all of ten minutes for her to get me to spill everything. I tell her everything that happened, without going into graphic details. No matter how much she asked me to give her all the details. When I finish, she just sighs.

"At least one of us is getting some."

I laugh. "You could get some, too," I say. "You're just depriving yourself."

She makes a face. "I told you. I'm celibate now."

I laugh even louder. "You're full of shit. You just haven't met the right guy."

Harlow sighs again. "You keep saying that and I'm going to think you're a hopeless romantic."

I shrug. "Nothing wrong with romance."

"Says the person getting laid."

I roll my eyes. "Quit your bitching. Besides, I don't know how long it's going to last. We haven't talked since he dropped me off yesterday afternoon. I know he had to work today, but it's been radio silence."

Harlow eyes me. "Have you texted or called him?"

I shake my head. "I was trying to give us both a chance to cool off after spending a week together humping like bunnies."

Harlow shakes her head. "You've got it bad," she says. "First you complain because he hasn't called you. Then you say you haven't called him because you want space. Which is it?"

I make a face at her. She's right, though. I can't have it both ways. What I want is Luke. I want him all the time. Which feels like too much, too fast. Especially since I have no idea how he feels about me. Harlow just gives me a sad smile when I tell her all this.

"There's nothing wrong with wanting a guy and being happy to be with him," she says. "Even if he ends up not feeling the same way, you can enjoy it while it lasts."

She's right again. It's annoying how she manages that.

"I know," I say. "I'm trying."

Just then, my phone buzzes with an incoming text and I see Luke's name on the screen. My heart immediately kicks into overdrive and a smile spreads across my face.

Luke: *Hey, Huff. How was your day?*

"Uh huh." Harlow's knowing tone makes me roll my eyes, but I can't wipe away the smile. I throw a pillow at her, but she just laughs.

"Shut up," I mutter before typing out a response.

Me: *Not bad. It's definitely a change from island life.*

Luke: *Tell me about it. I spent the entire day in meetings.*

Me: *Special torture!*

Luke: *Cruel and unusual punishment.*

Me: *Sounds like it.*

Luke: *What are you up to this evening?*

Me: *Nothing. Harlow's here now. We've been catching up on current events.*

Luke: *So, you're busy?*

Me: *Depends. Did you have something in mind?*

Luke: *Not really. I just miss you.*

I stare at the screen, reading those four words over again while my stupid, traitorous heart tries to beat right out of my chest. It's barely been 24 hours since he saw me. But he misses me. And he's not too scared to admit it, as I had been. I take a deep breath and blow it out before typing out a response.

Me: *So, come over.*

Luke: *Are you sure?*

Me: *Yes. I miss you, too.*

Luke: *I'll be there in an hour. I'll bring dinner.*

When I lower the phone, I find Harlow staring at me with a knowing expression on her face. I wish I had another pillow to throw at her.

"Shut up."

She laughs. "I didn't say anything."

"Your face did."

She shrugs. "I can't control what my face does."

She stands, clearly getting ready to leave.

"Wait, where are you going?" I ask.

"I'm leaving before all the smoldering sex stares start flying around the room and I get hit by one accidentally. I don't want pink eye."

I roll my eyes, but I'm laughing. "That's disgusting."

Harlow just eyes me. "Is he on his way over, or not?"

I nod, feeling guilty, though I'm not sure why. "But he's not going to be here for another hour. You don't have to go yet. I'm not the kind of girl who drops her friends to hang out with a guy."

"That gives you an hour to get ready," she says. "Hide anything embarrassing, shave all the parts that need shaving, brush your teeth. All that shit. Besides, I'm not the kind of friend who twat-blocks her friend when she's about to get lots of orgasms from a hot guy."

I roll my eyes at her crude phrasing, but she's not wrong. I had been wondering if I'd have time to shave my legs before Luke gets here.

Harlow grins. "See? I'm right. As usual."

"I hate when you do that," I grumble.

She just shrugs. "Have a good night!" Then she's gone.

CHAPTER 28

Luke

I don't know if going to see Piper is a good idea or not, but I don't care. I like having her around. I'd realized it as soon as I pulled away from her house after dropping her off at home yesterday morning. I'm happier with her around. But I couldn't just turn around immediately and confess my feelings. I'm not even sure what my feelings are. I just know that I like myself better when she's with me. I don't know what it means yet, but I plan to find out.

I'd managed to spend an entire day at work without calling or texting her, which had been made less difficult by all the meetings my father had scheduled for me. I swear, it's almost like he's punishing me for being gone last week. Even though it had been work-related. Not that much work was accomplished during my week at Art's beach house. But he doesn't know that. As far as my father and Wolfe Industries are concerned, Arthur

Mitchell is on the verge of signing with the company. In reality, I have no idea what Art's thinking about this deal. He's playing it close to the vest. But I know enough not to tell that to my father.

Not that it helped his demeanor at all. He'd still managed to be a complete jackass all day. I'm used to it by now, but today it's harder to swallow. Maybe it's because I've spent the last week around Art and Piper who care what I have to say and seem to value my input. Even when they disagree with me, they never belittle me. That time away only served to make coming back that much more unbearable. I'm counting down the days until I can quit Wolfe Industries and launch my own firm. I just need to bide my time a little longer.

With every mile that brings me closer to Piper, I feel more relaxed. By the time I park my car in front of her house, I'm fighting off a smile at the idea of seeing her again. I wonder if it was presumptuous of me to bring an overnight bag. Should I leave it in the car until I know whether she wants me to stay the night? I'm still debating what I should do when I hear my phone signal an incoming text. I look at the screen and laugh.

Piper: Are y*ou going to stay in the car all night?*

Still smiling, I grab the bag and walk to the front door. It opens before I can knock and Piper's standing there grinning. I look her up and down, taking in the skimpy pajama shorts and the thin top. I don't think she's wearing a bra.

"Damn, Huff," I say. "Is this how you greet all the men who show up at your door?"

She shrugs. "Just the UPS guy. But he knows all about you and he's not the jealous type."

I step inside and drop my bag before wrapping her in my arms.

"Good to know."

We spend the evening watching movies and most of the night making love. When my alarm wakes me for work, I call in sick to work for the first time in over five years and go back to sleep. I'm not looking forward to the inevitable explosion from my father, but I can't find it in myself to care. Today, I plan to spend the day with Piper doing whatever we feel like doing. She's like a drug. I've become addicted to her in less than a week and I've given up on pretending it's just a fling. I want her for as long as she'll have me.

When I wake up again, the sun is streaming through Piper's bedroom window and the bed is empty beside me. I sit up and scrub a hand over my face. The bathroom door opens, and Piper stands there wearing nothing but a towel. She's clearly fresh from the shower. I tamp down the disappointment that she didn't wake me to join her.

"Good morning," she says with a smile.

"What time did you get up?" I ask.

She shrugs. "Early. I run a coffee shop. People drink coffee early."

"Right."

"Besides, you looked like you needed the extra sleep."

I watch as she puts toothpaste onto a toothbrush and prepares to brush her teeth. That's when I remember that I didn't pack any toiletries when I'd rushed over here last night. I'd thrown a change of clothes into my bag and nothing else.

"Shit."

Piper looks over at me. "Something wrong?"

I climb out of bed and stretch. "I forgot my toothbrush."

I notice Piper's gaze lingering on me as I stand there in my boxer briefs. I wiggle my eyebrows at her. "See something you like?"

She laughs and shakes her head before turning back to face the sink. "There's a spare toothbrush in the bedside table on the right side."

While Piper brushes her teeth, I walk over to the other side of the bed and open the drawer. There's not a toothbrush in there, though. I stare at the contents for several seconds before comprehension dawns. Then, I smile.

"What's this?" I turn back toward Piper, holding the purple silicone toy out for her to see. I grin at her, waggling the vibrator back and forth.

Piper's eyes grow wide, and her mouth drops open as she lunges toward me, arm outstretched. I yank my hand back, holding the toy out of her reach. Her face is bright red. It's all I can do to stifle my laugh at her outrage. Does she have any idea how cute she is when she's embarrassed like this? How fucking sexy she is? It doesn't hurt that she's wearing nothing but a towel and is pressed up against me as she struggles to reach the toy in my hand.

"Give it back, Luke!"

I shake my head, a smile on my face. "I don't think so, Huff" I say. "I think I want to see what it does."

Her face shifts from embarrassed to annoyed. Rolling her eyes, she shoves me away from her and turns to stomp back toward the bathroom. She's leaving? Oh, no. That won't do at all. I reach for her arm.

"Wait," I say. "Where are you going? Stay and talk to me. I thought we were spending the day together."

She crosses her arms tightly over her chest, but she's stopped walking away from me.

"Not if you're just going to make fun of me for having a vibrator," she mutters, not meeting my gaze.

I go still. Is that what she thinks I'm doing? Nothing could be further from the truth.

"Piper," I say. "Look at me."

She blows out a long breath before turning those whiskey-colored eyes up to me. I'm struck by the mix of defiance and vulnerability I see there. I feel a sharp ache in my chest that nearly steals my breath. For a moment, all I can do is look at her. She's so damned gorgeous.

"What?" she demands, pulling me back to the present. Her annoyance makes me want to smile, but I manage to keep my expression serious.

"I wasn't making fun of you," I say softly. "I wouldn't do that."

Her eyes go to the vibrator still in my hand, then back to my face. Her expression is clearly questioning what I'm doing still holding the thing. I hold it out to her, letting her take it from me. She holds it to her chest, along with the towel that has started slipping lower. I hate seeing her guarding herself against me, hiding from me. I want to take that towel from her and toss it across the room, then kiss her until she forgets her own name. But I know that's not what she needs from me right now.

"There's nothing wrong with you having a vibrator, you know," I say.

Piper's gaze drops from mine, and I see her cheeks turn pink again. I reach out and touch her chin, tilting her face up until she looks at me.

"Don't be embarrassed. I'm sorry if it seemed like I was ridiculing you. I wasn't." I risk a smile. "Actually, seeing that in your drawer was kind of a turn-on."

Piper's brows draw down in confusion.

"The thought of you using that, touching yourself, getting yourself off, making yourself come? It drives me crazy," I say.

Her face relaxes a little and I can see a hint of desire edge into her expression. "Why is that?" she asks, her voice barely above a whisper.

Reaching up, I trail a finger down the column of her neck to her collar bone. "Because watching you come is one of the sexiest fucking things I've ever been privileged to witness."

Piper sucks in a breath at my words and the towel slips lower as her arms relax. I lean closer, my nose brushing her cheek.

"Everyone seeks pleasure, Piper," I whisper, my finger trailing lower. "It's natural and normal."

"What about you?" she asks, distracting me from my mission to get that towel away from her.

I pull back enough to look at her. "What about me?" I ask.

Her brow lifts in challenge. "How often?" Her gaze drops lower to where my hard cock is straining against the confines of my boxer briefs.

"Do I, what?" I ask, my lips curving into a smile.

She rolls her eyes. "You know."

"How often do I masturbate?" I ask, saying the words she can't seem to bring herself to say.

She can't quite meet my gaze when she nods. I can still see the blush staining her cheeks. Why is that so damned adorable? Piper is standing in front of me, practically naked. I've seen, touched and kissed nearly every inch of her. But she's somehow still blushing over talk of masturbation. Fuck, I love the contradiction.

I huff out a laugh. "Less frequently lately."

Her eyes widen a fraction, and she swallows hard. "When?" she asks. "When was the last time?"

I know what she's asking, but some little devil on my shoulder wants to make her say the words. I want to hear those filthy words come out of her pretty mouth. So, I can't help but tease her.

"The last time I did what?"

Her eyes narrow, but I can tell she's not angry with me anymore. This is just her normal level of annoyance with me. And that, I love to see.

"You're going to make me say it, aren't you?" she asks.

"Say what?" I ask, all innocence.

She's quiet for long enough that I think she's not going to say it. But then I see the moment her resolve hardens. She looks directly into my eyes when she speaks.

"When is the last time you stroked yourself?"

Holy hell, those words coming out of her mouth shouldn't be so sexy. Her voice is low, but her gaze doesn't waver. For some reason hearing those words from her evokes all sorts of filthy images in my mind. I don't need to think long to remember exactly when I last got myself off.

I keep my eyes locked on hers. "You know when. You caught me doing it."

Her sharp intake of breath makes my mouth curve into a smile.

"We came back from the fishing trip early and I saw you on the beach in that little red bikini that barely covered you. I stopped and stared for a full minute, thinking about all the things I wanted to do with you. I went rock hard in a second. I knew I couldn't face you like that, so I went upstairs. I thought a cold shower would solve my problem. But I kept picturing you in that bikini. I thought about how easy it would be to untie those strings and kiss every inch of your damp skin."

My fingers latch onto the towel where Piper holds it against her chest. She doesn't resist as I gently tug it away from her, baring her gorgeous body to my gaze. Her nipples pucker as the cool air hits them and I remember the way they feel against my tongue. Piper stands there, hands fisted at her sides, her gaze locked on mine. I take a small step forward, my hands itching to touch her, to feel her silky skin against my palms.

"I imagined burying my face between your legs and tasting you. I could hear your moans in my head." My fingers skim over the tops of her breasts, leaving goosebumps in their wake. "I imagined what it would feel like to sink inside your hot, wet, ready pussy." Piper's breath quickens and my other hand trails down over her hip toward the junction of her thighs.

"I couldn't take it anymore," I whisper. "I needed some relief."

Piper flattens her hands on my chest, smoothing them up over my shoulders. She leans into me, her cheek grazing my jaw. "What did you do?" she whispers, her breath hot against my neck.

I smile at her sudden boldness. I love that about her. She's shy, yes. But when we're alone, she lets me see a different side of her. One that isn't afraid to ask for what she wants.

"I reached down," I say, my hand moving closer to her pussy. "And gripped my cock in my hand."

My fingers dip between her legs, sliding easily through her slick heat. I love that she's already so wet for me. I swirl my fingers lightly over her clit, feeling her push her hips forward as if seeking more of my touch.

"I was so fucking hard," I whisper. "I stroked my cock, long and slow." I ease one finger lower to slip inside her. "Imagining that I was deep inside you."

Piper's hand drifts lower, down over my stomach to my hip. "Like this?" she asks.

She takes my cock into her hand and lightly squeezes the base. My eyes fall closed at the feeling of her fingers wrapped around my shaft. My hips buck forward on their own, thrusting against her hand.

"Just like that," I whisper as I slide a second finger inside her.

Piper lets out a little gasp but doesn't let go of my dick. In fact, she begins to stroke me in time with my fingers thrusting inside her. She makes a little twisting motion at the end of each stroke, teasing the sensitive underside of my cock. Holy fuck, that feels incredible. My fingers find that little spot inside her that I know drives her wild and I make sure to stroke it with every thrust of my hand. Piper's hand stills on my cock and her eyes slide closed. Little moans escape her. I know she's close, and I want it. I want her to come apart on my hand, in my arms, her pussy clenching tight around my fingers. I want to watch it.

I keep talking, telling her exactly what I'd fantasized about that day at the beach house. "I pictured your sweet pussy around my cock, squeezing me tight while I pounded into you, over and over. I could practically hear the moans you would make while I filled you. Faster and faster." My hand moves along with my words, thrusting into her faster as she clings to me.

"In my fantasy, you came so hard you screamed," I say, using my thumb to brush against her clit. Piper's mouth drops open and I feel the first tremors of her orgasm surge through her. A rush of moisture coats my hand and her pussy clamps down on my fingers as she cries out. A triumphant smile comes to my face as I watch her.

"There it is," I say, my voice a low growl. "Come for me, Piper. Come on my fingers."

I keep up the rhythm with my fingers, coaxing every last drop of pleasure from Piper's body. I love seeing her like this. Head thrown back, eyes closed, her body flushed and pliant in my arms. Watching her come, knowing I can bring her to such pleasure? It's the biggest turn-on I can imagine. Eventually, I ease my strokes, bringing her down slowly. Small tremors still wrack her body and she's breathing fast. When she opens those warm, whiskey eyes to look at me, all the embarrassment from before is gone and there's only need in them.

"I want you inside me," she says, her hand tightening once more on my cock.

"I love it when you're bossy," I say, leaning down to take her mouth in a searing kiss.

She pulls back and looks at me with one raised brow. "I can be bossy."

I smile. "Show me."

She pushes gently at my shoulders, guiding me toward the bed. "Sit on the edge of the bed."

I do as she says, waiting to see what she wants me to do next. Instead of giving me orders though, Piper steps forward and climbs onto my lap, straddling my hips. My cock strains up toward her wet pussy, practically begging to be inside her. I bring my arms around her, waiting for her to tell me what she wants from me.

"I think my breasts need your attention," she says in a surprisingly commanding tone.

I look at her breasts, only inches away from my face and grin. "I think you're right."

I lower my head and kiss the soft swell of her breast, moving lower until I can pull a pretty, pink nipple into my mouth. Piper gasps when I suck the sensitive flesh and my teeth lightly graze it. Her hips move against me, sliding her wet pussy against my painfully hard cock. I want nothing more than to lift her up and slam her back down onto my cock until I'm as deep inside her as I can go. But Piper's running this show. She's in control. It's both incredibly frustrating and incredibly sexy at the same time.

Her hands tangle in my hair and she pulls me away from her breast. "Now, the other one."

I can't help but notice her words are a little more breathless than they had been. Without hesitation, I move to the other breast and give it the same treatment, working it over until her nipple stands at attention.

Piper's breathing is rapid and she's grinding against me harder by the time I've finished with her nipples.

"That's enough," Piper says, reaching between us to grip my cock. "I want to ride you now."

The anticipation courses through my veins, hot and thick. I've never been more turned on than I am right now. Slowly, Piper lifts herself up and guides my cock to her waiting entrance. She lowers herself down, inch by inch until she's fully seated on me. She lets out a little sigh once she's completely filled.

"God, you feel so good," she says, grinding against me.

My hands move to her ass, and I squeeze the soft globes. She leans down to take my mouth in a kiss, her tongue sweeping against mine. Then, she braces her hands on my shoulders and begins to ride me. I let her set the pace as she lifts her body slowly up and down. She raises up until just the tip of my dick is still inside her, then slides back down until I'm as deep as I can get. It's incredible and agonizing and so fucking hot. I want so much to thrust up into her. To grip her hips and fuck her hard and fast until we both come. But I love watching her this way. She's strong and beautiful and in control. It's an incredible turn-on.

She keeps it up, riding me with agonizing slowness for several minutes. A fine sheen of sweat covers me as I fight the urge to take control. Just when I think I can't take anymore, Piper's eyes go to a spot over to my left.

"Pick it up," she says.

I follow her gaze and see the purple vibrator lying on the bed next to my hand. My gaze shoots back to Piper's face, a question in my eyes. She nods and smiles.

"I'm serious," she says, rising up before plunging back down. "Turn it on."

I snatch up the toy and study it, finding the power button easily.

"Hold it down for a few seconds," Piper pants.

I do as she says and the toy springs to life in my hands, vibrating at a steady rhythm as a low hum fills the air.

"Now what?" I ask. I know what I want to do, but I need Piper to say it. I need to hear the words.

"Use it to make me come," she says, a challenge in her eyes. She glances down at where we're joined. "My clit."

She leans her upper body back, her arms around my neck to keep her steady. It gives me the space I need to move my hand, and the toy, into position. The moment the vibrator touches Piper's body, I feel it. It's faint, but I can feel a buzzing vibration in my cock through her body. The sensation is a new one for me. I've never had a partner play with toys with me inside her. It feels...good. It's not overwhelming, but it adds a new layer of pleasure to what we're doing. Piper, on the other hand, feels a bit stronger about the toy.

"Oh, fuck," she moans, her hand tightening on my neck.

She keeps riding me, at least for a while. Eventually, her movements become stilted and jerky until finally, her body goes still. Her hands are still locked around my neck, but her muscles are rigid and she's gasping. Her inner muscles clamp down around my cock as she cries out.

"I'm coming! Oh, shit!"

I can feel her orgasm as it rips through her, making her spasm around my cock. Coupled with the faint vibrations of the toy and the sight of Piper as she comes, it's all too much for me. All at once, I feel my own orgasm barreling down on me, catching me by complete surprise. Piper grinds against me, her pussy milking my cock as I bury my face in her neck and pour out my own release.

Dropping the toy to the floor, I wrap both arms around her and hold her locked against me while the waves of pleasure overtake us both. I come for what feels like forever, holding Piper tightly against my body. I don't ever want to let her go.

I know that realization should scare me. It would have in the past. But instead, it fills me with a sense of peace. Being with Piper feels right. This feels right. Not the fake show we've been putting on for Art, but this. Everything else. When it's just me and her and we get to be ourselves together. Laughing, talking, teasing, making love. That's the part I don't ever want to let go of. I don't know what to do with this new understanding, so I push it to the side for now. There's no rush to figure everything out right now. For today, I'm content to keep her in my arms for as long as I can.

CHAPTER 29

Luke

Piper and I spend the day lounging around her house. I work on some promos for Piping Hot while she reads a book on the couch, her legs draped across my lap. It's relaxing and feels natural to be here with her like this. I try not to read too much into the feeling. I know that sooner or later, I'll be forced to examine just what it is that I feel for Piper, but right now I just want to enjoy this before the real world intrudes.

But the real world decides to intrude later that afternoon. I almost ignore the ringing of my phone. It's almost certainly someone from work. Or worse, my father. Piper glances at the screen and gives me a wide-eyed look.

"It's Art," she says.

I feel that same surge of excitement I get when I'm on the verge of closing a major deal. I can't deny there's a fair amount of worry mixed in. I'm still not convinced that Art is going to sign with Wolfe. But I think I made a good impression on him last week. And he'd loved Piper. Maybe this is it. Maybe he's going to give me the good news. I answer the phone.

"Art. It's good to hear from you," I say brightly.

I can't seem to sit still, so I stand and walk slowly across the room as Art and I exchange pleasantries. When I reach the other side of the room, I turn and walk in the other direction. From the corner of my eye, I see Piper stepping closer to me. I take a little step back, trying to focus on my conversation with Art. Piper follows me, stepping close enough to press her body against mine. I go still, shooting her a questioning look. She just smiles.

"I wanted to check in and let you know I haven't forgotten your proposal," Art says.

"Of course," I say. "I was starting to worry you had."

Art and I both chuckle at the joke, though it's not actually funny. I feel Piper's hand flatten on my stomach. I look down at her, surprised to see a mischievous gleam in her eyes. What is she doing?

"I had a few questions and concerns I wanted to discuss with you," Art says.

Piper's fingers dip into my waistband, tugging against the button.

"Of course," I say. "I'm available to answer any questions you have."

The button pops loose and Piper's hand slips inside my pants. Her fingers slide lower, brushing against my rapidly hardening cock. I reflexively reach out and grab her wrist to stop her and send her a look from under raised brows. What the hell is she doing? The look she gives me practically dares me to make her stop. But I've never backed down from a dare before. I'm not going to start now. We stay locked in a staring contest for several seconds before I loosen my grip on her wrist and let my hand fall away. Piper's smile is triumphant as she wraps her fingers around my length and squeezes gently. Then, she pulls my cock out of my pants and sinks to her knees.

Is she really going to do this? Now? While I'm on the phone with Arthur Mitchell? What happened to the woman who was too shy to tell me how she wanted me to fuck her? In her place is this brazen goddess licking her lips, a challenge in her amber eyes. She brings a finger up to her lips warning me to keep quiet. Anticipation coils low in my belly and my cock grows impossibly hard in Piper's hand.

She smirks up at me, clearly pleased by my response. Is this her way of getting back at me for teasing her about the vibrator? If so, I may have to do it more often. I dimly register that Art is still speaking and that he's asked me a question. It takes my brain a second to replay his words and form a response. He's asking me how Piper is doing these days.

"Piper's great, Art," I say. "Keeping busy."

Piper's tongue darts out to lick the underside of my shaft, swirling around the head. Fuck. That feels incredible.

"Good, good," Art says. "I trust her coffee shop is doing well? What's it called again?"

Piper closes her lips around my cock, sucking lightly. A groan rises in my throat, and I swallow it back down.

"Piping Hot Brews, sir," I manage through gritted teeth. I'm not sure if my voice sounds normal, but it's all I can do to form words right now. "The shop is coming along. We're working on a new marketing campaign."

Piper's head dips and she takes more of me into her hot, wet mouth. Her tongue swirls over me and her eyes never leave my face. I reach my free hand down and tangle it in her hair, needing to touch her, needing to do something with my hands. She lets out a little hum of approval and my knees nearly buckle when I feel it vibrate along my length.

Art is still speaking but I have no idea what he's saying. Something about the weather and the humidity.

"It's definitely hot right now." Art mutters his agreement, but my words are meant for Piper.

She takes me deeper into her mouth, increasing the suction. I feel the moment her throat opens enough to take me further. My grip on the phone tightens almost painfully. It's a wonder I don't crush it. But it's the only thing keeping me tethered to the real world while Piper works her magic on my dick. Had I thought she was shy in the bedroom before? The woman on her knees before me is anything but shy. She's magnificent.

"I called you for a reason," Art is saying. I try to pull my focus away from Piper's mouth on me long enough to understand that he's inviting us to dinner. Tonight.

"Be sure and bring that contract," he says, sending a new surge of excitement through me.

"Yes, sir," I manage.

"And that pretty girlfriend of yours," Art says. "I know she's awfully busy these days, but Mel and I would love to see her."

"Absolutely," I say. "She's very busy right now, but I'll see if she can come."

I stare down at Piper as I say it, knowing she understands the double meaning in my words. She gives me a little wink before taking me down her throat and holding me there. Fuck. I can't think. I can't do anything but stand there, my hand fisted in her hair while she holds me captive in her mouth. Mercifully, she eases back to take a breath just as Art ends the call. I make sure the line is dead before tossing the phone onto the couch behind me and digging both hands into her hair.

"You're going to pay for that," I say in a dark voice.

Piper grips my shaft in one hand and gives it a long lick while peering up at me. "Promise?"

I grin down at her. She really is going to be the death of me. But I can think of worse ways to go.

CHAPTER 30

Piper

Since Luke has to drive back to the city early, we agree to take separate cars to the restaurant to meet Art and Mel. Luke was filled with excitement when he left earlier. Even the thought of suffering through dinner with Mel hadn't been enough to dim his enthusiasm. This might be it. The goal he's been working toward all this time is within reach. I'm so happy for him. He's finally going to be able to get out from under his father's thumb. If I'm a little nervous about what it means for Luke and me going forward, I decide not to show it. We haven't talked about what happens after the need for our fake relationship is over.

I'd felt us growing closer over the last couple of days, especially after Luke talked to me about his family and his childhood. He's finally started letting me in, trusting me enough to know the man behind the carefully crafted image he's been forced to maintain. But we still haven't figured out what this thing between us is or what we'd like it to be. If he asked me right now, I'd tell him honestly. I want it to keep going. I want to see where it leads, and I want to call him my boyfriend. Officially, instead of pretend. But everything I know about Luke says he doesn't do relationships. I don't know if he's ever been someone's boyfriend in the real sense of the word. And I don't know how he'd respond to a discussion about it. I may have become more outgoing and adventurous in the bedroom, but I still find it hard to ask for what I want outside of it.

I take a deep breath and smooth a hand down the front of my dress as I take one last look in the mirror. I decide to put all that aside for tonight. We're so close to the prize now. I need to focus on helping Luke get that contract signed. Then we'll have time for relationship talk.

Luke is waiting for me near the front of the restaurant when I arrive. He looks handsome in the dark blue suit he chose for tonight. When he turns and sees me, I watch the way his eyes roam over me, as if they can see through my dress. An involuntary shiver runs through me. He looks as me like he wants to devour me, and that's more of a turn-on than I could have imagined. Too bad he's going home to his apartment and I'm heading back to Peach Tree after dinner. I take a second to wonder if we have time for a quickie after dinner but dismiss the idea. There's no way I'd want to leave after a quickie to go home to my empty bed. Especially not after having Luke in it for the last 24 hours. So, I just smile as I lean up to kiss his cheek.

"You look incredible," he says in a low whisper.

"'Thank you," I say with a smile as I smooth a hand down his lapel. "You look pretty dashing."

Luke smiles. "Well, I wanted to impress this girl I know."

"Oh? Is her name Melody?"

His smile shrivels up and he glares at me while I laugh.

"Keep it up, Huff," he warns.

"Planning to punish me?" I murmur.

Luke's smile turns wicked. "What if I am?"

The idea sets my imagination off with all sorts of naughty images and I suck in a breath. Screw waiting until after dinner. Now I'm wondering if we have time to go back to my car so Luke can show me what he means. But then I hear Art's voice echo across the foyer as he calls Luke's name.

"I guess I'll have to wait to find out," I say.

Then I turn and give Art a wide smile. Instead of a handshake, Art gives me a quick hug before shaking Luke's hand enthusiastically. I can't help but notice that Mel's greeting is far more reserved. Not that I'm complaining. I don't want her touching me or Luke. We're escorted to our table, and I'm surprised to find that Mel isn't putting herself into the chair closest to Luke. Instead, she stays close to Art's side. Maybe she finally got the hint after last week? I sure hope so.

We have drinks and appetizers as we make small talk. Art and Luke dominate most of the conversation and I find I don't need to contribute much. By the time the main course has been served, they've moved on to discussing the details of the contract Luke had presented to Art last week. I'll admit I don't understand some of the finer points they're negotiating, but things seem to be going well. I reach over, under the table to squeeze Luke's hand. This is happening. It's going to work. He turns and smiles at me and I wink back.

There's a lull in the conversation while the servers are clearing away the dinner dishes and refilling our drinks. That's when Mel speaks up for the first time tonight. She's been quiet for most of the night, only speaking when someone asked her a direct question. I hadn't thought much of it, but now I can see there's a gleam in her eye.

"Piper, how long have you and Luke been dating?" she asks. Her tone is casual, but her eyes are sharp.

I smile, trying to remember if Luke and I have ever given her or Art an exact date for our relationship. I don't think we have, but I can't remember for certain.

"You said you two met in college, right?"

I nod. "Sort of," I say. "My sister knew him in college and tried to get us together, but he stood me up."

Mel nods, taking a sip of her wine. "That's right," she says. "What college was that?"

Luke speaks before I can. "Dartmouth," he says smoothly.

Mel nods. "Right. That's where you went, Luke," she says. Her eyes narrow and she looks at me. "But that's not where you went to college, is it? You've never lived outside of this state, have you?"

My stomach drops and I freeze. I don't know what to say.

Mel smirks at me. "You see, I did a little digging after you spent the week in my home, Miss Brooks. You can't blame me for wanting to know more about who's sleeping down the hall, can you?"

"What's this, Mel?" Art asks, looking at his wife in confusion.

She gives him a placating smile. "Art honey, you can't blame me, can you? I was just looking out for you."

Art doesn't look happy, but he silences his objections. I look over at Luke. His jaw is clenched, and his fists are curled into fists under the table. This is really happening. It's all over.

"It turns out Miss Brooks went to the University of Georgia, not Dartmouth," Mel says. "She was lying about how they met. I wonder what else she lied about."

"I can explain," I say.

"Don't bother," Mel bites off. She isn't trying to keep her voice low. I can see the looks from other diners as she keeps going. "We know just what kind of person you are, Piper. You wanted to insinuate yourself among the wealthy elite, but now we know the truth. You're just another poor sap trying to ingratiate yourself with your betters. But it didn't work. We found out your lies, so you can leave now."

My face is hot, and my eyes are burning. I can feel the stares of people from neighboring tables. From the corner of my eye, I see some are holding up their phones, recording the whole thing.

"You don't know what you're talking about," Luke says. "Piper isn't who you're making her out to be."

I wonder why she isn't calling attention to the fact that Luke lied just as I did. But it's probably because she's still hoping to appeal to him in some way. But she's an idiot if she thinks she has a chance now.

"What the hell is going on?" Art demands, looking from me to Luke to Mel. "Someone explain. Now."

"I'd be curious to hear an explanation, myself," says a male voice from behind me.

As Luke turns to face the newcomer, I see a look of resignation fall over his expression.

"Son, who is this woman?" the man behind me says in a condescending tone.

Son? Fuck. Charles Wolfe is standing behind me.

I shift in my chair enough to see the imposing man standing behind me. The resemblance between Luke and his father is strong. They have the same height and build, the same dark blonde hair, and even the same blue-green eyes. But there's something cold and calculating about Charles Wolfe that Luke just doesn't have. They're so clearly related, but only a fool would look at them and think they're anything alike.

I hear Luke sigh beside me. "Dad, this is Piper Brooks. Piper, this is my father, Charles Wolfe."

He doesn't make a move to shake my hand. I give him a tight smile that he doesn't return. People are still staring at us. I wish he'd sit down. I wish I'd never come tonight. I wish a hole would open in the floor and swallow me whole. Anything would be better than sitting here with an entire restaurant seemingly hanging on every word of our conversation. Not to mention, I'm pretty sure this has blown whatever deal Art and Luke had been about to settle on to hell and back.

"You don't know the woman your son is on the verge of proposing to?" Mel asks, all fake innocence.

Shit. That was the wrong thing to say because Charles' eyes go wide, and he looks at me like I'm a bug he needs to squash. Then he looks at Luke who's now rubbing his temples like he's got a headache.

"Propose?" Charles says. "I wasn't aware you were seeing anyone."

"I don't run every aspect of my personal life by my father," Luke says.

I don't like the way his voice seems to have changed since his father showed up. He sounds colder, less like the man I've come to know in the past couple of weeks. Under the table, I reach out and put a hand over his closed fist, trying to offer him some comfort. But I don't know what to do or say right now. Everything he's worked so hard for is falling apart and it was my stupid, impulsive backstory that caused it. I could have kept things vague and avoided dating anything with a timeframe like college. Why had I been so stupid? These people are billionaires. Of course, they vet the people who come into their lives. Why had we thought we could get away with this?

"Which explains why I didn't know you've had a serious girlfriend since college until Mrs. Mitchell called me today," Charles says.

My eyes go to Mel who's sitting there smiling smugly as if she's just been vindicated. Fury rolls through me. She called Luke's dad and ratted us out. All because she hadn't gotten what she wanted, which was Luke in her bed. What kind of person does that?

I push my chair back and stand. When all eyes turn to me, I say, "I think I need to go now."

Luke shakes his head, but I hold up a hand to stall him. "No. Mel was right about one thing. I don't belong here." I turn to Art. "Thank you for being so nice to me. It's been lovely getting to know you. I'm sorry for"—I wave a hand to encompass the table and the people seated there— "all of this." Then I turn to go.

Unfortunately, the heel of my shoe catches on the leg of my chair as I turn. I have a moment of panic where I realize exactly what's about to happen. Then I tip sideways, reaching out a hand to catch myself. Luckily, a server is passing by at the perfect moment. Unluckily for both of us, he's carrying a tray filled with desserts. The man wobbles on his feet but stays upright. The tray however, tips to one side, spilling its contents down the front of a suit that probably costs more than my car. A suit that is currently being worn by none other than Charles Wolfe. My eyes go wide, and my mouth drops open.

The entire restaurant fills with murmurs and muffled laughter. I'm frozen in horror as I look at Luke's father who stands there glaring at me. If looks could kill, I'd be a dead woman. The server begins apologizing profusely, offering Charles cloths to wipe the bulk of the chocolate mousse and various sauces off his suit. There's no doubt that the suit is a goner, but I applaud their efforts to salvage it. Before anyone can stop me, I walk quickly from the dining room, escaping in the chaos. I'm dimly aware of Luke calling my name, but the sound gets further away as I walk and it's clear he isn't following me. I tell myself that's for the best. Now isn't the time for this. I've just ruined his career over the course of one dinner. I'm not sure if I want to hear how he feels about what just happened.

CHAPTER 31

Luke

I watch Piper as she walks quickly from the dining room, head down, ignoring all the idiots with their cell phones recording this nightmare dinner. I try to follow her, but the crowd of servers, restaurant managers, and guests seems to have multiplied around my father. For his part, my father is fuming. He's threatening to have the poor server fired and shouting at anyone who gets close enough to try and help him. I don't even look at Art and Mel. I already know what I'll see there. Disappointment, surely. Contempt, maybe. Instead, I bully my way through the crowd and finally break free of it.

I can't see Piper anymore. I walk faster now that the crowd is behind me, centered on the spectacle that is my father. I hope I can catch her before she leaves. I keep seeing the stricken look on her face and the way she'd looked over at me. She'd been so upset, her eyes bright with unshed tears. She blames herself for this mess, but she's wrong. This was my fuck-up. I should never have tried to involve her in my lies. There was no way this was going to work. I don't want her blaming herself for a ridiculous plan that was doomed from the start.

I make my way outside in time to see her car pull away from the curb and disappear into the Savannah evening traffic.

"Shit!" I yell, not caring who's around to hear me.

I dig for my keys in my pocket, only then remembering that the valet has them. I rush back to the valet stand and give him my ticket. It's okay. It'll be fine. I know where Piper is going. I don't have to catch her on the highway. I reach for my phone but realize I must have left it on the table in my haste to go after Piper. Can this night get any worse?

"Luke?"

I freeze at the sound of Art's voice coming from behind me. I'm not ready to deal with the fallout of my lies just yet. But it's not like I have anywhere to go to avoid him. I turn to see him standing a few feet away from me with his hands in his pockets. To my surprise, he doesn't look angry. If anything, he looks amused. When he finally speaks, he says the last thing I expect.

"I know you think I'm just some old, rich guy. So, my advice might not be what you want to hear. But I wasn't always rich. And I wasn't always old. Take it from me, son. If you find a woman who's worth it, don't let her get away. Or you'll end up like me one day. No kids, married to someone who doesn't even like you half the time, just wishing you could go back and fix things."

I look at him, shocked by how candid he's being. I'd wondered how much he noticed about Mel's behavior, but now I know for sure. He sees all of it, but he chooses not to confront her. Why? Is it easier to just ignore her infidelities? It can't be because he loves her. Maybe he's lonely. Whatever the reason, now doesn't feel like the time to ask him. Not when he's just found out Piper and I have been lying to him for weeks. And when my whole world feels like it's crumbling down around me.

I know I should apologize. Just because he isn't mentioning my lie doesn't mean he's not bothered by it. I have the awful feeling that I've disappointed him, which bothers me more than I expect it to. But Art isn't chastising me. Instead, he comes forward and gives my shoulder a squeeze.

"If I were you," he says, "I'd go after the girl. There will always be another business venture, another contract, another deal. But there's only one of her."

I can only stare at the older man as I take in his words. He's right. I know he is. I need to go after Piper. I need to tell her that she's more important than any business deal or contract. More important than my career or what my father thinks of me.

I nod. "You're right," I say as the valet returns with my car and hands me the key.

Art grins and turns to go. "Of course, I am."

I grip my keys tightly in my fist. If I hurry, I can be at her house in 20 minutes. If I ignore the speed limits, that is.

"One more thing," Art says, turning back to me.

I pause, giving him my attention. "I thought your proposal was sound. I'll have my people reach out to you sometime next week."

Shocked, I can only stand there and nod. "Thank you," I manage. "You won't regret it."

"What the hell was that?!"

My father's voice hits me with the force of a hammer, making every muscle in my body tense. Art and I shift our focus to the angry man striding across the parking lot toward me. Somehow, my father doesn't notice Art standing just a few feet away. All his righteous anger is focused on me and what just happened in the restaurant. I'm sure he's also pissed about his suit which is covered in dark stains. He stomps over until he's only a few feet away from me, his eyes shooting daggers at me.

"How you managed to fuck up this badly is beyond me," he says through gritted teeth. "Though I shouldn't be surprised. You always choke when the stakes are high."

His words are harsh, and I can feel the venom in each one. But somehow, they don't hold as much of the sting as they once did. Oh, I'm still pissed off and annoyed by my father's presence, but I no longer feel the need to soothe his ruffled feathers. I don't feel the strong urge to impress him. So, I stand there silently, letting him spout out every hurtful insult he can think of.

"This was the biggest deal of your career," he says. "The biggest for Wolfe Industries! It would have put us on the map, Lucas. But you went and hired some small-town whore to play pretend instead of—"

He never finishes. My fist plows into his face before he can say whatever horrible thing he was thinking about Piper. His hands fly to his nose where I see blood trickling down. He stares at me through shocked eyes that match the color of my own. I used to take pride in that, back when I was too young to know who he really was. When I was just a kid who wanted to be like his father. But now, it just pisses me off that I share even that little similarity with someone like him.

"You're going to regret that," he says, his voice sounding nasally as he tries to staunch the flow of blood.

I lean in closer, fighting the urge to hit my father again. "I regret a lot of things when it comes to you," I bite off. "But the only regret I have about that punch is that I didn't do it years ago. I quit. Run your company into the ground for all I care. You're on your own."

I turn to leave, only then remembering that Art is still standing there. He saw the entire scene unfold. Shame floods through me. I still don't regret hitting Charles, but I hate that Art witnessed the whole humiliating episode. He's wearing a look of disgust. For a second, I think it's directed at me, but then I realize he's looking at Charles. I won't think of him as my father again.

"I'm glad I didn't sign with Wolfe Industries tonight," Art says, looking Charles up and down in pity. "I don't want to align myself with someone like you."

Charles sputters for a moment, but he doesn't have a defense. Art heard everything he said about me. Worse, he heard the hateful things he said about Piper. Even if Art didn't like me, he adores Piper. Whatever good will Charles might have hoped for with Art was wrecked the moment he called her a whore. Remembering what he said has my fist clenching again. I should have hit him harder.

Art puts an arm around my shoulder, steering me away from Charles who's still just standing there gaping at us.

"Put some ice on that hand," Art says, nodding toward my clenched fist. I force myself to relax my fingers, wiggling them a bit. They're sore, but I can tell nothing's broke.

"Hell of a punch, son," he says with a grin.

That's the second time tonight he's used that word. Son. My brain trips on the word, so unused to hearing it with anything but derision and condescension. But Art sounded almost proud when he'd said it.

"Thanks," I say.

Art nods once more. "Like I said, I'll be in touch next week. Don't forget what else I said." He gives me a meaningful look. "Don't let her get away."

For the first time since my father appeared, I smile. "I don't intend to," I say.

"My advice?" Art says. "Go big or go home." He shrugs. "How do you think I made it this far?"

A small laugh escapes me. Art is known for taking big risks and reaping huge rewards. I don't know that Piper needs a grand gesture to convince her that I want to be with her for real. But I want to prove to her that her happiness is more important to me than my stupid career. And what's the one thing Piper wants more than anything? An idea starts to form in my head, and I feel my smile widen.

"I think I know what I need to do, Art," I say.

"Never doubted you for a second," he says, grinning.

"That makes one of us," I say. "But thank you. For everything."

"Let me know if you need help winning her over," he says. "I've got billions of dollars and I'm always looking for something to do."

I laugh. "I'll keep that in mind."

I hesitate before turning to go. Part of thinks I should just let it go. Leave well enough alone. But I can't, "You're not angry with us for lying to you?"

Art just smiles. "No. To tell the truth, it's the kind of thing I might have done when I was starting out. Like I said, go big or go home. I don't know the real reason you felt you needed to lie about having a girlfriend. I have my suspicions, but the reason doesn't really matter. I'm a romantic, son. I believe in true love. You and Piper might have started off pretending, but any idiot can see the truth." He shrugs. "I guess I just wanted to see what would happen."

I stare at him for several seconds. I wonder just when Art figured out Piper and I were lying to him and why he didn't call us out on it. It seems insane to me that he's not angry. Most people would be. But he's not. Before I change his mind by questioning him further, I decide to take him at his word.

"Thanks, Art."

He grins. "Don't mess this one up."

"I won't."

CHAPTER 32

Piper

Luke still hasn't called. He hasn't texted. The disastrous dinner was two days ago, and he hasn't called. If I was looking for a sign that he wasn't interested in staying with me after things with Art were settled, this is a glaringly obvious one. One of those glittering, neon signs that hurt your eyes if you look directly at it. Only this one is hurting my heart.

Why did I think this would work out? Why had I thought Luke was different? I can't even blame him. He never led me on. He never put a label on what we were. We were having fun. He never once lied to me. It's my own, stupid fault. I went and fell for my fake boyfriend. I feel like an idiot. But I guess that's just icing on the humiliation cake that I've been eating since the other night when Mel made her big, splashy announcement.

I've seen several video accounts of it on social media. A few people feel bad for me, but most are poking fun at me. They criticize my dress or my hair. Some commenters are convinced it's all staged for more views. At this point, I wish it had been staged. Then I might not feel like I have a great, big hole in my chest every time I remember the way Luke didn't try to stop me from leaving. Why hasn't he called? I sigh, swallowing back the tears that threaten. I cried enough yesterday. I'm finished crying. It's over now and I need to move on.

First things first, I need to shower. Then I need to get off my ass and go to work. Piping Hot Brews was closed yesterday, not that it matters. Harlow would have been my only customer, but she'd come over first thing in the morning and let me cry on her shoulder as I told her all about the night before. I spent all day wallowing and eating my feelings with Harlow supporting me the entire time. I'm glad to have found a friend like her in Peach Tree. Without her support, I don't know how I would have made it through this whole thing.

Sometime in the afternoon, Layna had called me. She'd seen the videos too. Of course, she had. I'm practically viral at this point. I'd managed to convince her—just barely—not to drive across the state just to be by my side. And not to kick Luke's ass. She'd threatened that, too. But I'd reminded her that he hadn't done anything wrong. We'd made an agreement and it's not his fault things blew up in our faces. She hadn't seem totally convinced, but she's letting the matter go for now. After talking to Layna, I'd turned my phone off so I wouldn't be tempted to replay the videos of my humiliation. Living through it once was enough.

But now I've got to face the music. Piping Hot isn't going to run itself and it damned sure isn't going to be successful if I'm hiding in my house all day. I need to get my shit together and go to work. The thing they don't tell you about running your own business and being your own boss is that you've got to hold yourself accountable. There's no one else to do it for you. Which sucks when all you want to do is stay home and watch cheesy romance movies and cry. There's no boss to call, wondering why you didn't come in to work today when you're the boss.

It takes me longer than usual, but I finally make myself shower and get dressed for the day. I even take the time to put on a little makeup and style my hair. Though I don't know why I bother with my hair since the humidity is bound to claim it as soon as I step outside. But I'm trying to make an effort at normalcy. It's as if I'm saying, 'See? My life is not falling apart at the seams. See? I can get up and get dressed and go to work, like a normal person who wasn't just humiliated online for millions of people's amusement.'

I sigh at my reflection. I look a little pale and the circles under my eyes aren't well-hidden by my concealer, but it's good enough. I straighten my spine and pull my shoulders back. I can do this. Hell, I probably won't see anyone all day, anyway. I can't remember if Stevie is scheduled to work later or not. It's possible I'll see her and maybe Harlow. But Harlow won't judge me, and chances are that Stevie won't notice what I look like.

I make my way toward the shop, walking my usual route. The town is the same sleepy, little town it's always been. Summer is in full swing, and the heat is almost unbearable today. I wonder how I'll feel about this walk in August when it will be even hotter. That's still a couple of months away. I wonder if I'll still be here by then or if I'll be forced to close. I push down the panic that comes with that thought and keep walking. There's no sense dwelling on what might be. I need to focus on the present. I shuffle through ideas for ways to put the shop on the map, lost in thought as I get closer. It's not until I'm about to cross the street directly in front of Piping Hot that I notice all the cars.

Dozens of cars line the street in front of the shop. They also fill the parking lot, leaving not even the handicapped spaces open. There's a line of people in front of the shop leading up to the front door. That's when I notice that people are packed inside the shop as well. My steps falter and I stand there, frozen on the curb.

"What the hell?" I mutter.

As I stand there staring, a group of four senior gentlemen cross the street toward me, walking away from the shop. All four of them are holding white paper cups with the shop's logo on it. It takes me a moment to realize where I know them from. They're the men who usually sit on the benches outside of the café sipping coffee and gossiping every morning. I've waved and smiled at them every day since moving here and they've barely given me a nod in response. Today though, they lift their cups in greeting, each one giving me a broad smile as they pass. The last one even speaks to me.

"Mighty fine coffee, darlin'," he says with a grin.

I manage to smile in return, but I can't force out any words of thanks. What the hell is going on here? Shaking myself from my stupor, I walk quickly across the street, avoiding the traffic that's never been here before. I walk past the line of people at the door, intending to go inside, but someone holds up a hand.

"The line is back there," a man says in a gruff voice, pointing back toward the parking lot.

A woman taps his shoulder. "That's her, idiot," she mumbles.

"I'm the owner," I stammer, wondering what the woman means. I don't recognize her, so I don't know how she could have known me. But I just shake my head and walk inside when someone holds open the door for me.

Inside the shop is organized chaos. Stevie is behind the counter making coffee. She's moving quickly, shouting things to someone. Harlow is behind the register taking orders and writing them onto the sides of cups. There's a pair of broad shoulders I don't recognize until Cole turns and shouts out a name, handing a cup to a young man in board shorts and a tank top. What is Cole doing here? What's Harlow doing here, for that matter? What the hell is going on? The man smiles his thanks at Cole and makes his way toward the exit. When he passes me, he stares at me for several seconds with his mouth slightly open. Then he pulls out his cell phone and holds it up.

"Do you mind?" he asks.

Confused, I just stand there while he comes around behind me and snaps a selfie of the two of us. I don't even have time to wonder why the hell he wants a picture with me before he's gone and the crowd inside the store has their eyes trained on me.

I suddenly feel like a zoo animal. The urge to flee is overwhelming, but I'm too shocked and confused to move. I feel an arm around my shoulder, and I startle at the contact. I look over to see Linc beside me. He steers me away from the crowd and down the hallway that leads to my tiny office.

"Hide in here until things die down," he says, depositing me into a chair. He looks down at me, concern in his kind eyes. "You okay?"

I nod, though I'm not sure I am. I'm not sure of anything right now. Seriously, what the hell is going on?

Linc must be content with what he sees in my expression because he nods. "I've got to go back up front and help the others."

I want to ask him what he and his brother are doing here, but I just nod. Words are failing me right now. Are all these people here because of a stupid video? Where did they come from? How did they find the shop? Linc turns to go as Harlow opens the door.

They stand there in the doorway, inches apart, looking at one another for several seconds. Linc points behind her toward the front just as Harlow gestures toward me. They both move simultaneously, trying to fit through the narrow doorway at the same time. Then they awkwardly freeze as they brush up against one another. They spend a few seconds where they each move in the same direction a few times before Linc puts his hands on Harlow's shoulders and gently urges her into the office while he moves into the hallway. He doesn't look at either of us before striding off toward the front of the shop. But I think his ears were pink. I look at Harlow. Her face is flushed, and she can't seem to meet my gaze.

"Um," I begin, pointing in the direction Linc just went. "What was that?"

She seems to shake herself and shoots me a bright smile that's clearly forced. "What was what?" she asks. "Holy shit, did you see how many people are out there? They love this place!"

I narrow my eyes at her obvious change of subject. But, since it's not the most pressing item on my mind today, I decide to let her avoidance of Linc go unmentioned. For now.

"Where did they all come from?" I ask.

Harlow shrugs. "All over," she says. "Some are on their way to the beach. Some are from Savannah. It doesn't matter where they're from. They're all here for you. For your coffee."

"But why?" I ask, needing to understand where the sudden influx of customers came from.

"Because of the sign," says a voice from the doorway. I look over to see Stevie standing there. "Are you coming out here anytime soon? It's madness out there. We need all hands on deck."

"What sign?" I ask, focusing on the first part of her statement.

Stevie gives me an impatient look that only a teenager can pull off. "The one on the water tower?"

I blink, still confused. "Which water tower?"

Stevie rolls her eyes. "*The* water tower. The giant peach? What other water tower do you think?"

I take a deep breath and remind myself that she's a teenager and I can't just grab her by the shoulders and shake her until she tells me what I want to know. "What sign?" I manage through gritted teeth.

Now, Stevie looks genuinely confused. "You don't know?

My head is about to explode. Something about my expression must finally get through to Stevie, because her eyes widen.

"Fine, fine," she says. "Sorry. I thought you were behind it. Someone hung a massive sign from the tower advertising this place."

I picture the giant peach-shaped tower on the outskirts of town and wonder about this mysterious sign. I have a feeling I know who's responsible for it. Luke felt guilty about our plan imploding before he could help Piping Hot, so he's trying to fix things.

Stevie turns her phone screen toward me. I can see the town's social media page is pulled up. It takes me a second to realize what I'm seeing. I grab Stevie's phone and scroll down the page to see that people have posted photo after photo of the massive peach-shaped monstrosity. After a dozen or so, I stop scrolling and just stare at one at random, taking in the giant, billboard-sized sign that someone hung from it.

"If you think this is hot, you should try Piping Hot Brews"

Confused, I look at Stevie. "That still doesn't explain this crowd," I say, looking around. "These people aren't all from Peach Tree."

Stevie just shakes her head as if I'm the most clueless adult she's ever met. "It's not just the sign," she says, scrolling through her phone again. "It's also the viral video."

I groan. Of course, they came to see the pathetic lady from the video.

Stevie hands me her phone again. "Over 200,000 views and counting."

I reluctantly take the phone, knowing what I'm going to see. But when I look down at the phone in my hand, I see Luke looking back at me. My stupid heart jumps in my chest at the sight of his handsome face. Those ocean eyes looking directly at the camera. God, I've missed him. I can admit it now. It's only been two days since I saw him, but I've missed his smile, those damned dimples, his commanding voice when we had sex. I've missed everything about him.

"Hey guys," he says. "I'm making this video because I need your help. I screwed up and hurt someone I really care about. I know how this app works, so story time!"

He flashes a big, bright smile at the camera and continues. "Not that long ago, I met his amazing woman. Despite me standing her up for our first date, she forgave me and offered to be my friend as a consolation prize. Now, this woman is gorgeous, funny, talented and makes the best coffee I've ever tasted. To say I was disappointed that she didn't instantly fall for my manly charms is an understatement. But I realized that being this woman's friend is far from a consolation prize. Plus, a person can never have too many friends. So, I agreed.

"When I had a work problem that I needed help with, she jumped at the chance to help me." The camera zooms in close to Luke's face, and he speaks in a hushed tone. "Not really. I had to bribe her a little, but when you hear what I wanted her to do, that part will make sense."

The camera pans back out and Luke resumes speaking at his normal volume. "You see, I needed someone to pretend to be my girlfriend to help me score points with a potential client. I know, I know. Lying is bad. It wasn't my finest hour. But I was desperate.

"So, I lied. Like I said, this amazing woman eventually agreed to help me. Even when it turned out to be more involved than we originally thought. But then I screwed it all up. I know you've all seen *that* video."

The video shifts to the one of me at dinner for a few seconds before shifting back to Luke. He's in a different location now. It's one I recognize. He's standing outside, underneath the giant peach-shaped water tower.

He takes a deep breath, and his face turns serious. "I made her think that my career was more important than her, and that's just not true. She's the most important part of my life. But I needed to find a way to let her know how sorry I am for hurting her. That's where you guys come in."

His gaze goes to the bottom of the screen and his eyes widen.

"Crap. Running out of time." He speaks faster now, his words stumbling over one another. "If you guys could make this video blow up so she sees it, that would be amazing. Oh, and one last thing. If you go visit Piping Hot Brews in Peach Tree, Georgia, you can have the best coffee of your life." He winks, and the camera pans out to include the tower and the massive sign hanging from it. Then the video pauses for a second before starting again from the beginning.

I want to be angry, but my lips curve into a smile as I shake my head.

"I can't believe he did this," I say. "I'm going to kill him." There's no real anger behind the words. Instead, there's just a soft, warm feeling in my chest that's spreading through my body.

"Make sure to thank him first," Harlow says.

When I look over at her, she shoots me a wink. Luke. That idiot. He's turned this place into a spectacle, thanks to that video and that ridiculous sign. I walk with the others back out front and stand behind the counter, looking around at the crowded dining room and the parking lot packed full of cars outside. He did this. For me. I try not to read too much into the gesture. He's just following through on his end of the deal. Right? So, what had he meant when he'd said I was the most important part of his life? And why can't I stop smiling?

"Read the comments," Stevie says, nodding toward the phone I'd forgotten I was holding.

I know how social media works. It's not always wise to read what the general public thinks of you. But I do as Stevie says and click the button to read the comments. To my shock, there are thousands of them. I scan through them, my smile growing with each one.

"She's crazy if she doesn't forgive you."

"If she says no, I'll be your 'friend'."

"This sounds like a love story in the making."

"Sounds like she's more than just a friend."

"I hope she forgives you! Waiting for an update."

"Is your friend blind? Because you're hot. I'd forgive you, if you know what I mean."

I read through a few more, but they all go on in the same vein. They are, for the most part overwhelmingly supportive. Most of the thousands of people in the comment section are encouraging Luke to 'win me back'. There are also quite a few that promise to be his 'consolation prize' if I don't come to my senses. My smile is so wide it hurts my face as I turn back to Stevie and hand her the phone.

"This is ridiculous," I say, blinking at the sudden moisture in my eyes.

"Maybe," she says with a shrug "But it's also really romantic."

Romantic. Is that what Luke's trying to do? Some grand, romantic gesture? This feels too big to win back a simple friendship. But then, we were never just friends. Not really. There's always been another layer there, whether it was the flirty texts or the fake relationship that led to us falling into bed together. Whatever we were, it was never just friends.

As Stevie heads back to her station behind the counter, I fish my phone out of my pocket and turn it on. I wait for the influx of notifications to stop before finding Luke's name and pressing the button to call him. He answers on the first ring.

"Hey, Huff." I smile at the ridiculous nickname.

"You did this," I say, instead of a greeting.

"I made you a promise." Luke's voice washes over me, instantly settling something inside me that I hadn't realized was quaking. Why did I never notice this before? Just hearing Luke's voice grounds me. It tethers me in a way nothing else ever has. Understanding dawns, and I feel almost light-headed with the giddy realization. I'm in love with him. I love Luke Wolfe. My heart trips in my chest and I give up the fight to keep the goofy grin off my face. I love Luke and I'm not going to let him go a second time.

"Besides," he continues, oblivious to my revelations. "I had a lot of time on my hands after I quit my father's company."

His words yank me out of my own thoughts. "You did what!?" I shout, drawing more stares from the crowd inside the shop.

All the implications for Luke fly through my head. His dream. His company. All the people who worked for him that will suffer under his father's leadership. The giddy feeling of moments before is gone, replaced by sorrow for what he's given up. My heart aches for him and what he's given up.

"Luke," I whisper. "Why?"

"I want to see you," he says, instead of answering my question. He doesn't sound like a man who's lost everything he ever worked for. Instead, he sounds light and carefree. Almost, happy? He's clearly in shock. Or denial.

"Where are you?" I'm walking toward the door before he can answer. I reach for my car keys, only to remember that I walked here from my house. Shit. I'll have to go home and get my car.

"Meet me under the sign," he says.

It takes me a second to realize he's talking about my sign. The one hanging from the water tower. My pulse quickens as I turn to look in the direction of the tower. I can only see the top of the giant peach above the trees, but it's not far. I debate going to get my car, but it's in the opposite direction. I can walk to the tower in less than 10 minutes.

"I'm on my way," I say, taking off at a brisk walk.

CHAPTER 33

Piper

With every step that brings me closer to Luke, I grow more certain. I'm in love with him. I don't know when or how it happened. But somehow, during the week I'd spent faking a relationship with him, I'd fallen head over heels in love with him. One week. That's all it had taken. My pace quickens. Before I realize it, I'm jogging. The giant peach-shaped tower looms larger in my vision with every step. I just need to get there. I need to tell Luke how I feel. It's early in the day, but it's already hot. The heat and humidity have my hair sticking to my neck, but I don't care. I break into a run. I need to get to Luke.

I force myself to slow to a walk when I turn onto the little dirt lane that leads to the water tower. I don't want to be so out of breath I can't tell him I love him. My heart hammers in my chest, but my breathing is slowing down to normal. The dirt road is lined with tall pines that make it hard for me to see the tower, but I know it's just ahead. I jogged this route a few times before the weather turned too hot. There's a turn at the end of the little road just before the clearing opens up. The tower is in the center of that clearing, surrounded by a fence that must be nearly 10 feet tall. I wonder how Luke got the sign up there. I'll have to ask him. Later. After I kiss him.

When I round the last turn and see him standing there next to the fence, my heart catches in my throat. He shouldn't look as good as he does in jeans and a t-shirt, but I can't stop the flutter low in my belly at the sight of him. It takes me a second to notice the bouquet of flowers in his hand. My steps slow as he takes a step toward me. Then, he's striding forward, meeting me halfway. I open my mouth to apologize about that stupid dinner.

"I'm sorry about—"

But I don't get the chance to finish because Luke's lips are on mine. His arms are banded tightly around me as he holds me against him. I wrap my arms around his neck and kiss him back with all the love I feel for him. When the kiss finally ends, Luke still doesn't release me. He hugs me to him, and I bury my face in his neck, breathing in his unique scent.

"I missed you," I whisper against his skin.

"Piper, I'm sorry," he says, leaning back just enough so I can see his face. "I shouldn't have roped you into this stupid scheme. Because of me, you were humiliated online, and you had to deal with that horrible woman. I should have just handled my own problems and left you out of it."

His hand comes up to cup my cheek. "But I don't regret it. I can't. Because it brought us together. That week with you was the happiest I've been in years. Maybe the happiest I've ever been."

My throat tightens against the emotion his words bring, and I try to swallow the lump there. I blink my suddenly damp eyes. "I don't regret it either," I say.

He grins. "Good. Because I'm in love with you, Piper. And I don't want to go back to a life without you in it."

Now, the tears spill over. Luke swipes them away with his thumb. "What do you say, Huff? Can I be your not-fake boyfriend?"

I nod as the smile spreads across my face. "I'd like that," I whisper.

"Good," he says. "Because I'm not letting you go again."

"I'm not going anywhere. I love you, too."

Luke's eyes soften with emotion and something like wonder. He shakes his head as if he can't quite believe what's happening. I pull him toward me for another kiss while my heart threatens to explode with pure happiness.

CHAPTER 34

Luke

It's been a week since I quit my job. It's also been the happiest week of my life. Not working for my father turned out to be one of the secret ingredients to my happiness. The other is Piper. She's been amazing. She's stuck by my side through it all, listening when I needed to talk and comforting me when I stressed about the future. Just knowing she loves me and supports me has been enough to relieve most of the stress from my shoulders.

But then Art had called me to set up a meeting. Piper had come along. Art had asked me about my plans for my future and my career. I'd told him what I'd only ever told my closest friends and Piper. I told him about my plans for a future away from Wolfe Industries. I'd also told him about the financial aspect that had been holding me back.

That's when Art had made his proposal. He'd offered to invest in my new marketing firm as a partial, silent owner. I'd been stunned and overwhelmed by his generosity, but it had been Piper who convinced me to agree.

"Everyone needs help sometimes," she'd said. "It doesn't mean your idea and your business plan isn't sound. You just need the money to make it happen. Don't give up on your dreams because of a setback."

Art and I finalized the contract this morning. Now, I'm spending the afternoon helping Piper at her shop. While business tapered off a bit after the video's popularity waned and the town removed my sign, Piping Hot Brews has had a steady stream of customers each day since. Time will tell if the success lasts, but it's great to see Piper without the weight of that worry on her shoulders. It's clear she loves this place and seeing it thrive makes her happy. Which makes me happy.

I take the cup Piper hands me giving her a wink before turning to call out the name written on the side.

"Dorothy!"

A petite, elderly woman with steel-gray hair approaches the counter. She's steady on her feet, though she looks like a strong breeze could knock her over.

"That's me," she says. "But it's Dottie, not Dorothy."

"Oh, I'm sorry," I say. "I think I read it wrong."

She waves a hand as if to dismiss my apology before taking the cup from my hand.

"Thank you, dear," she says in a small voice.

I smile. "You're welcome. Have a nice day."

She nods before taking a sip from her cup and smiling. "Delicious tea, dear," she calls out to Piper who gives her a little wave and a smile.

I walk over to where Piper is busy making a latte and drop a light kiss on her cheek.

"What's that for?" she asks, narrowing her eyes at me in mock suspicion.

I shrug. "I just like kissing you, Huff."

She rolls her eyes and gives a little shake of her head. "I've got to come up with a nickname for you."

I just smile as I take the finished drink from her. "Do your worst," I say.

Piper's smile is almost enough to make me ignore the waiting customers and even Miss Dottie herself and drag her back to the office so I can show her how much I love her. Instead, I give her ass a quick pinch as I walk past, making her jump.

"You guys are scaring the customers," Stevie says from her post at the register.

Piper points a stern finger at me. "Back to work, you."

I grin at her mock outrage. "I love it when you're bossy."

I laugh as Piper's cheeks turn rosy. I'm going to enjoy making that happen as often as possible for as long as she'll have me.

Maybe even forever.

End of Book One

A Word from Isla

Okay, I didn't set out to write a slow-burn book. I swear, I didn't. So, I'm sorry I made you wait so long for the spicy bits. Luke is a character with a lot to unpack and his story couldn't be rushed. I hope you enjoyed the ride and that it was worth the wait.

Next up is going to be Harlow's book. She keeps a lot hidden away so the guy who wins her heart is going to have to work for it. Luckily, I have just the guy in mind. Stay tuned!

Note: The peach-shaped water tower in the fictional town of Peach Tree, Georgia is inspired by a real-life water tower that's in a town called Clanton, Alabama. There's another in Gaffney, SC. You can find images of them online if you like. They make me laugh every time I see them.

Made in the USA
Middletown, DE
30 September 2023

39421255R00187